THE BOOK OF
CASEY ADAIR

THE BOOK OF CASEY ADAIR

Ken Harvey

THE UNIVERSITY OF WISCONSIN PRESS

The University of Wisconsin Press
728 State Street, Suite 443
Madison, Wisconsin 53706
uwpress.wisc.edu

Gray's Inn House, 127 Clerkenwell Road
London ECIR 5DB, United Kingdom
eurospanbookstore.com

Printed in the United States of America
This book may be available in a digital edition.

Library of Congress Cataloging-in-Publication Data

Names: Harvey, Ken (Fiction author), author.
Title: The book of Casey Adair / Ken Harvey.
Description: Madison, Wisconsin : The University of Wisconsin Press, [2021]
Identifiers: LCCN 2021008823 | ISBN 9780299333546 (paperback)
Subjects: LCGFT: Fiction.
Classification: LCC PS3558.A71855 B66 2021 | DDC 813/.54—dc23
LC record available at https://lccn.loc.gov/2021008823

The Book of Casey Adair is a work of fiction. While some of the
characters have real-life counterparts, their characterizations and the
incidents in which they are depicted are products of the author's imagination
and are used fictitiously. All other characters are drawn from the author's
imagination. The placement of letters is based on the order they would
have been received rather than the day they were written.

for

Debbie Michel

Laura Taylor Kung

Marcella Larsen

MADRID

1980–1981

We're all curious about what might hurt us.

—FEDERICO GARCÍA LORCA

Dear Poppy,

Or should I call you Penelope, as Prof. Stoddard insisted on doing for four years at Nearing? I'm writing this from a men's boarding house called Pensión Marianela, seven subway stops from the center of Madrid, where I've just moved in. I like it here so far. There seems to be a genuine camaraderie among the men in the pensión, so I'm hoping I might make a friend or two. I met my roommate, a handsome bearded doctoral candidate from Bilbao named Gustavo, who writes a daily Socialist newsletter at the university.

You've done so much traveling that it's become second nature, but for me just being on a plane was a new experience. I flew on a huge Boeing 747. When the airplane hit some turbulence, I gripped the arms of my seat, holding on for dear life. I was so shaken that the stewardess offered me some water.

There wasn't an empty seat on the plane. No surprise that so many Spaniards were on board, but I had no idea they smoked so much. The whole cabin was a gray cloud. The man across the aisle from me blessed himself as we took off. I flashed back to when I was in my first class to become an altar boy at St. Pius. A nun kept scolding me for not kneeling straight enough.

Spanish civil guards were everywhere in the customs area, looking like stone pillars. I pretended not to be nervous by keeping my body and face as still as possible, which I'm sure made me look guiltier than if I actually did have some drugs on me. A customs official asked me to open my backpack. The most scandalous thing in there was a copy of *Giovanni's Room*. I doubt he even knew what that was.

As soon as I stepped outside the airport, I stopped. What the hell was I doing in a foreign country where I didn't know anyone? I stood in a daze for a good five minutes before I waved a taxi. Even though I'm settled in now, I still have moments like that. I think I'll be better once I dig into my project.

How are you, Poppy? Sometimes I wish I were staying on for another year at Nearing with you, especially if I didn't have to study. Arriving in a foreign city where I don't know a soul has made me miss you and our alma mater. Tell me what your days are like.

Did I tell you I was going to visit Noah (my freshman year roommate) in New York City before my flight to Madrid? I don't think you knew him very well because he transferred to Queens College after his sophomore year at Nearing. His mom was always so nice to me. She used to call Noah "The Wisenheimer," which was a perfect nickname for him. He was always joking, always on stage. I really wanted him to take me to a gay bar in the Greenwich Village, but he had tickets to a preview of *42nd Street*. I suppose seeing a musical is the second gayest thing to do in New York City.

Will write more later. I want to get this in the mail to you today.

Love to you and your novio.

Casey

∿

THURSDAY, AUGUST 21, 1980   6:00 P.M.

I've never had much luck with journals. It might be because I've always tried to be too disciplined and have stopped after I missed a few days. But everyone told me I *had* to keep one while living in Spain. Maybe I'll just make an entry when I want to and not worry too much about how often I write.

Many of the men in the pensión are older than I am. A permanent fixture in the lobby is the manager, an enormous elderly man who sits with his cane hooked over the arm of his chair. He has thick white wavy hair, and chews on an unlit cigar stub. He greets anyone near him with "Buenos días, buenos días." That's why everyone calls him "Señor Buendía." He looked puzzled when I jokingly called him "Mr. Good Morning."

I hope I become friends with my roommate, Gustavo. We had a beer this afternoon. During our conversation he smoked three cigarettes, taking deep drags and exhaling through his nose. He's studying for his doctorate in political theory at the university. He doesn't think the democratic government is going to last much longer. Gustavo said he'd favor an overthrow of the monarchy in order to reestablish the Republic in Spain, but he's convinced the Fascists are the ones who will take over. As an excuse, he thinks they'll use a Basque separatist group (ETA) responsible for a string of bombings over the summer.

Gustavo was interested in my reason for living in Spain this year—to study how the theater changed after Franco's death. He thinks he might be able to connect me with some knowledgeable artists and writers. That would be a huge help. In the meantime, I'm hoping to see as much theater as I can, or maybe work in a theater. During the day I figure I can read plays and conduct some interviews.

∼

MADRID   AUGUST 27, 1980

Dear Professor Stoddard,

It occurred to me this morning that I never formally thanked you for your recommendation that made this year in Spain possible. I say "this year" although I just arrived in Madrid last week.

For the past few days, I've awoken early enough to see the men in blue overalls hose down the sidewalks. I never know where I'm going when I start my morning walk. I don't even bring a map. I just walk. I take it all in: the blind vendors selling lottery tickets, the white buildings that look like alabaster, the Gypsies selling their wares spread out on a blanket. The heat here is unlike anything I've experienced. I end up stopping at least every half hour for a bottle of Coke, which is sold in food carts on almost every street corner.

I'm still not used to so many older men without legs and arms. On the subway, seats are reserved for war amputees. I guess I shouldn't be surprised. It's not as if the Civil War happened a century ago. And the widows in black! It's hard to imagine going colorless the rest of your life because your husband has died.

I'm learning to enjoy evenings in Madrid, especially when it cools down and everyone goes outside. Tonight I spent some time at the Plaza de España, where families were strolling around the huge fountain honoring Cervantes. Children deliberately walked close enough to be sprayed, and then squealed in mock surprise when they got wet. Lovers held hands. I find Madrid very romantic, although it might be its foreignness that allures me.

When the families headed home, I found a café along the Gran Vía. (When you were here last it was called José Antonio. After Franco died, they changed the names of the streets that honored Fascists.) The food here is inexpensive, and you can get a three-course meal for about seven dollars. I eavesdropped as I ate, jotting down a word here and there I didn't know. My night ended at the Plaza Mayor, where I'm writing this letter. Do you go here when you're in Madrid? It's lovely. I haven't done much solo traveling (or traveling at all, for that matter), but between the sangria and the university musicians playing medieval music, it's hard to feel too lonely.

I'd love to hear about how you remember Madrid when Franco was alive. The city feels oddly laid back and very urban at the same time. People tell me Spain has changed a lot since it became a democratic country. I guess I'll find out more as I dig deeper into my project. I saw a terrific production of *Luces de bohemia* the other night. Two hours of a blind poet walking around Old Madrid right before he dies. I left the theater in complete despair. I remember reading it in your class. You said it was one of your favorite plays.

I hope you are well, Professor Stoddard. I think of you often.
Sincerely,
Casey Adair

∿

NEARING, VERMONT   SEPTEMBER 1, 1980

Casey, my dearest—

"Penelope?" The only time I've ever heard you utter that name was during freshmen orientation, before I asked for a new nametag. If you started calling me Penelope now, it'd be like talking to Granny or Professor Stoddard. Stick with Poppy if you know what's good for you.

I was thrilled to get your letter and have read it three times, but I do think you grossly overestimate my travel experience. I'm from

Toronto, for Christ's sake. It's not as if I had to get on your Boeing 747 to fly into Burlington, Vermont, at the start of every semester. In fact, the plane seats all of twelve people. I'm not even sure it has a second engine. So enough nonsense about me being worldlier than you. I have never been to Madrid, as you know.

Ernesto is busy with his senior thesis on the South American painters Wifredo Lam and Fernando Botero. They couldn't be more different: Lam paints what I can only describe as insect-like figures and Botero paints these darling cartoon-like portraits of really enormous people. I think Ernesto should focus on just one of them, but I wasn't an art history major at Nearing, so I've kept my mouth shut. Besides, at least when it comes to art, he's a whole lot smarter than I am. He's actually pretty brilliant. He's applying to a bunch of PhD programs in art history, but his father wants him to go to business school. I'm hoping he gets into Harvard or Yale. If I don't return to Canada over the next few years, I'd at least like to stay in New England.

Ernesto reports that assisting Professor Stoddard isn't as demanding as he feared. Stoddard gives him a list of things to do Monday morning, and Ernesto checks off the items by Friday afternoon. They hardly ever talk. I've only said hello to Stoddard once or twice on the quad. He seems even more remote than usual. He walks with his head down, sucking his cigarette. The man is so thin you have to wonder if he's eating anything at all.

I don't think you and I ever decided on a date for me to visit Madrid. I know we mentioned Christmas as a possibility, but it looks like it'll have to be after that. Ernesto has invited me to visit his parents in Oaxaca for the holidays. (And yes, Mexico's another place I've never been to.) I'm trying not to place too much importance on the trip since we've only been seeing each other for five months. I haven't even broached the subject with Mummy and Daddy. They're still hoping Ernesto is just a phase.

You asked me how I spend my time. A typical day is working in that cute little bookstore in town, then if it's nice out I play tennis with one of the admissions interns. Otherwise, I read before cooking dinner for Ernesto and me. Yes, it's all very *Ozzie and Harriet*, but it's temporary. I have more time than Ernesto, after all.

I'm sorry The Wisenheimer didn't take you to a gay bar in New York. I'm sure you'll find one in Madrid. I want to hear about all the Spanish boys who can't stop flirting with you.

Write to me this very second.

Smooches,

Poppy

∾

SUNDAY, SEPTEMBER 7, 1980   11:00 P.M.

This morning I decided to go to the Parque de Retiro and read Lorca's *Blood Wedding*, which opens next week. I found a bench by the lake, which is overlooked by an equestrian statue of King Alfonso XII atop a semicircular colonnade.

When I heard someone say, "Documentación," I looked up and saw two civil guards like the ones in the airport with their tricornered patent leather hats. If it weren't for their machine guns, they'd have looked like the chorus in a Gilbert and Sullivan production.

The taller of the two repeated the request. Documentation? I told them my passport was in my room. Would he accept a U.S. driver's license?

"El cinturón."

What would they want with my belt? As I was taking it off I realized that I was wearing a money belt filled with bills. I'd gone to the bank on Friday to withdraw 50,000 pesetas. Stone faced, the officer unzipped the belt and started counting. The next thing I knew he was shoving me into the backseat of a van where another civil guard sat behind the wheel. The driver demanded my address and told me I would have to produce my passport when we arrived.

The two escorted me inside the lobby of the pensión. Mr. Good Morning was sitting in his usual chair. A guard explained to him what he wouldn't explain to me: that between my hanging around Retiro Park and the money I was carrying, he suspected I was a drug dealer. Or maybe a prostitute.

"Casey lives here," Mr. Good Morning said. "He's a respectable young man."

The guards stepped back and whispered to each other before they addressed me. They said that they were willing to believe Mr. Good Morning, but ordered me to carry my papers wherever I went.

I thanked Mr. Good Morning and went upstairs to my room where Gustavo was sleeping. I turned on the light and told him what had happened. My Spanish came out all jumbled. I can't remember every single word of our conversation, but I want to at least write down what I *think* we said. I remember things more clearly if I hear people talk, even if the words aren't exact. I'm an actor. I see life in scenes.

"Fuck, Casey." Gustavo reached for his pack of cigarettes on the bedside table. "If they're picking up innocents like you, what are they going to do with a guy like me?"

"They mistook me for a drug dealer." I couldn't find it in me to talk about the prostitute part. "I guess I'll just carry my passport from now on."

"Bullshit," Gustavo said. "You know where you carry your papers? Franco's Spain, that's where. I need to write about this in tomorrow's newsletter at the university."

When he rose from his bed, I tried not to stare at his naked body, compact and tan, short black hair fanning from the center of his chest. He got dressed and walked to his desk. He asked me a lot of questions, taking notes.

"We can't let them get away with this," Gustavo said.

"Please don't use my real name," I said.

"All right."

"Because I'm really not that political."

"That will change, my friend," he said.

~

WEDNESDAY, SEPTEMBER 10, 1980   5:00 A.M.

Gustavo was up all night, writing his piece on my detainment but mostly working on his dissertation. I couldn't sleep. I came down here to the lobby about two hours ago, and nodded off in the chair that Mr. Good Morning uses. I've never seen anyone else sit here, but it's the only chair in the lobby that's cushioned, so I took it, even though the cushions were flattened from his weight.

I thought about writing to Poppy, since I was awake, but I decided not to. I'm feeling a little annoyed with her, even though I know I'm being unfair. She's right that we didn't make firm plans for her coming to Spain, but I was really hoping we would spend Christmas together. One of my first days in Madrid I went searching for an American restaurant so we could have a traditional Christmas dinner.

I suppose it's to be expected that she'd rather be with Ernesto. But for so long the two of us were together, like boyfriend and girlfriend without the sex. At Nearing we did sleep together once and when Poppy told her mother the truth—that we just slept—she believed her daughter immediately and said, "Casey's so harmless." By "harmless" I think she meant not very masculine, wimpy, sexless.

Maybe this should be the year I stop being harmless.

~

Moncloa Underground: Alternative News
from the University of Madrid
More Echoes of Franco, by Gustavo Ibarra
September 10, 1980

Ever since the government of Adolfo Suárez barely survived a vote of confidence last spring, I have been writing about signs of a possible coup. Today I have another story to tell. An acquaintance of mine, a young American who is studying in Madrid, was recently detained by two civil guards in Retiro Park with no justification whatsoever. My friend was put into a van and driven to his boarding house, where fortunately the manager spoke on his behalf. My friend was released, but ordered to carry his passport at all times.

There is no law that requires us to carry documentation in Spain. Whether guards like these are rogue officers or following orders, we are seeing a pattern in Spain, and that pattern has echoes of the Fascist Franco regime. I've said this over and over, but it bears repeating: Our democracy is hardly five years old. It is fragile and we must defend it.

Last week I wrote about a staff writer who was questioned by a guard for simply handing out this newsletter on campus. In August I interviewed Santiago Brouard, Deputy Mayor of Bilbao, who said he was an assassination target because he supports a sovereign Basque Country. I've reported on faculty members in Galicia who face intimidation if they take a hard, anti-Fascist stance. And now my friend, detained for no reason.

Do not be fooled. They can change the names of our streets as a cosmetic erasure of fascism, but Franco's iron hand is still very much with us.

As always, we must be vigilant.

~

Professor Warren C. Stoddard
Pearson Hall, Nearing College
Nearing, Vermont 05251

SEPTEMBER 10, 1980

Dear Casey,

You certainly could not have written at a more inconvenient time. Autumn is extremely busy for those of us on the Nearing faculty, and this year was even more so. Adriana Abato—you remember her, don't you? The Italian professor?—went into labor a month before her due date, and I spent the first few days of the term scrambling to cover her classes until her maternity replacement arrived from Bologna. Then there was the usual madness of the opening weeks of the semester: over-enrollment, under-enrollment, course switching, the late arrival of my introductory Spanish text, meetings about grade inflation, meetings about how best to support the freshmen class. I miss the days when students arrived, we handed them their schedules, and then waited for them to sink or swim. Almost all of them swam. The more we coddle, the more they sink.

Amidst all of this, my mother decided that she could no longer stay at the nursing home I'd found for her. I drove to Burlington last weekend and picked her up. She's now here with me in Nearing and we start the nursing home search all over again next week. I've had to hire a local woman to be with her while I'm at the college.

The one good thing here in Vermont is that it is getting cooler. Autumn is my season. I agree with T. S. Eliot about April being cruel. And summer? Let's just say I've never been one for family clambakes.

In answer to your questions: (1) I haven't spent much time in the Plaza Mayor being serenaded by medieval musical groups. (2) Yes, I imagine Madrid has changed since Franco died. It would only stand to reason that you are finding the city somewhat more liberating than I did.

And with that I shall return to my work. I wish you good luck in all you do this year and beyond.

Yours sincerely,
Prof. Warren C. Stoddard

∼

FRIDAY, SEPTEMBER 12, 1980   8:00 P.M.

Today is the eighth anniversary of my father's death. I decided to spend it alone by taking a long walk around Retiro, where I visited the Palacio de Cristal. It's mostly made of wrought iron and glass, and looks like the most beautiful greenhouse in the world. The few people inside left soon after I arrived, as if cued to exit a stage. I sat cross-legged on the floor and against a low windowsill. I then did what I always do on this day: I cleared my mind to think about my father.

It's easy to romanticize a person from the past, especially when that person is someone like my father. But it's true: everybody loved him. I was invited to everyone's birthday parties because he came with me, along with his guitar. He brought the guitar to the leather tannery too, where he'd play for the guys during lunch breaks. I suspect he grew up thinking he'd be a professional musician, but when my mother got pregnant with me, they married quickly. Gigs around the North Shore couldn't pay the bills.

My father went to Mass every day, but it was the Saturday night folk Mass he looked forward to the most. He'd play and sing with a group of friends, all progressive Catholics. He had to buy a second copy of

Dorothy Day's *Loaves and Fishes* because the binding of the first copy broke. He campaigned for Father Drinan, who like my father opposed the Viet Nam War.

My mother was religious too, but after my father died she left Catholicism and joined an evangelical church whose members were followers of Jerry Falwell. With my father gone, she embraced everything he opposed. It was as if the pain of losing him was so deep that she had to expunge any trace of him from her life.

I know my father would have accepted me if he'd lived long enough to discover I was gay. He might not have understood, but that wouldn't have mattered to him. But without my father, I was left to tell only my mother, which I did three years ago in a letter. I expected yelling and tears and quotes from the Bible. What I got felt worse. She wrote back to me, but didn't acknowledge my news whatsoever. In time, our letters and phone calls grew more and more infrequent. I spent summers doing groundskeeping work at Nearing so I wouldn't have to go home. She came to graduation, waving to me as we approached the stage, then congratulating me after the ceremony, an envelope in hand that contained a card and a check for fifty dollars. I didn't know if the money was a bribe to change my ways and come back to the fold, or severance pay for being let go. Then she abruptly left. She knows I'm in Spain and has the address of the foundation, but doesn't know where I'm living.

Sometimes I imagine the letters my father would have written me if he were still alive. He would have wanted to know everything about living abroad. He might have even saved enough money to visit, or maybe I could have saved some money for him. I can see him now as he says goodbye to my mother at Logan Airport, his lanky body towering over everyone, his guitar hanging off his shoulder, on his way to Madrid.

∿

Dear Professor Stoddard,

Thank you for your letter, which I received after visiting the Prado this morning. What amazed me was the sheer size of the paintings, especially the ones by Velázquez. I'm used to seeing them in books or the slides Professor Lakhensingh (hope I spelled that right) showed us in my art history class at Nearing. And Goya's *El tres de mayo* is even more moving than I expected. I think that's my favorite painting ever. I've heard that *Guernica* will return to Spain now that Franco has died, but I'm not sure when. I hope I'm here when it does.

I'm making steady progress on my research. I went to a play last night called *Asa Nisi Masa*. In the first act, the cast of five played on a jungle gym grunting and screeching. No real words were exchanged. The second act was a repeat of the first, only halfway through the actors took off their clothes, so now there were naked people grunting and screaming and swinging from the jungle gym. I suppose that after years of artistic oppression, you have to let loose. It was just your cup of tea.

I'm off to the theater in an hour or so. Tonight it's Lorca, whose plays (I learned from you) were pretty much verboten during the Franco years. Now he's being revived, as are many playwrights who were banned under Franco.

All best,

Casey

PS: How is your mother?

PPS: I hope this letter has arrived at a more convenient time than the last one did.

∾

SUNDAY, SEPTEMBER 21, 1980   2:00 A.M.

There were only a few guys at dinner tonight. Mr. Good Morning was sitting with a man from London whose name is John but whom everyone calls King Juan Carlos because they think he's as snooty as the King. And he is. He corrects my Spanish even when it doesn't need correcting.

I sat with Gustavo and a blond guy about my age I'd seen around but had never met. (There are so few blond Spaniards. How could I not notice him?) He's an architecture student at the university. He looked dressed for a night out—a collarless shirt with blue and white vertical stripes, tight black jeans, black leather boots with an embossed wingtip design. Sexy as hell.

He introduced himself as Octavio. He'd brought a bottle of red wine that he shared to accompany our fried eggs. Dinner at Marianela is always some sort of egg: omelets, hard boiled eggs, fried eggs and an egg and potato salad mixed with peas called *montaña rusa*. (Why Russian mountain? Maybe it's because the salad is piled very high, and *montaña rusa* is also the Spanish word for roller coaster?) Dolores, an elderly lady with thick ankles who shuffles in her slippers, usually serves us. She always wears a gray uniform with a white collar, and a torn black cardigan even if it's warm.

At dinner Gustavo talked about a protest against Spain joining NATO on Sunday.

"You two should come," he said.

"It's not my thing," Octavio said.

Gustavo waved a dismissive hand. "We didn't wait all these years to get rid of Franco just get in bed with a bunch of fucking imperialists. Spain shouldn't enter any new alliances with the United States. We need to chart our own path."

"I'd rather go dancing tonight and sleep late in the morning," Octavio said. "You want to go dancing, Casey?"

"Sure."

"Come with me tomorrow, Casey," Gustavo said. "Please."

Although I don't completely understand the issues surrounding Spain and NATO, I was touched Gustavo invited me. It felt like a significant moment in our fledgling friendship.

"I can do both," I said, even though I wondered if attending a demonstration would be the sort of thing that could get me in trouble with the Civil Guard. Gustavo finished his wine and eggs and left the dining room.

"Now about that dancing," Octavio said. "There's this new bar in Chueca. And just so you know, only men will be there."

My first gay bar. The only gay bar anywhere near my college was fifty miles away and I didn't have a car.

Dolores, who also works as a maid in the pensión, wheezed as she bent over and balanced our plates perfectly on her arm. I wonder if she has emphysema. When she left, Octavio told me she was pretty deaf. I asked Octavio why Dolores was working at her age. He said she lived here in a basement room for free. If it weren't for Marianela, she'd be out on the street.

I ran upstairs to change into a pair of clean blue jeans and, in an attempt to play the mysterious foreigner, a Nearing College T-shirt. My loafers were no match for Octavio's boots, but they were better than sneakers.

The metro was packed: everyone was going out after dinner. As we got closer to the Chueca stop, I looked at the male passengers, wondering if any of them would be going where we were. A few of them did get off with us, and one of them followed us to a bar called Black & White, on the ground floor of a stone building.

In keeping with the name of the bar, the walls were black, the furniture white. Octavio and I ordered beers, then sat at one of the small white tables. I watched the men, some with their arms around each other, others kissing, and let myself feel at home. Although the name of the bar was Black & White, I felt like I'd just *left* a world of black and white and was now seeing in color. Maybe for the first time.

I didn't look like most of the men, all muscly in their tight tank tops. And hardly anyone was wearing a belt. I excused myself and went into the men's room. I knew I couldn't change looking like a scrawny boy in front of these men, but I could at least look like I had some fashion sense. I unbuckled my belt and put it on top of the toilet tank mounted high on the wall, with a chain dangling that you pulled to flush.

Octavio appeared just as I exited the stall and led me to the dance floor. A silver disco ball spun from the ceiling while a DJ in cutoffs played records. The room was big enough to fit about a hundred guys, some shirtless, revealing torsos so perfect it was hard to believe they were real. The sweat on their chests looked like it had been applied with a spray bottle.

We must have danced half an hour before Octavio signaled us to go back upstairs. He said he had to leave, and that he wasn't returning to the boarding house. I didn't ask why. He walked me to the metro and then went on his way.

I'm back at Marianela. I'm exhausted, but there's no way I can miss Gustavo's demonstration tomorrow.

I'm trying not to think about where Octavio is right now.

Oh. And I forgot my belt at the bar. I'll swing by some night next week.

～

MONDAY, SEPTEMBER 22, 1980   1:30 A.M.

I only slept about three hours last night before the NATO demonstration, so I was in a daze following Gustavo through the Moncloa district to a university basement office. About thirty people—mostly students—were making signs, not just against Spain's participation in NATO and the increase in U.S. military bases in Spain that would follow, but also in support of improved working conditions for miners in Asturias and Galicia. At the end of the room Galician musicians warmed up their flutes and bagpipes and drums. I leaned against the wall feeling like a parishioner who didn't know the words to the opening hymn.

Gustavo thrust a stack of poster board into my arms and told me to write, "Yankees Go Home" in red, white, and blue.

I knew it was the U.S. military that Gustavo wanted to leave, but I couldn't help but think the word "Yankees" included me. I told myself I needed a thicker skin to do this work. I started writing while Gustavo dashed from table to table checking the signs, instructing the protesters to underline a word or make the letters thicker. After a while he whistled through his fingers, unfolded a large hand-drawn map of Moncloa and thumbtacked it to the wall. With a red magic marker he highlighted the route of the march: from the university we'd pick up Calle de la Princesa a few blocks away, then head straight to the Plaza de España and gather in front of the statue of Cervantes. He announced that there were about two hundred people outside, a pretty good crowd considering this was the first march opposing Spain's entry into NATO.

We followed Gustavo to the street and distributed the signs. Everyone started chanting and waving their flags. That's when I started to wake up. Wake up and wonder what the fuck I was doing here. I was sent here to study theater, not protest the Spanish government. The agreement I signed with the foundation must have included a clause about not making political trouble. What if I got arrested? I wanted to be back at Black & White dancing with Octavio.

Gustavo ran up the steps of the university building and cheered us on through a megaphone. He waved for five of the protesters in the front to join him. They unfolded a long white sheet with that read "Bases, out. As well as war," which makes more sense in Spanish because it rhymes: "*Bases, afuera. Así como la guerra.*" Along the perimeter of the sheet the words *NATO N-O!* were repeated in blue lettering. Gustavo encouraged us to yell the slogan, cupping our mouths with both hands.

At first the march to the Plaza de España was more like a celebration. People gathered on their balconies and waved and clapped; others joined us as we walked. At the end of the line the Galician musicians played what sounded like Irish folksongs. Some protestors jumped out of the procession to dance.

Cars started piling up in back of us. Drivers honked. We were louder than the horns for a while, but as the traffic grew, the horns drowned us out. The municipal police arrived in black helmets, brandishing clubs and carrying body-length plastic shields, making them look more like robots than humans. As the chanting switched from rhyming slogans to angry declarations of "NATO No!" the demonstrators became a mob.

I tried to thread my way to the sidewalk, but the mob was closing in. I pushed as hard as I could to get off the street. One woman fell back into another woman's arms. Someone elbowed me in the stomach. It wasn't strength that kept me pushing; it was panic. I stumbled onto the sidewalk just in time to see Gustavo, blood dripping down the side of his face, pushed to the ground by two cops. They handcuffed him behind his back and pulled him up.

I ran toward the back of the crowd, and kept running until I reached the metro to Marianela. On the train I sat next to a young man and woman clutching hands. It looked like one of them was trying to keep the other from leaving, from abandoning the other. Seeing them only made me more aware that I'd behaved like a coward. But what was I supposed to do? Run up to Gustavo and get myself arrested too?

In the lobby of Marianela sat Mr. Good Morning as usual, but today he had an accordion on his knee, serenading as if he were in a Parisian café. It felt like background music to the wrong movie. He nodded and smiled at me, but I whipped by him and went straight to my room. I collapsed on my bed, keeping one foot on the floor to steady me.

It's now after midnight, and I have no idea how Gustavo is. I shouldn't have left. My father wouldn't have left. He would have stayed with his friend.

~

NEARING, VERMONT   SEPTEMBER 16, 1980

Casey, my love—

It really was wonderful hearing from you. I know it sounds nice to be on the Nearing campus with no classes, but if you want to know the truth, I'm bored. I do like working in the bookstore in town, and I get a 50 percent discount on three books every month. Last week I read a new novel called *Housekeeping* by an author I'd never heard of, Marilynne Robinson. It's about a lot of things, but what stood out for me was the idea that sometimes we patch together families that don't always look like the *Leave It to Beaver* sort. It got me thinking about you and me, how I do think we're sort of a family without an official name. Anyway, I loved the book. I don't know if you can find a copy in Madrid, but if you can't, I'll send you mine.

I'm getting anxious about visiting Ernesto's family in December. His mother has been writing me almost daily. She keeps telling me how excited she is to meet Ernesto's novia. Sometimes I think his mother believes we're already engaged. Ernesto assures me that his mother is just a warm, loving woman, who always wanted a daughter. She has doted on any girl he's brought home. He says I should relax.

The foliage and the cool September evenings in Vermont remind me of you, especially our first year at Nearing. Do you remember how we'd walk around campus after leaving the library until one or two in the morning? I wasn't on to you then. I kept hoping some spark would ignite between us, but alas, it was never meant to be. I only hate you a little for that, by the way.

I've been toying with the idea of flying to Madrid from Mexico after Ernesto and I visit his parents. Maybe right after Christmas?

Write to me soon. Or sooner, if you can.

Love you,

Poppy

~

WEDNESDAY, SEPTEMBER 24, 1980   4:00 P.M.

On Monday morning, Gustavo sent a woman to the boarding house to request 50,000 pesetas for his bail. I turned her down, explaining that the foundation had strict rules about how I used the money, and that I was obliged to account for all of it. Gustavo must have found the bail somewhere else because later that day he returned with a row of stitches above his eyebrow.

He was furious that I didn't help him, that I "abandoned the fight," as he said. Yesterday I put a pack of Fortunas—he usually can't afford cigarettes with red tobacco—on his desk, but he never said anything. And after lunch today I invited him for a beer but he said he was too busy. It kills me that we're not talking, but there's not much I can do until he cools off.

I met Octavio late yesterday afternoon at Café Comercial. It's one of the oldest cafés in Madrid and very elegant: marble tabletops, fluted wood columns, huge mirrors, crystal chandeliers. Galdós set a scene of one of his novels there, which to me made the place all the more bohemian. I felt as if I should have worn a beret and smoked a cigarette while talking about surrealism in Spanish literature.

Octavio waved as I entered the café through the revolving door. We embraced. Spanish men hug each other as easily as American men shake hands. I'm still not used to being held this way.

A cigarette was burning in an ashtray on the table.

"You look good in glasses," I said.

"I was up late last night," Octavio said. "I couldn't bear to stick contacts in my eyes."

He ordered us a half-liter of red wine. The waiter, bow-tied and aproned, nodded grimly.

I told him about the demonstration and Gustavo's arrest. I skipped the part about how pissed off Gustavo is at me. Octavio said politics, as well as Gustavo (as hot as he was), bored him.

"I'm going to see a performance of *Fuenteovejuna* at the National Theater tonight," I said. "Want to meet up at Black & White afterwards?"

"I'm booked. And by booked I mean I have an appointment. Shit, why is it so hard for me to tell you? I earn money by being good company to lonely old men, mostly wealthy clients in the Salamanca neighborhood. They're all Fascists, but I ignore their politics. Sometimes they tell their wives they're out of town and we go to a deluxe hotel. I've been in the best hotels in Madrid."

I had no idea what to say. He explained that his work paid his tuition bills. He hoped my knowing he hustled wouldn't get in the way of our friendship. All his friends knew. Even his sister knew.

I asked him what would happen if one of his parents knew.

"I haven't talked to them in years. They washed their hands of me once they found out I was a poofter. I haven't lived with them since I was sixteen. That's when my father caught me jerking off to a magazine photo of Burt Reynolds."

"He threw you out just for that?"

"It was the final piece of evidence. My father suspected I was gay before I was even a teenager. When I was ten, he convinced a bunch of the kids in the neighborhood to beat the shit out of me so I'd toughen up."

I reached across the table to touch his hand, but he withdrew.

"I was pretty disposable. He has seven other children. I'm the youngest. Number eight. That's how I got my name."

I stabbed at a sardine. When the juice dribbled down my chin, Octavio reached across the table and dabbed it dry. I thanked him for being so sweet.

"So, what about you? What's your story, Casey?" He pronounced my name—as he always does—elongating the first syllable as if the "a" were an "i": "Caiiiii—see."

It was hard for me to switch gears from talking about Octavio's life to mine, but I gave him the short version of my family history.

Octavio lifted his glass in a toast. "Such a pity," he said in mock distress. "We're both orphans!"

When we left the café, Octavio set off for his appointment and I went down the street to retrieve the belt I'd forgotten at Black & White. It was an after-work crowd, there for beer and camaraderie.

But in the basement men's room it was all groaning and banging. Standing on the toilet to reach my belt on the tank, I saw two men in the adjacent stall, jeans down to their ankles, one behind the other facing the wall. I'd never seen two guys fucking before. My porn has been limited to *Penthouse Magazine* when on occasion they'll show the butt of some guy engaged in straight sex.

One of the guys flipped his head back and saw me. I grabbed my belt and jumped down; he knocked on the stall.

"Come play with us," he said.

I left the men's room, having no idea what I'd even do if I joined them, and went back to Marianela. I took off my clothes and climbed underneath the blankets. I jerked off envisioning the guys in the men's room, but Octavio's naked image came to me, like an intruder, pushing away the strangers, beckoning me.

∼

MADRID   SEPTEMBER 26, 1980

Dear Poppy,

I'm so happy you might visit around the holidays after all. Let me know when you've decided so I won't make any plans. Not that my life is "crowded with incident," as Mr. Wilde would say. Just thinking about you playing Lady Bracknell at Nearing makes me smile. I'll never forget your entrance and your line to me: "Good afternoon, dear Algernon, I hope you are behaving very well." You said the word "hope" like a hiccup, because idle Algernon was so, well, *hopeless*. That's not to be confused with *harmless*, of course, which I'm working on not being.

I've made the acquaintance of a young man from Valladolid named Octavio. He's extremely cute. He's much more experienced than I am. I hope we'll end up friends, at the very least. He really is *gay*, Poppy, both sexually and in the sense that he doesn't seem to have a worry in the world, despite a childhood right out of Dickens.

I've been seeing lots of shows. A couple of weeks ago, my roommate gave me the name of an expatriate who returned to Madrid from New York once Franco died. She's written a number of books about Spanish politics and works with the Cultural Attaché here. She invited me to a party a week from Saturday. Some actors and playwrights should be there.

How is Ernesto? Sorry to hear you're not very enthusiastic about Christmas in Mexico. I bet Ernesto is right: that's just the way his mother is. Relax. You'll be as diplomatic as Gandhi and everyone in his family will love you.

Love,

Casey

PS: I looked in the English language section of a bookstore here in Madrid, and could not find *Housekeeping*. Would you bring me a copy when you visit?

PPS: I've written this letter to an accordion serenade. The manager here fancies himself a virtuoso.

∾

SUNDAY, OCTOBER 5, 1980   10:00 A.M.

Last night I went to the party of Gustavo's expatriate friend, Elena. I was the first guest to arrive. Elena told me to make myself at home while she tended to the flowers I had brought. An elegant woman in her sixties, she wore a dark blue dress and a cream-colored scarf with pink and red rose petals. Gray hair tucked back behind her ears and her silver hoop earrings. Her face—thin, long—looked like it could never appear completely happy or completely sad, but always at ease.

I looked around the apartment. One wall was covered with photos, including one of Lorca in a bow tie, his hair slicked back and his widow's peak as prominent as ever. The other walls were built-in bookcases with a sliding ladder. Elena had read everything from *In Search of Lost Time* (in French) to *The Family of Pascual Duarte* (in Spanish, of course) to the poetry of Eugenio Montale (in Italian).

Soon the guests arrived, one right after the other, until I was surrounded by about twenty people, many wearing casual shirts and multiple scarves. They were dressed to have fun, while I stood there in my beige pants, white shirt, and tie. I wanted to die.

Gustavo was one of the last to arrive. He'd told me he'd been invited before we stopped speaking to each other, so I wasn't surprised. What did surprise me was when he smiled and gave me a thumbs-up sign right before he flirted with a cute young waitress who passed around tapas: cod on toast, potato tortilla, prawns, ham croquettes, and even octopus, which tasted surprisingly mild and was only a little chewier than a scallop. A man played Granados on the baby grand piano in the corner.

When Elena directed me to Núria Espert, the First Lady of Spanish Theater, I forgot every Spanish word I'd ever learned. I could barely introduce myself. She kissed me on both cheeks. Her skin was like rice paper. She had eyes that make you feel like she was looking into your soul without judgment.

"I'm trying to avoid Lorca's sister-in-law over there," she said. "I'm doing his *Doña Rosita* in the spring and I've heard she thinks I'm too old."

We talked a little about Lorca, his talent for writing great female characters. She invited a man to join our conversation, introducing him as José Luis Gómez, Director of the National Theater, who won an award at Cannes a number of years ago. He asked me to call him by his first name; Núria Espert then asked me to use hers, too.

"I told him I'm avoiding Laura," Núria said.

"Don't believe the rumors," José said. "You're the perfect age for the part."

"José and I have talked a lot about Rosita's age," she said to me. "She's supposed to be in her twenties or early thirties, but that just doesn't seem old enough to be a spinster these days."

"You'll be splendid," José said.

He asked me what kind of theater work I had done. I told him that I'd studied Spanish theater in college and was especially interested in Lope de Vega and Lorca.

"And what about acting?" José asked. "What's your experience on the stage?"

"It's been mostly American and English theater," I said.

He presented me with his card and said it really didn't matter that I hadn't acted in any Spanish theater. He told me to call him in mid-January, when he was holding auditions for *As You Like It*. He was looking for some young actors. I could audition with whatever piece I'd like, even something in English.

"I'm interested in your acting ability," he said, "not your ability to speak Spanish. I want to see what you feel in a role, not how you pronounce every single word. A philosopher once said that people who are truly bilingual don't speak two languages; they have two hearts. Those people are very rare. You should audition where your heart is. Audition in English. I'll understand what you're feeling."

I agreed to call him in January, which feels so far off that I bet he won't even remember me. And even if he's still interested in me after I audition, it'll probably be a walk-on role. But I could never turn down a first-hand look at what the National Theater is doing.

∾

SUNDAY, OCTOBER 12, 1980   7:00 P.M.

I hope I'll be able to concentrate enough to write tonight. Mr. Good Morning is playing his accordion again, this time "Jalousie" over and over. It's like being trapped in the Lawrence Welk Show.

Gustavo is finally talking to me again. The day after the party, he suggested we have a drink, so this afternoon I invited him to the Café Comercial. It was busier than it had been when I'd met Octavio there. We sat across from each other at a small round table. His stitches had been removed, and now there was a thin pink scar above his eyebrow. I ordered us glasses of cognac.

"God, Casey. Couldn't you ask for something more proletarian?"

"I was hoping you'd see this as a peace offering. A new start. I'm sorry if you felt I abandoned you at the protest."

Gustavo lit a cigarette. He apologized for not speaking to me. He was a Spaniard, he said, *and* he was an activist—no wonder his passion could sometimes be explosive.

There would be more anti-NATO demonstrations and he wanted me to march with him again. As an American, I apparently brought credibility to the cause. The others were impressed when I showed up.

I told him I'd think about it, then asked what was going on with him about his arrest. The courts took forever, he said, but the organization had a great lawyer that worked pro bono. He gave Gustavo strict instructions to behave the next time he marched. Better yet, he shouldn't march at all, but for Gustavo that was out of the question.

Then he said (and these were his exact words), "I have to ask you something. What's up with you and Octavio? You do know that he's a fag, right?"

I thought I'd heard wrong. This was the left-wing Socialist who last spring gave his blood, sweat, and tears to support the collective bargaining rights of municipal workers. I tried to think of other words that sounded like *maricón*, the word for fag. The only thing I could come up with was *marisco*, the word for shellfish. I was sure he hadn't called Octavio a shellfish.

"I didn't know," I said, hating myself.

"Because I just want you to know that if you are a fag, I'm not into that."

"Don't worry."

Gustavo did the rest of the talking as we drank our cognac. I just listened because I couldn't bring myself to say the one thing that I should have. I paid our bill and told Gustavo that I wasn't going right back to the pensión. I walked around the corner to Black & White, hoping to see Octavio.

I'd had two glasses of wine before he arrived, a chic leather bag over his shoulder. He came right over to me and kissed me. I ordered Octavio some red wine. I looked at him while he sipped, trying to expunge my guilt with a third glass. He told me about a paper he was writing on Gaudi, whose work, he said, was like Disney on hallucinogens. He suggested we go to Barcelona some weekend and see the Sagrada Familia.

The other night at dinner in the boarding house, Octavio had had a little too much to drink and blurted loudly, "We should fuck sometime" I looked around to make sure no one had heard him, then laughed it off because I thought he didn't mean it. But I did envy the way the word "fuck" came out of his mouth as easily as the word "talk."

Now I took a long sip of wine and said, "Barcelona sounds great. But don't you think it's time we fucked?" I took his hand and led him downstairs and into a stall. I didn't say anything; I just dropped my pants and pushed myself against the wall, fingers splayed. He suggested we shut the door. I told him to leave it open. He liked whatever had gotten into me, he said. When he asked me if I'd ever been fucked before, I told him no.

Octavio went to the sink and lathered up his hands from the soap dispenser. "This should make it less painful," he said, slowly inserting a finger.

I told him it felt great even though it really hurt like hell. But I wanted it to hurt. After my being such a coward with Gustavo, I deserved for it to hurt. Octavio moved his finger in and out; I breathed to his rhythm. When he entered a second finger, I told him I was ready.

But I wasn't. I liked the warmth of Octavio inside me, but I couldn't wait for it to be over. I didn't let on. Gradually the pain turned to a feeling of fullness. When Octavio reached around and stroked me, I sensed the first inklings of pleasure. I came and Octavio pulled out immediately.

"What about you?" I asked.

"Not today," Octavio said, pulling up his pants. "I have to save myself for tonight."

When I cleaned myself there was bright red blood on the toilet paper. I guess even gay men bleed when they lose their virginity. I flushed the toilet paper before Octavio could see the blood.

We went back upstairs and sat. I told him he was a wonderful lover, all the while thinking about the blood.

"You don't have to flatter me," he said. "I hated my first time. It was like I'd had this itch for years that I wanted scratched, but it was scratched way too hard. I waited a long time before I did it again."

"OK. I guess it did hurt a little."

"You gave yourself away when you bit your fist."

In about an hour he had to meet his client who always liked him to bring a present. He'd given Octavio ten thousand pesetas to spend on him however he'd like, but he was running out of ideas. I told him I didn't have a clue what he should buy.

"I'll find something," Octavio said. "Can we do this again in a more romantic setting? Somewhere other than a bathroom? And not at the pensión, either. A friend of mine has an apartment he lets me use once in a while."

We agreed on next Saturday night.

On the way back to the pensión I decided I wanted to have dinner alone in my room, so I bought some bread and some cheese and a bottle of wine, the sort of thing I imagined I might share with Octavio on our date. I'm hoping the wine will keep my mind off what Octavio and his client are doing right now.

∿

Dear Gustavo,

When we were talking about Octavio yesterday afternoon, I misled you. Actually, "misled" is not the right word. I did not tell you the truth. The fact is, I did know about Octavio being gay. It was cowardly of me to pretend otherwise. You should know that I am also gay.

You don't need to worry about me ever making the wrong assumption about you. I would never put either of us in such an awkward position.

Sincerely,

Casey

∿

Dearest Casey—

It was so great to receive your letter and hear about everything going on with you in Spain. I don't think I can keep up with you. I don't know which to ask about first: rubbing elbows with the Madrid glitterati or your love life with Octavio. I guess I'll save the best (and juiciest) for last and start with the party hosted by the expatriate who has returned to Spain.

So, tell me all. Who was there? What did they wear? Did you bring Octavio? I would imagine bringing a man to the party would have made you very chic. You must be surrounded by gay directors and actors over there. Do you have photos? I'm sure you were adorable.

Now to real heart of the matter: Octavio. Are you dating yet? Have you slept with him? What's he look like? Hair colour? I picture him with a moustache. Does he have a moustache? Matinee-idol handsome is what I'm imagining. And the two of you at theatre premieres in tuxedoes dazzling everyone.

Life with me is fine. Well, maybe a little less than fine. Ernesto's mother continues to worry me. A few weeks ago, she asked for my measurements. She wanted to make me something. I thought, there's no real harm in that, right? The other day I received a package from her (her name is Rosa, by the way) and inside was this gorgeous handmade dress, which I loved. But then she said she made one for herself as well. I hope she doesn't expect us to dress as twins for Christmas.

Oh, Casey. I'm starting worry this trip is happening too soon. What am I getting myself into?

Love,

Poppy

PS: How is your accordion-playing serenader these days? Are you dancing the Beer Barrel Polka in the lobby with all your Spanish boyfriends?

∼

Dear Poppy,

Well, Rosa sure sounds like a piece of work. Matching dresses? Maybe she's just frightened of her only son getting married to some gringo. She wants to make sure you two get along so she'll be close to him. I say give her a chance. You're not dating her; you're dating Ernesto.

First the good news. I have been seeing more of Octavio. In fact, I'm going out with him this Saturday night. The only hitch is that he's also dating other men. They're much older than I am, so I try not to see them as competition, even though I am hit with pangs of jealousy now and then. I need to be patient with myself.

Usually we just go to a café called El Comercial. It's filled with old European charm, although the waiters aren't very friendly. The coldness takes some getting used to, especially after the many nights you and I spent in the Miss Nearing Diner chatting with Barbara and Lois on the night shift. Remember our first night there—it must have been three in the morning—when you ordered "two eggs any style" with a completely straight face?

The other day, Gustavo asked me if I knew that Octavio was a *maricón*. I assumed that homosexuality would be no big deal at worst, and another cause to fight for at best. I told him that I *did* know about Octavio and that I was gay as well. This afternoon when I came back from the theater, he'd removed all his stuff from our room. Not a pair of socks in sight. Maybe the manager will just leave me alone and let me have a single. I'm sounding dispassionate about the whole incident, but the truth is, I'm really hurt. I thought Gustavo and I could become good friends.

Elena's party was wonderful. I stayed later than I thought I would. We had cognac and talked about anything and everything: it felt like one of the late-night philosophical discussions you and I had at Nearing after too many glasses of wine. I could have listened to her for hours. Like Gustavo, she thinks a coup attempt is a growing possibility. The economy is tanking, there have been more bombings in the Basque Country, and no one is on Prime Minister Suárez's side.

I have no idea what a coup would even look like, Poppy. If I were you, I'd start giving Mr. Cronkite a visit on the nightly news to see if you'll be living in a dictatorship or a democracy when you come to see me. And by the way, have you chosen your dates yet? I'm keeping the two weeks after Christmas free, not that I'd have any big plans otherwise.

Love,

Casey

PS: Yes, the accordion man plays on . . . and on and on and on.

~

THURSDAY, OCTOBER 23, 1980   8:00 P.M.

On Saturday, Octavio and I had our date at a restaurant called Botín, near the Plaza Mayor. He insisted on paying. It didn't feel right dining off the money he'd made having sex with other men, but the menu was way out of my price range. The restaurant is the oldest in the world, which isn't hard to believe because it's in a cave shaped like the cover of a stagecoach wagon. The description on the menu said that it's been a stopping ground for writers and artists from all over, like John dos Passos, Hemingway, and Fitzgerald. Galdós mentions it in one of his novels. Everything they serve is traditional Spanish cuisine, so I let Octavio order for us. Our entrée was a roast suckling pig that brought me back to my high school days reading *Lord of the Flies.*

I'm not used to long meals, and certainly not used to three-hour meals. Two bottles of wine. Five courses. Aperitifs. Dark espresso. At around midnight, Octavio and I ventured outside. A cab was already waiting for us. Octavio told the driver to head toward Serrano Street, where he'd arranged for a room.

Serrano Street, in the Salamanca neighborhood, is one of the priciest streets in Madrid. In the storefronts were the latest in fashion, home décor, foods, and liqueurs. When we were dropped off, I asked Octavio if we could walk a few minutes first. I told him I was feeling woozy from the wine, which was true, but I also wanted to talk to him before we went to the apartment. I didn't need to know who the apartment belonged to—I'd already figured it was a client's—and I'd filed that fact away in a part of my brain that said "Do Not Open Until Christmas." I wanted to ask Octavio about more basic things, like how the eighth child of a poor family found this world of the wealthy.

Octavio said that once he decided what he needed to do to live in the city, it took only a few weeks. He found out where the closeted rich guys hung out, asked one of them to buy him a drink, and that was it. Word of mouth took care of the rest.

He touched the small of my back and motioned toward the building where the taxi had stopped. I followed him under the green awning of what looked like a presidential palace. In the lobby, Octavio greeted the concierge, an older Moorish-looking man dressed in a blue suit and bowtie.

We rode the elevator to the top floor. We were still kissing when the doors opened in front of the penthouse. The living room was decorated in variations of white. In the dining room hung a photograph of Pope John Paul II. The bedroom was as large as a fancy hotel room. The patchwork quilt didn't make the room feel any cozier. I sat on it just to create some wrinkles.

I pointed to a photo in a silver frame on the dresser. "I guess this is your guy and his wife."

"I wouldn't exactly call him 'my guy.' Maybe I think of you as my guy."

I tried not to take Octavio's comment too much to heart because I knew it would be easy to fall in love with him.

"He's really good looking," I said. "What's his name?"

"Victor," Octavio said. "And his wife is Teresa. I saw her once. The two of them were at a zarzuela I was attending with another client."

"What did you say?"

"Rule #1 of hustling: never acknowledge a client in public."

"I never thought about that."

"You're so green. It's sexy." He then recited the lines of a poem by Lorca:

Green, how I want you green.
Green breezes. Green branches.

The ship out on the sea
and the horse on the mountain.

He led me to the bed. We undressed each other one slow button at
a time. When we were naked, I asked Octavio to just be still: I wanted
to take in his body the way I couldn't at Black & White. I ran my hand
along the stubble of his pubic hair. Apparently his clients liked him
shaved.

I took him in my mouth, flicked my tongue. I repositioned myself
so that he could do the same. I tried to tell him how nice it felt, but I
still had him in my mouth, and the words came out all gargled, like
when you're with the dental hygienist and you answer a question
with instruments in place. It felt good to laugh.

Octavio rolled me over and massaged me: head, neck, shoulders,
back, ass. He tongued me before he entered me; I didn't know people
even did that. He asked me to get on my back. He slid in slowly, and
there was some pain, but then there was less pain, and then the itch
wasn't being scratched too hard, and then it felt very good, then it
felt like he was fucking every part of my body. When I grew warm
inside, I asked him to stay there for a while, not moving, until I said,
"My turn."

I did exactly what Octavio did, and while I'm sure I wasn't anywhere near as good as he was, he held onto the pillows and groaned,
and then we were done. I pulled the quilt over us and slipped my
head under Octavio's arm. We didn't say anything for a while, but then
I did.

"Did you think of Victor?"

"I can separate business from pleasure."

"That's good," I said. "How many clients do you have?"

"Seven."

"Wow. Do you have a favorite?"

"One more time. It's a *job*. I don't have favorites."

I didn't say anything more, and soon Octavio fell asleep. I lowered
my hand as close to his chest as I could get without touching him. I
moved my hand up and down as he breathed, then I kept it still while
he inhaled, and I felt his chest. I let my hand rest there.

I made sure I didn't mention any of Octavio's clients in the morning, not even when I saw a volume of Lorca's poems on Victor's nightstand and wondered if Octavio's recitation last night had been memorized for him and not me. Was the book one of the gifts he'd given to Victor?

We took the subway back. It was Sunday morning; the train was empty.

I haven't talked to Octavio since then. He's been working, and I'm trying not to think about him working.

~

MONDAY, OCTOBER 27, 1980   11:30 P.M.

Today I spent some time in church because it was quiet and I needed to think, and in a country so Catholic, this seemed like the place to do it. (My father would sometimes visit our church on off hours, just to be alone.) I went to the Church of San Manuel and San Benito. It's like nothing I've ever seen. Churches in the United States—or at least Catholic ones on the North Shore—are far less adorned. The outside of St. Pius has a few decorative touches, but the church itself is made of brick. San Manuel and San Benito looks like a cathedral in comparison, with its huge dome and adjacent tower. It feels even bigger inside: my steps echoed as I approached the candles by the altar, its cupola painted sky blue with gold stars. I lit a candle, sat, and thought about what's been going on lately.

Gustavo has returned to our room at the pensión. Mr. Good Morning informed him that there were no other spaces available at Marianela, and that he'd have to wait until January if he wanted a new roommate. So two days after he moved out, he moved back in. We hardly talk. And he behaves differently. He now wears underwear to bed and gets dressed in the bathroom instead of our room. I'm always on guard. All I can do is pretend things are normal and not change my routine. But I'm anxious most of the time he's in the room, as if I'm being followed in a store for shoplifting. I need to constantly tell myself I have nothing to be ashamed of.

But is the same true of my relationship with Octavio? The last thing I expected while living in Spain was to be dating a hustler. Part me wants to embrace our relationship, feel its power, maybe even let its sophistication define me. I want us to be like George Peppard and Audrey Hepburn in *Breakfast at Tiffany's*. Instead, the day after we slept together, I didn't know whether I should send Octavio flowers or a check for his going rate. I didn't give him anything, which I bet was the only gift he wanted.

I looked around me in church. I looked at the magnificent apse, sky blue with its gold border and design. At the enormous Palladian stained-glass windows. At the ivory statue of Christ, calm yet majestic. It struck me as almost unbearably sad that I no longer believed in the Catholic Church, no longer saw the building I was in as a place to ask questions and get answers. I don't know if I would have been able to talk to my father about my lack of faith, although I might not have lost faith if he were still around. I used to believe because he believed. In a way, my religious belief was a belief in him.

A priest appeared at the altar and walked to the wooden booth on the side. He told me he would now hear confessions. I rose from the pew and walked out the door. I had nothing to confess.

~

Moncloa Underground: Alternative News
from the University of Madrid
Reagan's Election Is Good News for Francoists, by Gustavo Ibarra
November 5, 1980

Make no mistake: last night's landslide victory of Ronald Reagan is also a victory for fascism in Spain. Manuel Fragas' Alianza Popular will be more emboldened now. The military knows that the United States will almost certainly close its eyes to any right-wing insurrection.

Consider the current US Ambassador to Spain, Terence Todman, who is pushing our country into an immoral alliance with NATO. As US ambassador to Costa Rica, he closed his eyes to the rule of thugs throughout South America. He has spoken of having patience when it comes to democratizing countries now under military dictatorships. He continues to support aid to countries like Paraguay, despite the brutal regime of General Alfredo Stroessner. Even *The New York*

Times has called some of Todman's words "a direct attack on the State Department's human rights activists."

At least under Carter, Todman met some resistance. When Reagan is sworn in, Todman will have an ally in the White House. Is there any question whose side Reagan and Todman will be on if Spain falls yet again under the rule of the military? Do any of us really think the US will stand firmly on the side of democracy?

My friends, there is a scent of a coup d'état in the air.

∼

Casey, dear—

Your letter was a Godsend, coming after a tremendously long day working at the bookstore. I put it in a box where I'm keeping all your letters from Madrid. Yes, I'll be keeping an eye on the political news coming out of Spain. I know a coup d'état would be horrible for the country, but there'd be something romantic about being there if it should happen, like out of a Hemingway novel, don't you think? Even as I write this I know it sounds silly. It would only be romantic if we knew the coup failed. But that's true of all history, isn't it? We can look back on it sentimentally only because we know we got through it. That is, for those of us who did get through it.

Is there something you're not telling me about your relationship with Octavio? It seems as though he's a real player—the last thing I would ever say about you. I don't think you need to feel bad about being jealous. I'd be jealous if Ernesto slept with other women, no matter how old they were. Try to keep your head above water, if you can.

I'm sorry to hear that Gustavo moved out. It was cowardly and bigoted of him. And you really don't know how the rest of the residents feel about living with a gay man. They could all harbour Gustavo's prejudice even if they seem nice. Forgive me, but I do worry about you. Please be careful.

Oh! I bought my airline tickets and I'll be arriving on December 27 (TWA flight 904) and leaving January 5. Yes, I'll miss New Year's Eve with Ernesto, but I told him that he and I would have many more together. And it's my once in a lifetime opportunity to usher in 1981 in Madrid with you. He seemed okay with it, although he's not the most communicative man I've ever met.

And what the hell is wrong with you Americans? I've never been so proud to be a Canadian as I was last night with Ronald Reagan's trouncing of poor Jimmy Carter. When you return from Spain, you should move to Canada where we at least have Pierre Trudeau. Do you know he met with John and Yoko on their world peace tour? John said that if all politicians were like Trudeau, there would be world peace.

Write to me yesterday.

Poppy

～

SUNDAY, NOVEMBER 16, 1980   6:00 P.M.

Last night Octavio and I went to the Café Comercial for some pre-dinner cocktails, then walked to the Plaza Mayor. It started to rain, a light shower at first but then so hard that it was impossible to stay dry, even with Octavio's umbrella with its chestnut handle and a gold band. (He told me it was English—a Brigg umbrella—given to him by a client.) We ran down a street off the plaza and found Casa Ciriaco. On the walls were mementos of bullfighting and pictures of famous clients, including the philosopher Ortega y Gasset, whose black-and-white photograph hung over our table. I remembered reading him at Nearing but I'd forgotten what his beliefs were so I asked Octavio. He said Ortega y Gasset believed that to remain in the past means to be dead, that we can only understand when we allow ourselves to be surprised and to wonder.

Octavio told me I had to have *pepitoria de gallina*, a hen cooked in sauce with egg and almonds. It's a specialty of the restaurant. We finished the bottle of wine before our meal arrived, so Octavio asked for another. As we were eating, a quartet of medieval musicians entered the restaurant, shaking the water off their long hair like dogs after a swim. Between songs, Octavio leaned into me. He had to leave at 10 on the dot, he said. He couldn't clear his calendar.

37

I sipped some wine, trying to tear myself from a spiraling dread. I wanted to respond as if I weren't surprised or bothered. I wanted to be the mature lover.

"Of course," I said, but the quiver in my voice gave me away.

"I really am sorry. You know you're welcome to come along. Victor loves having two young men with him. I've done it a couple of times before." Octavio nodded toward the photograph of Ortega y Gasset. "Be open to surprise. Think it over while I go to the loo."

I'd fantasized about having sex with a bunch of guys, but the idea of having sex with my lover and an older man and getting *paid* for it? That felt over my head, even cloaked in philosophy. I declined Octavio's offer.

He paid the bill and we went outside. The rain had stopped, and I asked him if I could walk him to Victor's place. We didn't talk much along the way. In front of the apartment building, he gave me a long, slow romantic kiss. I pulled back, afraid someone would notice us. When I asked him if he'd like to go out next weekend, he told me he'd have to check his calendar back at the pensión.

I waved as he entered the building. Octavio greeted the concierge, just as he'd done when the two of us had stayed at Victor's place last weekend. He pushed the elevator button to the penthouse, his back to me.

I didn't want to go home, so I walked to the Gran Vía. Near the Plaza de Cibeles, I came upon a tavern called El Museo del Jamón. The Museum of Ham? I went inside, where pig carcasses hung high along the walls. I ordered a beer and some cheese, even though I wasn't at all hungry.

I've just walked my lover to the apartment where he's having sex with another man. I thought of nothing but that sentence. It made me want to be with Octavio even more. I finished my beer and ran back to Victor's building. The curtains on the top floor were drawn.

I sat on the steps under the awning until the concierge asked me to leave. I walked around the block, stopping again at the apartment building. I couldn't bring myself to go home.

I stayed until the staying became waiting and the waiting became morning.

I hung back, watching Octavio leave the building. I didn't approach him. For now, it was enough just to see him again.

I watched him flag a taxi and ride away.

I don't know what is happening to me.

~

Dear Poppy,

Yes, Americans are crazy for electing Reagan. Even my home state of Massachusetts voted for him, and we were the only ones who supported McGovern in '72. It actually snowed on election night in Madrid, the first snowfall (about ½ an inch) in about ten years. It felt like an omen, although of what I had no idea.

The American Embassy invited Americans in Madrid to watch the returns at a fancy hotel near the Puerta del Sol. Televisions were perched all around the ballroom. The embassy held a straw poll. We voted in makeshift booths as soon as we arrived. They announced Carter the landslide winner (many of the people there were appointed by his administration) before the polls closed in the United States. If only our vote had been a sign of things to come. Well, I guess the landslide was.

The next day on the front page of *El País* (the pro-democracy newspaper founded after Franco's death) was a drawing of the world. Above the United States was the word *REAGAN!* while across Europe, many silhouetted people ran away from North America eastward, some with their hands up. I felt like running with them.

I'm still struggling to figure out what my relationship with Octavio is or should be. He's asked me out again this weekend, and I told him I would go, but I'm feeling more and more uneasy about how casually he dates other men. The easiest thing would be to run away, not let myself become vulnerable, although it may be too late for that. So despite my anxiety, I've decided I'll stay the course to see where Octavio and I are headed. You know that class on New England poets we took at Nearing? My favorite poem we read was by Emily

Dickinson. (Remember that guy who sat in back of me and announced that many of Dickinson's poems could be sung to "The Yellow Rose of Texas"?)

Exaltation is the going
Of an inland soul to sea,—
Past the houses—past the headlands,
Into deep Eternity.

Bred as we among the mountains,
Can the sailor understand
The divine intoxication
Of the first league out from land?

I didn't get the poem the first few times I'd read it, but after a while I finally decided that the poem was about falling in love, or at least the beginning of falling in love. So I expected to feel that "divine intoxication" when I started to fall for a guy. There is that, of course, but it's more complicated. Intoxication, yes. And dread. And jealousy. And not knowing who I am anymore.

In case I don't hear from you before you arrive, I'll be waiting for you at Barajas Airport.

Love,

Casey

PS: How is Professor Stoddard these days?

PPS: I find it endearing that you still spell words the Canadian way (*theatre* and *colour*) even though you went to college in the States.

~

SUNDAY, NOVEMBER 23, 1980   10:00 P.M.

When Poppy and I went out for dinner for my birthday last year, she sent back a bottle of wine. She leaned into me and said, "You know that's not like me, but the wine was so bad that I had to do it." What I didn't say was that sending back the bottle *was* like her. When she was waitlisted for a Caribbean history class at Nearing, she called the professor every day until he let her enroll. And when we took the bus to Toronto for spring break our junior year, she was convinced the taxi driver at the bus station would rip us off by taking a longer route to her house. She gave him block-by-block directions to the Rosedale neighborhood.

Poppy doesn't think of herself as assertive in the same way I don't think of myself as irrational, someone who could fall into an all-consuming, sleep-depriving, what-the-fuck-am-I-doing love. Maybe I'm still not that type of person. But when do I stop being one type of person and become another type of person? Does waiting outside all night for a glimpse of Octavio tip the scales? What about agreeing to spend the night with him and Victor because I knew it would please him and yes, I'll admit it, because being with him under any circumstance feels better than not being with him at all? Sometimes I wonder if I'd be better off with somebody far less experienced, like The Wisenheimer.

We started last night with a campy Spanish movie called *Pepi, Luci, Bom* about a masochistic housewife, a lesbian punk rocker, and a revenge-seeking woman who grows marijuana in her apartment. It was shot in 16mm by a new gay director named Pedro Almodóvar. It gave us a lot to talk about when we grabbed some tapas and drinks. I knew Octavio had to see Victor later in the evening, and I told him I understood, but after we separated on the Gran Vía, I turned around and ran after him and I asked if I could go, too.

He patted me on the back as if I'd just batted in the winning run in a playoff game. As we walked, I asked him if there was anything I needed to know. He said he'd guide me, but that after a while it would all seem natural. I didn't believe him.

He led me into the apartment without knocking, telling me that Victor was already in bed. I realized that the two of them had a routine—something Octavio and I didn't have—and that I was disrupting it. On the dining room table were a bottle of champagne and two glasses. Octavio removed a third from the hutch, placed it on the tray, then carried it into the bedroom.

In the bedroom the lights were dimmed; piano music wafted softly from the stereo in the den.

"I've brought a guest," Octavio said to Victor. The white coverlet was pulled just above his waist. "An American."

Victor and I exchanged greetings. He was as handsome as he was in his photo. Maybe handsome isn't quite the right word. He was distinguished, with his salt and pepper hair, prominent nose, and long face. He motioned toward the tray. Octavio poured champagne for everyone.

When Octavio brought Victor his glass, they kissed. This saddened me: I'd envisioned their evenings as more sexual than affectionate, their naked mingling driven by the sole objective of orgasm. I hadn't prepared myself for tenderness. But there was tenderness last night, mostly between Octavio and Victor, and occasionally between Victor and me, like when, once undressed, I positioned myself to his side, and he simply took my hand in his, as if welcoming me into the family.

Octavio eventually paid attention to me, but I knew he was performing for Victor. All I wanted to do was kiss Octavio, which I did a few times, but mostly I was on the sidelines. From start to finish the encounter lasted about an hour but felt much longer: I half expected to see the sunrise when we were through. Victor fell asleep shortly after we were done. Octavio whispered to me that he was obliged to stay with him until morning. (He might not have used the exact word "obliged," but I wish he had.) I dressed quickly, ran my fingers through my hair in the bathroom mirror, and left at a little after one.

A handful of taxi drivers combed the streets looking for passengers. I thought briefly of going to Black & White, but I decided to take the hour's walk back to Marianela. I wanted to take the city in, to let its outer beauty draw my attention. I wanted to enjoy the surface of things, whatever could be touched and known for sure. I crossed the street to get a better view of the Metropolis Building at the foot of the Gran Vía. Light bathed the façade and the winged goddess atop of a black dome, draped with gold garland. I wanted to stay in that spot forever.

My mind soon circled like a vortex back to Octavio. I tried not to imagine his arms around Victor, the two of them in a spoon position. I wanted that position saved for us, even though he had only held me that way once.

When I returned to Marianela tonight and opened my door, Gustavo swirled the chair from his desk, holding a bottle of wine that he offered me. The gesture wasn't completely unexpected: he'd started to be a little friendlier lately, asking me to accompany him downstairs to dinner, inviting me for a beer in the bar next door. But until the other night we'd never discussed how he'd been for two days. I interpreted his occasional kindness as a tacit acknowledgment of his regret.

As he handed me the bottle, he apologized, telling me he'd discovered that two of the guys he worked with in the anti-NATO movement were lovers. He said they were honorable men, and then, as if he knew I was asking myself why my honorability alone wasn't enough to change his opinion, he said that he believed I was a good man.

"I'll forgive you for leaving the protest if you forgive me for being an asshole," he said.

"Agreed," I said, although I didn't think the comparison was fair.

After a glass of wine he said, "In a way, I really envy you. You can have sex whenever or wherever you want. You're all guys. Guys always want to have sex. So if you're a guy who wants to have sex with another guy, then it's really easy."

I told him it was a little more complicated than that.

I really envy you. I asked myself if I should be grateful for having so many sexual possibilities open to me. I wish I could embrace my luck.

And I'm already worried about a second time with Octavio and Victor: whether I'll do it again, whether I'll be more active if I do, and whether or not I've become one type of person, when I've always believed myself to be someone else.

∽

OAXACA, MEXICO   DECEMBER 5, 1980

Dear Casey,

I'm mailing this letter from the Oaxaca post office special delivery. They tell me it should reach you in two days. God, I hope they're right.

Where do I even start? Ernesto and I flew into Mexico City Monday afternoon and spent the night in a hotel near El Zócalo. The room was next to a noisy elevator, and I didn't get more than three hours' sleep. Ernesto insisted on paying for everything, which not only meant cheap digs, but also a full day's bus ride from Mexico City to Oaxaca that I couldn't bear. On our way to the station I told the cab driver to detour to the airport. I insisted on paying for two airline tickets, which Ernesto didn't like at all, even though I told him they were an early Christmas present. It's not as if he doesn't have the money to splurge. His father owns three hotels in Oaxaca. And his house is nothing to sneeze at, either.

When we got to Oaxaca, neither of us were in the best of moods. On top of it all I had a splitting headache. Ernesto's teenage brother Carlos had decorated the guest room (where I was sleeping alone) with streamers and a huge poster that read, "Welcome, Poppy!" I did my best to appear grateful. I understood how sweet the gesture was, but I just wanted to be alone.

I'd brought some cute gifts from Canada for Ernesto's family: a calendar with scenes of the Rockies, maple syrup cookies, a stuffed moose, a pint of Crown Royal, and a miniature inukshuk (one of those monuments of piled flat stones). I gave them out at dinner, and they were a great hit, especially the moose, which everyone thought was a real hoot. I started to feel settled in. *Phew.*

Well, that feeling didn't last very long. When the next morning Ernesto's mother invited me to Mass, I realized he hadn't told her I was Anglican, even if in name only. I broke the news to Rosa. The split second before she cheerily suggested I meet her *after* Mass and go for a walk, her eyes widened with such heartbreaking disappointment that I almost agreed to convert to Catholicism right then and there. I felt dreadful.

After Mass we strolled around the main plaza, where there was a flea market of sorts. We sat on a bench near a gazebo, and I thought, *This will be okay. Ernesto's family is kind and caring. Rosa and I will work it out.* But then, Casey, *then* I mentioned I'd be leaving two days after Christmas to visit you, and her face fell like an avalanche before she could recover.

Later that afternoon Ernesto and I had a major fight. I asked him if he'd told his family *anything* about me except that I was wife material.

He said something vague, then explained that his mother misinterpreted me at the plaza. He said she thought you were another *boyfriend*, Casey. I really don't believe that. I think the very idea of her son's girlfriend jetting off to a foreign country to spend time with a man put her in a panic. Even if said man is gay, which she obviously doesn't know.

Ernesto's parents heard us arguing, and his father—who up until now had been pretty quiet—sat us down in the living room and tried to negotiate a truce. Of course he had no objectivity whatsoever and bristled at any criticism of his wife. We finally did make peace, but I feel like my every word is scrutinized, my every move assigned a numerical score from a panel of stone-faced Eastern Europe Olympic judges.

Oh, Casey, help me. I cannot do this—any of this. I can't stay here. I can't stay with Ernesto, who is now trying to counter his parents' coldness towards me by doting on me every minute we're alone. He's trying to save our relationship by wrapping me in a blanket of care but the blanket covers me head to toe with no space to breathe. I've decided to leave Oaxaca on Monday and fly to Madrid. So I'm crossing my fingers that the post office was right and that you'll have this letter in two days.

I'll be on Iberia 115 from Mexico City, arriving Tuesday morning at 6:30. I'll be staying at the Reina Victoria, not too far from the Puerta del Sol. I don't expect you to meet me at the airport given this short notice, although I can't imagine a better welcome to Madrid. But please come by the hotel as soon as you can.

I so want to see you. Everything feels so fragile right now except our friendship.

Much love,

P.

∼

MONDAY, DECEMBER 8, 1980   10:00 P.M.

At breakfast Octavio told me he was leaving this afternoon to visit his brother in Valladolid. He'll be gone for three weeks. He waited until the very last minute, right as Dolores was clearing the plates. And he didn't even tell me alone: Mr. Good Morning and snooty King John were at our table. I told him I hoped he'd have a great time, which I guess is really all I have the right to say at this stage of our relationship. I also said that I'd be really busy with my theater project over the next few weeks, going to a lot of openings and preparing my first report for the foundation. This isn't really true. Very few plays open around the holidays and what I need to submit to the foundation is minimal—a summary of expenses and a brief description of what I've been doing in Madrid, no more than a page.

I don't understand why he had to withhold the information until a couple of hours before he left. Or why we haven't had sex or even kissed since our *ménage* with Victor. We didn't even embrace when he left. I don't have his address or telephone number.

Shortly after breakfast, Mr. Good Morning called my name from the bottom of the stairs. When I ran down, he was holding a letter sent special delivery that he'd signed for on my behalf. It was from Poppy, telling me she has decided to fly to Madrid earlier than expected. She and Ernesto aren't getting along at all, but I couldn't tell if they've officially broken up. I do want to see her, but this is sudden. If this were a play, I'd advise the playwright not to immediately follow Octavio's surprise exit with Poppy's dramatic entrance. You have to save something for the second act.

~

WEDNESDAY, DECEMBER 10, 1980   1:15 P.M.

Yesterday morning I took the bus to the airport to greet Poppy. As soon as she came out of the customs door, she looked at me and burst into tears. I'd never seen her cry like that before, her words barely comprehensible, muffled in my shoulder.

"I'm okay," she said when she pulled away from me. "I think I've just been waiting to see you before I had a real meltdown."

We took a taxi to her hotel, a beautiful white stone building with so many windows it almost looked like a glass palace. We followed the bellhop to the room where Poppy and I sat on the edge of the bed.

I asked her if she wanted me to leave so she could rest, but she begged me to stay.

"I am not going to sleep at all until tonight," she said. "Think of something we can do today while I take a shower."

I came up with a mental list of possibilities—Parque de Retiro, the Prado, a stroll down the Gran Vía to the Plaza de España, the Plaza Mayor—then turned on the TV.

"Jesus Christ," I yelled. "Poppy, get in here."

She came up behind me wrapped in a towel.

"That's not possible," Poppy said, as she looked at the screen.

But it was. John Lennon had been shot Monday night in New York City, in front of his apartment building. Yoko was with him. They'd just returned from a record studio when a guy named David something was waiting for him with a pistol. Lennon was pronounced dead on arrival. And a detail that feels like a touch from a Chekhov play: Howard Cosell told the country what happened while broadcasting *Monday Night Football*.

Poppy fell to her bed, burying her head on the pillow. I sat in the chair, face in my hands, pinching the skin along my temples to keep away the grief. I was six years old when The Beatles were on Ed Sullivan for the first time. My father let me stay up beyond my bedtime to watch them. When I went to school the next morning I found out that many of my friends weren't allowed to watch. I remember thinking I had the coolest father in the world.

My father started buying their albums, and he let me play them constantly. I studied the clues of Paul's death. He was barefoot and out of step with the other Beatles on the *Abbey Road* cover. I compared photos of early Paul with photos of the late sixties, trying to find the subtlest difference to verify the rumor that he'd been replaced with his lookalike, a man named William Campbell. I rotated the song "Revolution 9" backwards, listening for the words "turn me on, dead man." I ruined my *Magical Mystery Tour* album by playing "Strawberry Fields Forever" over and over because I'd read that John said "I buried Paul" at the end.

And now John was dead. I poured some coffee for Poppy. I told her we'd take it easy the rest of the day. I ditched my original list of activities and proposed we have lunch and take in a movie later in the afternoon. Carlos Saura's flamenco interpretation of *Blood Wedding* had just opened, and I thought seeing it might be a way for Poppy to forget about Lennon without forgetting she was in Spain.

The movie made me feel better, not because it was uplifting—it was a dark interpretation of a dark play—but because of its artistry. What surprised me was how homoerotic the movie was, especially the dance between the two male leads. Chests puffed out and wearing tight black pants, they performed not just a dance of death but also a dance of Eros.

I tried to explain this to Poppy as we left the theater and walked to the Café Comercial for drinks but I don't think she was listening. I assumed her mind was on Ernesto and John Lennon, but I also wondered if she would have grasped what I was telling her about the homoerotic subtext, even if she'd been paying attention.

In the café, Poppy ordered a bottle of wine. They were playing Beatles records: "Come Together," "Strawberry Fields Forever," and Lennon's "Nobody Loves You (When You're Down and Out)." By the time "With a Little Help from My Friends" played, the café was full. A man near the window stood from his chair and began to sing, encouraging us all to join him in the refrain. Soon others were on their feet, singing *Oh, I get by* . . .

Everyone was silent after the song, the sort of silence that follows a eulogy. We seemed to be waiting for someone to tell us what to do until the music started again. Poppy and I drank more wine. She said that she was glad she'd come to Madrid early. The whole Ernesto situation was a nightmare. She waited until yesterday morning to tell him she was leaving. He wasn't happy, but he didn't seem that surprised, either.

I told her about how Octavio left with little notice and wondered aloud if he'd held off informing me for the same reason Poppy waited to tell Ernesto. He didn't want a scene.

"I think I've fallen for him," I said.

"Give him some time. Give *yourself* some time. He sounds like a speed skater while you're learning how to walk on ice."

"I didn't know how to tell you this," I said, "but his dates with older men aren't really *date* dates."

I looked at my fingers as I explained who these men were. I didn't tell her about my evening with Octavio and Victor; I had the feeling I'd soon regret telling her anything at all. She said that the thought had crossed her mind. After she told me I deserved better, she took a long sip of wine. The silence that followed was our sign to leave.

I walked Poppy to her hotel. We passed through the Puerta del Sol, where a candlelight vigil was being held. She suggested we go to her hotel room. The view would be perfect.

Poppy retrieved her key from the concierge and asked that a bottle of champagne be sent up. Once in her room, she opened the drapes and we looked down at crowd, bigger than I'd imagined. The candles made the Puerta del Sol looked like an illuminated Seurat painting.

"Tuesday in the Square with John," I said.

The hotel waiter rolled in a small cart with a bottle of champagne and two flutes. He poured us each a glass before Poppy signed the bill. When we toasted each other, I detected some flirtation in her voice.

We returned to the window. The crowd was now swaying as everyone sang the *Na-na-na-na-na-na-na* notes of "Hey Jude."

"Do you remember where you were when you first danced to this song?" she asked. "It was great if you liked the guy you were dancing with because it went on forever. But if you were stuck with someone else, then you were really stuck."

I told her I'd never danced to it. I wanted to unsay the words as soon as they came out of my mouth because I thought they sounded like an invitation. Poppy thought so, too.

"You won't be able to say that after tonight." She sipped her champagne before putting her glass down. I did the same.

As we danced, I tried to keep my distance without seeming unfriendly. I really *was* glad Poppy was here. I just didn't want to go down a path I couldn't retreat from.

But eventually I did go down that path. *We* went down that path. It would be easy to put the blame on Poppy, but that would be unfair. Sure, she's the one who initiated the kiss, but I could have broken away.

I could have said I was tired, made an excuse to return to Marianela, but I didn't. It was easier to have sex with her than to miss Octavio and grieve John Lennon.

It's funny how people think that all gay men can't perform sexually with women, because I didn't have a problem. What was missing was desire; what was left was intimacy without the erotic. It was love-making of a strange sort, like a higher level of affectionate conversation. When we finished I found myself wondering if what we'd just done could be enough to make a life together. By the time sunlight was streaming through the window, I had my answer: *Of course not.*

I snuck out of Poppy's room without really sneaking out. I knew she was awake, and she knew I knew she was awake, but I pretended I needed to be quiet as I gathered my clothes and shut the door behind me.

Poppy and I are supposed to meet at the Prado this afternoon. I'm glad we'll be standing in front of paintings and not in front of each other, because I have no idea what I'll say to her.

∿

Sr. José Luis Gómez
Director, Teatro Nacional
Teatro María Guerrero
Tamayo y Baus 4
28004 Madrid

DECEMBER 12, 1980

Dear Casey,

I hope you are enjoying your time in Madrid. I was very glad to meet you at Elena's party in October. I'm holding an informal party on New Year's Day at 18:00. Many of the same people will be there. I hope you can join us.

I also want to confirm the audition dates for *As You Like It.* They will take place on Monday, January 19 and Tuesday, January 20, starting at 15:00. We will meet in the Sala de la Princesa at the Teatro María Guerrero. Kindly call my secretary to make an appointment.

I look forward to hearing from you, and wish you a happy Christmas.

Sincerely yours,

José

~

I went to the communications center today and tried to call Octavio. I had no idea what his number was, so I asked for the phone directory for Valladolid, where his brother lives. I sat at a desk, poring through all the Romeros, and wrote down about fifty telephone numbers. Then I requested a phone, looked at my list, and started to call, asking whoever answered if Octavio was available.

I thought I'd had luck when a woman told me Octavio was in his bedroom and that she would get him. My ears started to pound. When Octavio said hello, it was an elderly voice. I hung up and kept going down the list.

I reached the real Octavio about halfway through the names. This time, the woman who answered said he was right there in the kitchen, and she handed him the phone.

"Hello?" said Octavio, *my* Octavio.

I hung up. I'd been thinking so much about how I was going to get in touch with him, that I'd lost track of why. What was I supposed to say? I scribbled his telephone number and address in Valladolid. Head down, I walked to the cashier to pay my 1,100 pesetas. I left the building feeling like I'd just seen a pornographic movie and everyone who went by me knew.

I wrote Octavio a letter this evening—well, actually three. Each letter felt more desperate, and I willed myself to rip them up before I humiliated myself further by putting them in the mail.

It would be cruel to use Poppy as a confidant for my love life now. Not that she's been making any overt gestures to sleep with me again, but our night together hovers over us, as if one of us received bad medical news that we don't dare discuss. She says things like, "I'm really happy to be here with you." It's not the sort of thing we ever had to say to each other. We just knew it to be so.

∿

Dear Casey,

By now you've probably decided not to see me again after my quick exit from Marianela. All I can say is that I'm sorry. I wanted to tell you earlier, but I just couldn't. The only excuse I have is that all my life I've kept secrets. As a teenager, I kept my sexuality from my family. Now I keep how I pay the rent from pretty much everyone.

I hadn't planned on making money the way I do. When I left home, I came to Madrid and found a job at a supermarket on Bravo Murillo. That went well for a while, until I was accused of taking money from the till that I didn't take. I didn't know what to do after I was fired. I'd been living from paycheck to paycheck. So I did what I had to in order to make money. I grew used to it. I enjoy some of the perks. But I can't do this forever. The Victors of the world will someday replace me with a new model.

There's something else to confess. I'm not an architecture student at the university. I don't head off to classes in the morning and I don't cram for exams like I say I do. There's no degree in my future. I needed to tell the men at Marianela that I did *something* during the day (Señor Buendía has always seemed especially curious), so I told them I was in school. Until now, Casey, I didn't feel the need to tell anyone at the pensión the truth.

I plan to stay at my brother's for Christmas and will then return to Madrid. I'm hoping you'll go on a date with me, just the two of us, no Victor, no work that would take me away.

I miss you. I miss Madrid. I miss going to Black & White and hanging out in the café. I'm ready to leave Valladolid. My brother is okay about me being gay, but his wife isn't. She makes sure I'm never alone with the kids. I guess that's okay. I'm not a great fan of kids anyway, or maybe it's more accurate to say they make me sad. I look at my niece and nephew (four-year-old twins) and I think about how much could go wrong for them, how most of us barely make it to adulthood alive, let alone in one piece emotionally.

I'll sign off now. Hope you and Poppy have a great time together.

Octavio

$\sim$

MADRID   DECEMBER 20, 1980

Dear Octavio,

I'm glad you were honest with me, even if some of what you said was hard to hear. To know that you are not an architecture student makes no difference to me. It's the deception that bothers me. At the same time, I can't imagine what it has been like for you at the pensión, having to maintain your façade. But it's also hard for me to figure what's real about you. When you left every morning carrying books, are you saying it was completely for show? Did you read any of them? You seem to know something about architecture. Did you learn enough to get by in case anyone at Marianela asked you a question?

We all keep secrets. Some are bigger than others; some are more literal than others, like misrepresenting your profession. And sometimes there are good reasons to keep these secrets. I'm going to tell *you* something I've been hiding. Even as I wince at what your response might be, I need to say that I think I've fallen for you. And even now I'm being cautious, trying not to use the word that might scare you away.

Hugs,

Casey

$\sim$

WEDNESDAY, DECEMBER 24, 1980   11:30 P.M.

It strikes me that until now I have lived most of my life afraid. I was taught to live my life afraid. After my father died, my mother was in a constant state of worry, whether it was over a high heating bill, a missed call, my arriving home ten minutes late. But I always got the feeling that none of these things were the cause of her anxiety; they were an excuse for it. My lateness didn't really worry her. She saw it as an opportunity for *me* to worry about *her*. And so I did.

I've been worrying a lot these days. About Octavio. About Poppy.

Poppy and I don't seem to be able to agree on much lately. It doesn't help that I keep fantasizing about being in Valladolid with Octavio, while she is trying to figure out what to do post-Ernesto. She won't write him so much as a postcard, which seems harsh. Maybe I empathize with him, being abandoned like that. Poppy tells me that she'll return to Toronto after her visit here and spend time with her family.

Tonight we ate in the dining room of her hotel. I wasn't in a very Christmas Eve mood. Poppy ordered us cognac after the meal, and we sipped it quietly, pretending to be relaxed in each other's presence. I can't remember a time when I had to think of something to say to Poppy, but that's how the rest of the evening went, until she asked about New Year's plans.

"I want to go to the Puerta del Sol and do the grape thing at midnight," she said.

The "grape thing" is the Spanish tradition of counting the twelve seconds before midnight while you pop grapes into your mouth— one for each month of the year.

I agreed right away. She then talked about wanting to rent a car and drive to Ávila or Toledo on New Year's Day. I wasn't sure how to tell her that José Luis Gómez had invited me to a theater party and that I was hoping that Octavio would have returned by then, and that he might come with me.

When I didn't respond, she suggested I sleep on the idea. We agreed that I would swing by the hotel tomorrow at noon.

~

Professor Warren C. Stoddard
Pearson Hall, Nearing College
Nearing, Vermont 05251

DECEMBER 17, 1980

Dear Casey,

I've enclosed a collection of poetry I've written, hoping that you might give them a careful reading before I send them off to be bound. As I remember, you were an outstanding student of poetry. Didn't you write that excellent paper on the use of vowel sounds in Garcilaso de la Vega's sonnets?

I do completely understand if you are too busy. I also understand that this request comes somewhat out of the blue. I really don't know many people who read Spanish, appreciate poetry, and might understand the nuance of my words.

I wish you a Merry Christmas and a Prosperous New Year.

Yours sincerely,

Prof. Warren Stoddard

~

Dear Professor Stoddard,

Your book of poems arrived on Tuesday, just in time for Christmas. I've already read it cover to cover. I have lots of questions, like why you decided to give yourself a pseudonym. Don't you think this should go out into the world with your real name? I'm aware that writing about matters of the heart makes one very vulnerable. But still, "Leonardo Martín," I hope you get over your reservations. Maybe you could come to Madrid and do a reading?

At the risk of crossing some unspoken boundary between a former student and his professor, I must tell you that these poems rang true to me, especially at this point in my life. The whole notion of changing oneself for the sake of love intrigues me.

I'll end by simply saying that your words spoke deeply to me, and I think they would speak deeply to many others as well.

As for any suggestions, I have none whatsoever. Your manuscript is perfect.

With thanks and appreciation,

Casey

PS: I can't help but feel a little surprised at receiving this, since only a few months ago you told me my letters were a nuisance. But I'm very happy, even if I don't understand.

~

Dear Casey,

I've asked the valet at my hotel to drop this letter off to you. I'm sorry I can't tell you personally that I'm flying home to Toronto today. God, you must think I'm an outrageously horrible human being, skipping town on you the way I left Oaxaca and Ernesto. And on Christmas Day, no less. I hope you'll be able to forgive me.

I'm terribly confused, Casey, and I need some time to figure my life out. I thought that after leaving Ernesto, spending time with you in Madrid would make things better. And in some ways it did. But in other ways it hasn't helped at all. I didn't come to Madrid hoping for a romantic holiday with you. I just wanted to be with you, to spend long evenings talking about everything from politics to books to movies. I wanted to gossip with you. I wanted us to be like we were at Nearing, only in Madrid.

But that didn't happen. We are both at such wrenching times in our lives. I have no idea what to do now that I've left Ernesto. And you and Octavio: I know you love him. I could see every time you talked about him. But I also could tell that you are afraid. I wish you would listen to that fear.

There's been so much on our minds, Casey: Ernesto, Octavio, our unexpected night together, even John Lennon's death. It's like we never had a chance to be our usual selves with each other. I'm leaving because I don't want to spend another night with you trying to fill in silences. I don't want to have another dinner with you imagining Octavio across the table instead of me.

I know you and I will get back on track soon. I will continue to write, and I hope you will as well. Please come to Toronto when you return from Spain.

Love you, Casey—

Poppy

PS: I've asked that valet to deliver Marilynne Robinson's *Housekeeping* with this letter. It's been in my suitcase all this time. I'd completely forgotten about it.

∾

Dear Casey,

Merry Christmas from Valladolid, my friend. I'm hoping you didn't have to spend Christmas Eve alone eating the traditional pork and purple cabbage with Mr. Buendía and King John.

My brother's mother-in-law watched the twins so we could go to Midnight Mass at the cathedral in the center of the city. Felipe assured me that our parents were attending Mass on Christmas morning. They know I'm here, and Felipe says my mother would like to see me, but that my father forbids it. It feels awful when your very presence creates a scandal.

I loved being in the cathedral on Christmas Eve again. It's so gorgeous. You asked me in your letter if I knew anything about architecture at all. Well, I really *do* love studying buildings. Many of those mornings I left Marianela with my arms full of books, I headed to the library and did read about architecture. I guess me telling you I was a student wasn't a complete lie. I'd sit at a long oak table and study the glossy photos of works by Gaudí and Bofill. It's the precision of architecture that I admire, the exactness I find comforting. Maybe that's because my life is such a mess. I still don't consider it out of the question that I could legitimately study architecture someday.

I plan to return to Madrid this weekend. It's a little earlier than I anticipated, but I can see the toll my being here takes on my brother. Having to negotiate the holidays around my father's refusal to speak to me hasn't been easy for him. I thought I'd give him a break so he could enjoy New Year's Eve without worrying about a family blowup.

We will see each other soon, Casey. I have a list of things I want to do when I get back. Will you accompany me?

Hugs to you.

Octavio

~

SATURDAY, DECEMBER 27, 1980   8:00 P.M.

Octavio sent me a letter not once mentioning that I told him I've fallen hard for him. I feel as if I've just proposed marriage and he's responded by shaking my hand. What is the pull that he has over me? The basics of my attraction to Octavio—he's male, he's handsome— are obvious. It's our sexual relationship that's trickier to figure out. I'm not sure if it's sex with Octavio that I like or sex with a man that I like. I suppose it's a little of both, but seeing how inexperienced I am, it's hard to tell where my desire turns into love. Sometimes I lie in bed naked, pretending he's next to me, and I can't tell where my body ends and his begins. This makes no sense because the last time we had sex we were with someone else, and I felt fully apart from him. Octavio's and Victor's bodies were the ones intertwined, the ones that looked inseparable.

There's also something in Octavio's profession—and in me participating in it with Victor for a night—that has felt defiant and, yes, shameful. It's something I've often felt before, but now there's an added touch of danger to it. There's something seductive about this type of shame. There's also something comfortable about it. Once I reached puberty, my mother removed all mirrors from the bathroom except for those that reflected the body above the neck. Then she sat me down and warned me never to look down when I was showering. Never look down? I had all I could do to keep my eyes off the other boys in the gym showers. She instilled such shame in me. But now that I'm many miles and years away from home, who's shaming me now? I wonder if I'm asking for shame so that once I willfully assume it, I can just as willfully cast it off.

I received a surprising gift from Professor Stoddard. He's written a book of love poetry that he plans to publish. I read some of the poems three or four times. He never specifies the gender of the object of his affection. The book is dedicated to a man named Emory, so I'm assuming Stoddard has chosen to come out to me. I'm honored he told me, but puzzled at why he chose to reveal so much of himself to me after his chilly correspondence in the fall.

I haven't done much work on my project over the past few weeks, except for seeing a couple of plays (a sociopolitical drama by Alfonso Sastre and a zarzuela) and doing an interview with the head of a theater company who quickly dismissed me when I told him I had no experience with the "Living Theater" in New York City. I'd never even heard of the Living Theater, although I pretended I had, nodding my head eagerly, wishing to be anywhere but where I was. I was relieved when he ended the interview.

With Octavio's letter and Poppy's departure, Madrid seems new and strange again. When I walked past the statue of Quixote last night, it looked foreign, distant. It no longer comforted me. It didn't help that it was cold and hardly anyone was out. I felt like I was seeing the city the way Stoddard might have seen it when he was last here.

But mostly I've been spending time in my room. Gustavo is away for the holidays until tomorrow. I'd hoped to catch up on some play reading, but whenever I sit down and open a script, I barely make it past the first page without my mind wandering off. Octavio and Poppy. Poppy and Octavio. Octavio and Poppy and Poppy and Octavio and Octavio and Poppy.

I've been so distracted that Mr. Good Morning's Christmas repertoire on the accordion has hardly bothered me.

～

MADRID   DECEMBER 30, 1980

Dear Casey,

I arrived really late tonight. I didn't see a light on in your room so I figured you were asleep. I decided to write this note and slip it under your door for you to read in the morning. I'm happy to be back in Madrid, even happy to be back in Marianela. I'm not quite ready to go back on the Marianela Egg Diet, but I'll get used to it.

I know I never said anything about the most important part of your letter, when you confessed that you had feelings for me. I was touched by your words. I hope you can understand that I don't think one size fits all when it comes to relationships. I'm not talking about my clients. They don't mean anything to me. But we're in Madrid. I want to experience as much as I can here. I want *you* to experience as much as you can.

I've missed you, Casey. I'd like to go to dinners with you. To have great sex with you. But let's not give ourselves to each other completely. Not yet. We're still young.

xoxoxox,
Octavio

~

Dear Casey,

After my disappearing act last week, I won't blame you if you tear this letter to shreds. I really am sorry. I came to Madrid to celebrate the holidays with you, not to ruin them. I wanted to make a graceful exit. I figured you already have enough theatrics in your life. I was trying to avoid a scene.

Have you ever seen the movie *Summertime*? Katherine Hepburn plays a single woman who falls for a married Italian man on a vacation in Rome. She ends up leaving him, but before she does, she says the most heartbreaking thing. I'm going to paraphrase here, but she tells the guy that she's always stayed at parties too long because she didn't know when to leave. "Now, with you, I've grown up," she says. "I think I do know when to." I suppose I didn't want to stay at your party too long. I hope I've grown up a little, knowing when to leave, especially if I feel like I'm at the wrong party.

I didn't fully understand how hard you'd fallen for Octavio until I saw you. His absence seemed to take up all the emotional space you had inside you. I know I was vulnerable anyway, given the breakup with Ernesto (which is official—more later). Our sleeping together the night of John Lennon's death made me even more of a basket case. I don't blame you in the least for that evening. I know I was the one who initiated things. I was needy and lonely. I know we can put the evening behind us, or maybe even look back at it with bemused affection someday, as adults. Lesson learned. Don't sleep with your gay best friend. We both know it's more than that, though. For the first time in our relationship, we weren't there for each other. Well, I guess we were there for each other, but in a way that was all about pretending.

Returning to Toronto has been good for me. I'm feeling less tense, and the past few nights were the first I'd slept soundly without cocktails. Mummy can drive me crazy sometimes, but the control she exerts over the household is in its own way comforting. I'm sure she's relieved at my breaking up with Ernesto, but she isn't saying anything. Why did I ever think that it would work out?

I'm speaking with the owner of a bookstore called The Book Mark tomorrow to see if I can find some part-time work. It's in Etobicoke, which is a hike from Rosedale, but I think I might enjoy getting on the Bloor Street bus just like everyone else going to work.

Now for Ernesto. I called him the day after I returned. I'm not an expert on breakups, but this was pretty painless. I think it was actually more painful for me than for him. He seemed far more wrapped up in applying to grad school than in our relationship. He said he wasn't surprised and that it never would have worked out. "*No hay remedio*," he said, an expression I was only vaguely aware of. Literally it means, "There's no remedy," but I think a more colloquial translation would be, "The damage is done."

Please write to me, Casey. I shudder to think that damage has been done to our friendship. We'll work things out, right?

Love,

Poppy

∼

WEDNESDAY, JANUARY 14, 1981   10:00 A.M.

At his New Year's Day party, José Luis Gómez told me he was looking forward to seeing me audition. I spent last week searching for a good piece (decided on Tom's final monologue from *The Glass Menagerie*), which I now rehearse when Gustavo isn't in the room. My audition slot happens to be the day of Reagan's inauguration. It will be good to have a distraction.

Everyone at the party was talking about politics. They're worried about a coup, which could be either bloody or relatively smooth. I do wonder what might happen to Gustavo if the Fascists should take over. I haven't had much contact with him lately. He's so true to his beliefs that I doubt he'd flee the country and live as an expatriate somewhere.

He's more likely to stay in Spain and be a political prisoner. I'm afraid he'd put his life on the line.

Octavio and I have fucked just once since he returned from his Valladolid, using Victor's apartment again, without Victor. That's it. I never know when to expect to have sex with him. I need more than a guidebook to Spain this year. I need something like *Let's Go: Gay Sex*. I didn't invite him to José's New Year's Day party.

Sunday afternoon Octavio took me to a bullfight. One of the blindfolded horses threw his rider, then galloped full speed across the bullring. Everyone knew he was going to run right into the wall. People screamed, oddly believing they could somehow warn the horse before it was too late. Just before the horse did hit it, the noise died down. I closed my eyes, but even though our seats were on the upper deck, I still heard the horse's thud. He labored to stand for a few seconds, only to collapse. They dragged him out of the bullring. A few minutes later I heard a gunshot.

I wanted to leave after that, but Octavio was energized. I even detected a smile while the horse was galloping toward his death. I asked him why he'd be happy at a time like that and he said it wasn't about the horse getting hurt. It was about the horse being in danger. That's what got his blood flowing.

I told him I thought that was cruel.

"No it isn't. I kept hoping that the horse would slow down or start running in circles. The best kind of danger is when you become absolutely sure that the danger is real, that something bad is going to happen, but then at the last minute—no, at the last *second*—something changes."

The other night, he asked me if I wanted to see a movie, and I told him the truth, that I had a ticket to the theater (a mediocre production of *Evita*). I asked him if he wanted to meet up afterwards, because— and this was only true in the sense that I could make it happen—I was busy all week, giving me hardly any time to see him until Saturday. He agreed, inviting me to his room after the play. We just talked. Sometimes I think he has sex with me just to keep me interested in him. I just don't know why he wants to keep me interested. I doubt I give him the danger he craves.

∿

Dear Poppy,

I'm sorry it has taken me so long to return your letter. I was relieved to receive it, but wasn't sure how to respond. I want to work on our friendship, too. You are right when you say that my mind was on Octavio while you were in Madrid. I wish I could have been a better host. I wish I'd been there for you.

About our sleeping together: We were both lonely and hundreds of people were under our window with candles. Maybe we can acknowledge that we needed to be with each other for that one night. And you're right: what happened *is* more than just that night, but I think it's a good place to start if we want to go back to normal. Let's just move on from that night, okay? I hate that we're not connected like we used to be. I loved the Hepburn quote about never knowing when to leave parties. I only hope you know when to come back to one.

Today I stood in a neighborhood bar watching the presidential inaugural events on one side of the split screen and the hostages exiting an airplane on the other. It was you who told me about the hostage taking in November of our junior year. I was studying for a microeconomics exam in the basement of the Mattison Library. You dragged me to the student union where we watched the news on TV. I want to remember more moments like this with you. I want *you* to tell me when the world changes.

I auditioned for the Director of the National Theater this afternoon, and he offered me a small role in *As You Like It*. My participation would be like an apprenticeship and I'd learn a lot. I'll also be understudying Orlando. I'm nervous, but I accepted the offer right away.

Please write to me soon.

Love,

Casey

~

MONDAY, JANUARY 26, 1981   10:00 A.M.

Mr. Good Morning's accordion is in for repairs again. I suppose I should be grateful for little favors. The other night when I told him that I had gone to a production of *Evita*, he responded by playing "Don't Cry for Me, Argentina." I don't like that song to begin with. On the accordion it sounded like a Muzak version of Muzak.

After dinner last night at Marianela, I tried to get Octavio to talk about us. Everyone except Snooty King John had left. He was over in the corner, sipping cognac that he brings with him to meals.

I told Octavio that his response to the bullfight disturbed me and that I couldn't understand wanting to see an animal in such a panic. He reiterated that he was reacting to the danger he was feeling. He really didn't want the poor horse to die.

I asked him if I was dangerous enough for him. He told me he didn't want danger from me.

"I want Casey," he said.

"Are you saying that's enough for you?"

"I didn't say that. I see the world in bits and pieces. When I go to the theater, I sometimes have a hard time figuring out what's going on. I look at the costumes and think, wow. I look at the scenery and think, wow. I hear the dialogue and think, wow. And then there's the lighting, the actors themselves. But here's the thing: Most of the time the elements don't mesh for me. They never quite fit together like they do for everyone else in the audience. But I'm happy enough keeping them separate."

"So what does that make me in your movie?" I asked. "A prop?" I wanted to suggest that he saw me as Pasha's broken eyeglasses in *Doctor Zhivago*, but I knew he wouldn't get the reference.

"Please stop, Casey."

That ended the conversation. Dolores started collecting our dishes, and Octavio left for a new customer, someone Victor had referred to him.

I don't know how much longer I can feel so unmoored. For now I'll focus on rehearsals for *As You Like It*. I've started learning Orlando's lines already. Like most of Shakespeare's male lovers, he's not that interesting. Octavio would probably say I was typecast.

~

Casey, dear—

I was so very happy to receive your letter. I feel like we're getting back to normal, don't you? Yes, it might take us a while to return completely to our old selves, but it's what we both want, so I don't see why that can't happen.

I have some news about Ernesto. After I returned to Toronto I received a letter from him. I thought we'd already ended things formally over the phone, so I had no idea why he was writing me. I put it on my bureau and stared at it for a good fifteen minutes before I dared pick it up again. Then I held it to the light to see if I could get even the slightest hint about what was in the letter, but to no avail. Finally I just tore it open. The first place I looked was at the end, just to see how he said good-bye. He closed with a simple, "Love, Ernesto." I could feel the relief descend upon me. He did say that my departure had embarrassed him in front of his family. He also said that he wished I had treated his mother with more respect. (I really did do my best.)

He's returned to Nearing and is putting his nose to the grindstone to finish up his honors thesis on the two South American painters. He's spending a lot of time with Prof. Stoddard, helping him get ready for the term. Stoddard's mood improved dramatically over the holidays. Ernesto has no idea why, but we know it can't be love, right? Remember him saying, "Love means nothing and money is everything"? Maybe he inherited some money. Who knows? If I find out anything more, I'll tell you right away.

I'm enjoying my life in Toronto right now. Daddy is helping me with the rent on a one-bedroom just north of Bloor. I'm working in a bookstore again. It has real character, unlike those ubiquitous Barnes and Noble stores you have in the United States. The building is an Ontario cottage, and the owner lives upstairs. The bookstore itself is as it was when people lived in it: a series of rooms, with a small one in the rear, where tea is served from two until four every afternoon.

The people I work with are just darling, although most are older than I am. I should say that *all* are older, since the one man my age was fired yesterday. On Thursday the police raided four of the gay spas in the city and arrested almost 300 men. It sounds brutal. They used axes to bust in, and then beat many of the men. One of the cops supposedly said that it was a shame that the showerheads at the baths weren't hooked up to gas. Can you believe it? There were photos in the paper of men wearing nothing but towels around their waists, some with bloody faces. Anyway, my colleague at work was arrested, so he was fired.

Over the weekend there were protests about the raids along Yonge Street that turned into riots. I could hear the sirens from my apartment. The *Globe and Mail* says that about 3,000 people showed up. Everyone marched to Queen's Park and then tried to break into the Ontario Legislature. This afternoon I had lunch with some girlfriends and no one could talk about anything else. One of them has a gay brother and went with him to the protest. She said that a bunch of guys stood on cars yelling, "More cocks, less cops!" (I'll refrain from criticizing the use of *less* rather than *fewer* and instead ask how this sort of chant gets your average Canadian on your side.) And the bigger crowd shouted, "No more shit! No more shit!" (Not the best slogan for a headline.)

We all agreed that the cops just should have left the gay people alone in their bathhouses, but no one can understand why the gays had to resort to violence at Queen's Park.

I wish you were right here next to me to explain it all.

Please write to me.

Love,

Poppy

~

WEDNESDAY, FEBRUARY 4, 1981   10:00 P.M.

The revival movie theater has been playing *The Graduate* this week, one of those movies everyone assumes you've seen even if, like me, you were too young to get into the theater when it first came out. The Simon and Garfunkel soundtrack made me feel as if I'd already seen the movie. We used to sing their songs in eighth grade music class with Mr. Brennan, who played his accordion on a stool in front of the room. The movie was subtitled instead of dubbed, which I loved. Hearing Dustin Hoffman and Anne Bancroft speak made me want to be back in the United States.

The details of the movie could not have been more foreign to my life. I'm not Jewish, wealthy, or heterosexual. But I can identify with Benjamin's confusion about his future. I'm almost halfway through the fellowship year and have no idea what I'm going to do when I return. Sometimes I'm not even sure what I'm going to do next week.

And then there's the relationship between Benjamin and Mrs. Robinson, which will go nowhere, that can't be counted on, that could end at any minute. The parallels to my life are too striking. I ended up seeing the movie two afternoons in a row. I keep thinking of the last scene, when Benjamin screams Elaine's name at her wedding and she screams back and flees with him on a bus. When they are finally with each other, you have to wonder if they're really happy, if the whole lure of the relationship was not being able to have it. I've been wondering whether I'd be overwhelmed with joy if Octavio yelled my name and pulled me on that bus, or, once we were driving away, I'd see him in a different light. I can't answer, but even the possibility that I might not want to be on that bus with him has helped me feel a little less desperate.

I'm happy that life in Madrid isn't all about Octavio. Rehearsals are taking up a lot of time. I do lots of watching and listening. The actor playing Jacques is remarkable. I hang on his every word, even when he recites the "All the World's a Stage" monologue, which I've heard a thousand times. But he makes it sound fresh each time he says it.

The big political news is the resignation of Prime Minister Suárez. It wasn't unexpected. There's always the possibility that a change in leadership could stabilize things, especially if the new prime minister (who won't be chosen for another few weeks) can crack the astronomical unemployment rate and bring a diplomatic resolution to the Basque separatist conflict. Gustavo says some instability would be a good thing, that it would create real opportunities for change.

Even as I write this, I know how selfish I sound, but with all the instability in my personal life right now, I don't want to deal with any political instability. It's all too much.

~

Professor Warren C. Stoddard
Pearson Hall, Nearing College
Nearing, Vermont 05251

FEBRUARY 7, 1981

Dear Casey,

I was happy to learn that you were in receipt of my collection of poems, which, I'll remind you, only a few people have read. I would like to keep it that way, despite your flattering suggestion that I not publish these poems under a pseudonym. I wasn't certain you'd like them or even understand them, for that matter, but I'm glad I trusted my instincts and that you found them sufficiently moving and well-written. Thank you for your kind remarks.

I am also writing to let you know that I plan to leave Nearing at the end of this academic year. At age sixty-one retirement is premature, but I've been at Nearing for over thirty years. Enough is enough. A new dean arrived at the college in the fall with grandiose plans that have thus far turned out to be so much fanfaronade. He was the language department chair at Dartmouth where he was a fan of John Rassias, whose method of teaching language has become the latest educational fad. The literature says that his method "teaches the soul, not just the intellect" and that its practitioners use "choreographed drills" to reinforce language patterns. Right up my alley, wouldn't you say? When Dean Aldrich explained that he wanted to introduce this method to Nearing, it was for me the proverbial straw that broke the camel's back.

My mother died in November, two months after I'd moved her into a new nursing home. While I was saddened, I also recognized that her death has freed me up to do whatever I'd like after retirement. I have tentative plans to relocate to Boston where my friend Emory lives. If I remember correctly, you are originally from that area as well.

It's been dreadfully cold this winter in Vermont. I don't mind, however. Temperamentally I'm much better at bundling up than I am at wearing polo shirts and shorts.

Yours sincerely,
Warren Stoddard

~

John Lennon has been dead for almost two months, but I can hear him everywhere. Saturday night Octavio and I went to Black & White, and they played a whole set of Lennon songs, from "Starting Over" to "Whatever Gets You Thru the Night," even though you really can't dance to them. After about fifteen minutes the guys got restless and started chanting "disco, disco, disco." It felt like the musical version of Gustavo's protest marches.

Octavio and I didn't stay out very late. He had an appointment with a new client near the Paseo de Recletos, so he took a taxi and I took the metro back to Marianela. As we hugged, a rush of anger hit me by surprise. How screwed up was this? I get the date with Octavio while some old guy gets the sex?

We could have spent the night together because Gustavo's in Valencia for a few weeks making plans with a group to oppose a possible Fascist takeover. Before he left, he gave me his number there in case I ever wanted to call. I was touched by this unexpected gesture.

I've liked having the room to myself these past days. It's given me the space to go over my blocking for *As You Like It*. By the time Gustavo returns at the end of the month, we'll be in dress rehearsal, so his timing has been perfect.

The production is going to be dark. José has set the play during World War II during Hitler's rise. We saw the costume sketches for the first act during our read-through, and they are mostly black, gray, and silver. It's a very militaristic look.

After rehearsals we usually head to a local bar for drinks and some tapas. Everyone goes. There's none of the hierarchy that exists in theater in the United States, where the line between the stars and the minor players is clear. We really are an ensemble.

The other night I saw a play called *Crazy for Democracy* that lampooned post-Franco Spain with skits and music. It was terrible, but the theater was packed. It was frightening.

It's time for dinner (more eggs) downstairs. Then I hope to go to bed early because I have to be at the theater at 9:00 tomorrow morning for costume fitting.

~

FRIDAY, FEBRUARY 13, 1981   9:00 P.M.

Suárez's resignation last month hasn't stabilized the politics here. On Tuesday a politician named Calvo Sotelo was named a candidate for prime minister. (The guys at Marianela call him "Calvo Sin Pelo," which means "Bald Without Hair," which he is.) He represents the right wing, although he isn't a member of the Falange, the really far right party that supports a return to the Franco years. At first some thought that Sotelo's candidacy would satisfy the Falangists, but that doesn't seem to be the case.

A member of the Basque separatist group ETA was tortured and killed by the government in Carabancal. There's now a general strike in the Basque region. The government has tried to calm things by firing a number of police chiefs, but that has only led to some resignations in the Interior Ministry, in support of those who tortured José Ignacio Arregui. A right-wing newspaper has called the firing of the police chiefs an act of weakness on the part of the government that must be stopped.

I find myself missing Gustavo during all of this. I wish he'd get back from Valencia so I could talk to him. The guys talk about politics at Marianela, but they usually don't let on whose side they support. I know where Gustavo stands, which is becoming more and more where I stand. I knew politics would play a role in my study of the theater when I accepted this grant, but didn't expect to be this emotionally engaged.

Sometimes I feel Spanish politics is beginning to push Octavio out of my affections, like a second lover. He himself couldn't care less what happens. It's maddening—but also a relief to be critical of him. It makes my attraction to him feel less obsessive than it was only two months ago, when I waited all night outside Victor's apartment for him, or when I went through a phone book calling everyone with his name. I'm glad those days are gone. At least I hope they're gone.

~

Dear Poppy,

Thanks for your letter—I got it last week. I planned to write back to you immediately, but time slipped by. I'm rehearsing about eight hours a day, because as an understudy I need to attend all rehearsals, taking notes on every gesture and movement of the actor playing the role. This is the first time I've felt connected to a community in Madrid. I really don't fit in with the guys at Marianela, unless you count Octavio. Actually, you should scratch that. I don't fit in with Octavio these days.

We go out only now and then, and have sex even less than that. He's always "saving himself" for his clients, or is exhausted or—and this is the reason that gets to me most—he wants to keep our (ever diminishing) sex life fresh. He tells me he doesn't want us to get bored with each other, but what he really means is that he's getting bored with me. I no longer wait up for him, hoping he'll knock on my door, so maybe I've begun to wrestle free from the hold he has on me.

I was horrified to hear what's been happening to gay men in Toronto. I always thought of Canada as far more accepting than the United States, which doesn't seem to learn from its mistakes until it's too late. I'm glad the men in the bathhouse pushed back, even if it did involve some violence at Queen's Park. You said that you didn't think the storming of Parliament was doing anything to help our cause, and I might have agreed with you before I arrived in Spain. But I've learned from Gustavo that sometimes you have to fight fire with fire. I don't think it's fair to judge these guys. They are responding to police brutality, not instigating it. The police invaded their private space, bloodying their noses and pulling them naked out into the street on a February night.

And on that cheery note I'll say goodbye and await your next letter. Tell me about the bookstore, about any more demonstrations regarding the raid, about any new boyfriends. Tell me everything, just like you used to do.

Love,
Casey

~

We are living in the middle of a coup attempt, right now, as I write. Late this afternoon, about 200 civil guards and soldiers stormed the Spanish Parliament and began shooting. A Francoist named Antonio Tejero led the charge, taking over the podium in the middle of the formal vote for the new prime minister. About 350 members of parliament are now being held hostage. No one at Marianela owns a TV, so we've been listening to the radio all night in the lobby.

The Francoists have announced the formation of a new government in Valencia, where military tanks are patrolling the streets. I worry about Gustavo being there. If the military decides to track down those they believe are dissidents, I'm sure he'll be on a list. One of the leftist guys at Marianela—a student of comparative literature at the university—has already packed his bags and plans to flee to Portugal with his brother, who is driving down from Zaragoza.

I now know there's at least one Fascist among us: Mr. Good Morning can't seem to hide his glee at the coup. Around 8:00 he started singing "Marcha Real," the national anthem of Spain, while playing his accordion. He sang along until Antonio, a paunchy man from the Canary Islands who works for the telephone company, lunged toward him, ripping the accordion from his arms and throwing it on the floor. "Enough!" he yelled. "Enough of that Fascist bullshit!"

Antonio explained to me that for most of its existence, the anthem hasn't had any official lyrics, but Franco introduced his own at the end of the Civil War. That's what Mr. Good Morning was singing. When Franco died, the government returned to the anthem without words.

Octavio has shown so little interest in the coup that I'm wondering if he might be sympathetic to the Francoists. I know some of his clients are Fascists. But he gave me the impression that he simply put up with their political leanings. What if it's something more than that? Now the very idea that I might have been the lover of a Fascist makes my stomach turn. I don't think I can ever sleep with him again. Maybe a crisis can help clarify things. I'd rather it not be such a costly one, though.

I'll go back downstairs now. King Juan Carlos II (the real King, not the snooty American) is supposed to address the country tonight, but no one is certain what he'll say. I hadn't realized that even though he supports a democratic government in Spain, he was actually a protégé of Franco's when he was a young man. That makes some people nervous about his speech.

~

TUESDAY, FEBRUARY 24, 1981   8:00 A.M.

Rafa, the owner of the small bar next door, opened up around 11:30 last night so we could watch King Juan Carlos address the nation on his black-and-white TV. Guys stood or sat at tables in small groups, smoking and talking low, shaking their heads. Rafa had taken out some checkerboards and Parcheesi boards, to take our mind off things while we waited, but no one wanted to play.

When King Juan Carlos finally came on at 1:15 this morning, he was in full military regalia. I didn't know if he was nodding to the military insurgents or trying to reinforce his role as Head of the Armed Forces to try to stop the coup. His speech lasted little more than a minute, but the intent was clear: he was on the side of the democracy, and vowed to resist. I was waiting for everyone to cheer, but people were still too tense. No one was certain if the military would follow the King's orders. I don't think we'll feel safe until Tejero is arrested.

After the announcement we all had one last drink and then Rafa told us he was closing. I returned to Marianela and slept from three this morning until about six. I thought about Gustavo as soon as I woke up. If I don't hear from him soon, I'll go to the communications center and call.

On my way out to get the newspaper this morning, I saw Antonio from the Canary Islands—the one who had smashed Mr. Good Morning's accordion—with two suitcases. He told me that Mr. Good Morning informed him that as manager of Marianela, he had the right to terminate any agreement with any resident. I told Antonio how sorry I was.

"Who cares?" he said. "As if I wanted to stay in this Fascist boarding house any longer."

"I hate Señor Buendía," I said.

I really meant it.

∾

Moncloa Underground: Alternative News
from the University of Madrid
The King's Speech
Special Edition, February 24, 1981

I address the Spanish people with brevity and concision:

In the face of the exceptional circumstances we are living under right now, I ask for your calmness and trust, and I hereby inform you that I have given the Captains General of the Army, the Navy, and the Air Force the following order:

Given the events taking place in the Palace of Congress, and to avoid any possible confusion, I hereby confirm that I have ordered the Civil Authorities and the Joint Chiefs of Staff to take any and all necessary measures to uphold constitutional order within the limits of the law.

Any measure of a military nature that needs to be taken must be approved by the Joint Chiefs of Staff.

The Crown, symbol of the nation's permanence and unity, will not tolerate, in any way whatsoever, the actions or behavior of anyone attempting, through use of force, to interrupt the democratic process of the Constitution, which the Spanish People approved by vote in referendum.

∾

The coup attempt has ended and so has my relationship with Octavio. It's official.

Tejero called the coup off this afternoon, after many of his henchmen abandoned the cause. There are no longer tanks in Valencia, but I still don't know if anything has happened to Gustavo.

We now have a clearer idea of what went on inside the Congress of Deputies. The insurgents forgot to turn off one of the television cameras when they burst in, so much of the attempt was recorded. We all went back to the bar earlier this evening to watch the video of General Tejero, in his patent-leather tricornered hat and push-broom moustache, standing in front of the Spanish Parliament, waving his gun like a child who'd been given his first military toy.

Tejero then starts shooting wildly at the ceiling, commanding everyone to get on the floor "in the name of the King." Everyone obeys except Prime Minister Adolfo Suárez, who calmly folds his arms across his chest in defiance. It's the bravest act I've ever witnessed. He just sits there, arms crossed. It's an image I'm sure my father would have loved.

Before dinner tonight I asked Octavio if he would meet me in my room so I could talk to him. He sat on Gustavo's bed and I sat on mine. He lit a cigarette. I'd planned what I was going to say: *How could you be so nonchalant in the face of your country falling back into the hands of a dictator? Don't you know what that would mean for people like you and me?*

What I said was, "Fuck you."

He thought I was playing a game, because he couldn't stop smirking. He put down his cigarette, pressed his lips together, twisted his finger around a lock of hair.

"What do you mean, Casey?" His smirk turned into a smile. He joined me on my bed, put his hand on my leg.

I don't know if what I said after that made any sense to him. It hardly made sense to me. I tried to explain that the last twenty-four hours were eye-opening for me and that it was impossible for me to understand his indifference in the face of what had happened.

Octavio blew into his cupped hands as he thought about a response. Then he flicked his tongue to the back of his mouth, pushing it against his cheek as if trying to dislodge an annoying bit of food.

"You think my clients are going to let anything happen to me once it's even harder to find men to fuck? I wouldn't be surprised if things got *better* for me if the Fascists take over. Men would be afraid to meet other men at cafés or in the parks. I'd be their only hope."

Mr. Good Morning started playing the accordion downstairs, with a few missing notes. It wasn't the national anthem, but "Jalousie," his unfortunate signature song. I'd have thought that the music might have made me feel like things were getting back to normal, but it had the opposite effect. Octavio's words sounded all the more callous as Mr. Good Morning played. I could feel myself withdrawing from him even though part of me was resisting, like when you realize you've just caught a cold but instinctively do everything to fight it.

"Make love to me," Octavio said, moving his hand to my thigh.

Not fuck me. *Make love to me.* Words he thought would bring down my guard. And they almost did. For a moment, I contemplated reciprocating his touch, but I found it in me to lift his hand off me instead. Something else seemed to lift from me as well. My breathing eased.

I told Octavio to leave.

Right now, I don't feel as lonely as I would have imagined, although I'm sure that will come in due time.

∾

Dear Casey,

The newspaper is filled with stories about the spectacle in Spain right now, and I'm worried about you. I know I'm overreacting when I picture you in handcuffs, being carted off by those horrible civil guards who almost arrested you in the park because you weren't carrying your passport. But I'm sure your theatre project is just the sort of thing that threatens the Fascists. I'm sending this special delivery so you can let me know as soon as you can that you're all right.

There is *some* news other than the spectacle in Madrid. The raid on the bathhouses is still a hot issue here. It has galvanized the homosexual community. There have been meetings attended by hundreds of men who want an investigation into police behavior. They're calling the cops the Gestapo for wielding crowbars and clubs, dragging men out into the street before they could even put a stitch of clothing on. On CBC last week a man said that his parents had spent time in a concentration camp in Nazi Germany. After the raids, he said, he knew how they felt when they were prodded like cattle into a death train. I think he went too far by comparing the raids to the Holocaust. That sort of language turns off people who otherwise might be sympathetic. But the raids have tapped into a well of anger. Some are saying we're witnessing the beginning of a movement.

Please write immediately to let me know you are safe.

Love,

Poppy

~

If nothing else happens during my year in Spain, today alone would have been worth the trip. This afternoon a pro-democracy demonstration was held in front of the Congress of Deputies. I joined a group at the Puerta de Alcalá behind an enormous banner that read "Liberty, Democracy and the Constitution." This march felt different from the one I attended with Gustavo last fall, which was made up of mostly students in jeans and T-shirts with political messages. Today there were lots of people my age, but there also men in suits, elderly Civil War widows in black, parents with baby strollers.

When we reached the Parliament steps, I could barely see the stage that had been assembled. The crowd trickled down the side streets off the square. One of the journalists announced that over a million people had showed up.

At first, standing in the middle of so many people felt claustrophobic. But when I listened to the speakers rallying and the crowd cheering, claustrophobia gave way to a feeling of liberation. And it wasn't just the march for democracy that moved me. I thought of the protesters Poppy had written about in Toronto. I decided I was also marching for them.

I thought about how excited Gustavo would have been to see so many people taking to the streets. After the demonstration, I threaded my way through the dispersing crowd and walked to the communications center with Gustavo's number. When a woman answered, I asked her if she knew where he was. I told her I was Gustavo's roommate. "He's in the hospital," she said. She gave me the number.

I called right away and blurted, "It's me. Casey. Are you all right?"

He sounded pleased to hear from me. He explained calmly (I wondered if he was on medication) that there'd been an incident the night of the coup and that he'd been hurt. An eye injury. He didn't want to go into detail but said he was expecting to be discharged soon. He'd return to Madrid in a few days.

I'm trying my best to believe him.

$\sim$

Dear Poppy,

Please relax. I am fine. But Madrid has been tense. The first few days after the coup attempt, drivers honked their horns at the least provocation. I bumped into an older man on the metro and from the look he gave me, you'd have thought I put a gun to his back. Yesterday morning at breakfast one of the guys at Marianela walked into the dining room and yelled, "Get down on the floor!"—what General Tejero had said when he and his henchmen stormed the Parliament. It was meant as a joke, but it didn't go over well. One of the university students chewed him out.

But I've also felt calm slowly descend on Madrid. Yes, people are anxious, edgy, agitated. But I do believe there's an awkward relief that has started to seep into us, that relief you get when you receive bad news then slowly realize it isn't the worst news possible.

We had a rehearsal on Sunday, hours before the coup was officially called off. José Luis Gómez said there was no way some renegade civil guards were going to force Spanish artists back into the closet. We ran the first act yesterday, and I felt like there was a pall over every line, every movement. Duke Frederick now has a push-broom moustache, just like General Tejero's.

Thanks for the update about the Toronto raids. I find myself wishing I were there at the protests and the meetings. If nothing else, I think my year in Spain is allowing me to see myself as a player in some bigger scheme—this is vague, I know, but I'm not quite sure how to phrase it yet. I guess I just feel something boiling inside me, even if I don't know exactly what it is. Yesterday I went to a pro-democracy rally where a million people showed up.

Gustavo has taught me that political movements, if they are to be successful, sometimes have to go to extremes to get people's attention. So comparing the bathhouse raids to the Holocaust might not be as crazy as you think. I'm not even sure it's that far-fetched. When you described naked men being lined up by police, I couldn't help but think of concentration camp detainees lined up the same way.

Octavio and I have split up, if we ever were in fact together. It all came to a head the night of the coup attempt. We haven't talked since then. We avoid each other at dinner, which means I eat way too many meals with Mr. Good Morning and snooty King John.

I'll end now and put this in the mail special delivery, so you can stop picturing me in a jail cell being tortured by the Fascists.

Love,
Casey

∾

As You Like It
Presented by the National Theater of Spain
Director's Notes by José Luis Gómez

I so vividly remember the first time I saw a play by Shakespeare. I was a young man from Huelva, spending a summer here in Madrid. I took acting classes and devoured every piece of theater I could afford. On the night before returning home, I waited in line for a standing-room-only ticket at this very theater. The play was *As You Like It*.

The play was presented as a fairy tale. The duchy where the play begins was almost comically evil; the Forest of Arden, where the leading characters flee, could not have been more idyllic. The only real complications had to do with mistaken identities. Love wins easily in the end. The audience went home happy.

I came to understand that this version of *As You Like It* was a reflection of its time. Under the weight of Franco's censorship laws, there was little room to explore the injustice of Duke Frederick usurping the position of his older brother. Nor did this production dwell on the deep injustice Orlando faces from *his* brother. Theater at that time was not a place to consider politics, unless to support the dictatorship.

Many of us have feared a return to fascism for some time, which is why, many months ago, I chose to set *As You Like It* right before the Nazi occupation of France during World War II. I need not dwell on the parallels between our version of the play and our present political climate. My vision for the play has sadly proven all too prescient.

I write these notes shortly after our democracy, restored a mere five years ago, was threatened by Fascist civil guards. This is the same military body that assassinated García Lorca, our greatest twentieth-century playwright, whose work we presented in this very theater only weeks ago. As artists and supporters of the arts, we must stand in solidarity against the forces that would rob us of our democracy. During the Franco era, some of the riskier productions didn't list a director on the program. The cast took all responsibility collectively, in order to keep the regime from imprisoning individual artists. We must remember how we once found strength as one voice because, sadly, we need to speak in that one voice again. We must do this in memory of Lorca.

Thank you for joining us.

~

WEDNESDAY, MARCH 4, 1981   1:00 P.M.

As You Like It opened last night to a full house and ended with a standing ovation. It was hard to tell whether it was the quality of the show or José Luis Gómez's anti-Fascist interpretation that made the audience rise to their feet. Maybe it was both, and people stood because they were moved by both the artistry and the message. People gasped at the sight of mustachioed Duke Frederick. A few people even hissed.

Gustavo came back from Valencia in time to be there. He loved every anti-Fascist minute of the play. Before the show, he handed me a package. Inside was a leather-bound and gold-embossed edition of Shakespeare's sonnets in Spanish.

I opened the book and read his inscription:

But if the while I think on thee, dear friend,
All losses are restored and sorrows end.
Sonnet 30, lines 13–14

I remembered a word I'd learned from the mother of The Wisenheimer, my freshman roommate. Whenever his parents drove up from New York City, they'd invite me to dinner with them. Mrs. Bergen bought me notebooks with the Nearing insignia on the cover, sent me birthday, Valentine's Day, and Christmas cards. In May, when I presented Mrs. Bergen with a bouquet of flowers, she held the flowers against her breast, smelled them and said, "I am *verklempt*," the perfect word for what I felt when I opened Gustavo's gift.

This morning Gustavo gave me details about what had landed him in the hospital. He and some of his cohort took to the streets as soon as the tanks started rolling in Valencia. They stood in front of one of them, defying the driver to run them down. When some pro-Fascists saw Gustavo and his friends, they started hurling anything they could get their hands on: bottles, garbage cans, oranges from a nearby tree, and rocks, one of them sharp enough to cut through Gustavo's eyelid and slice his eye. His retina detached from the impact. The doctors operated, but they weren't completely successful. Gustavo is now partially blind in his left eye.

He doesn't seem bothered by the effects of the injury. At times he's even poetic about it. He says what happened to him is what happens to a country before a dictatorship takes over: the Fascists blind you with propaganda, and everyone walks around not knowing everyone else has been blinded. Paranoia sets in that the Fascists then exploit. Sometimes he wishes he'd lost an arm or a hand, because that way people would be able to see what the Fascists did to him.

Between the politics here in Spain and Poppy's reports of the demonstrations in Toronto, I'm fired up, but not as much as Gustavo. Sometimes I envy him, believing in a cause so deeply that he'd willingly risk physical harm to defend it. I envy the comfort of knowing something to be so true that not much else matters.

~

Dear Casey,

Thanks for letting me know that you're all right. I hadn't read anything about violence in Madrid, so my fears weren't rational, but I still worried about you. Maybe that's a good thing, a sign that we're back into our old friendship and that my trip to Madrid is behind us.

I'm learning more about the bathhouse raids, which the police have labeled "Operation Soap." People aren't letting the issue die. A minister at the Metropolitan Community Church is on a twenty-five-day hunger strike. Yesterday Margaret Atwood spoke at a "Gay Freedom Rally." She was moving and hilarious. One thing she said was, "So they raided the bathhouses. What do the Toronto police have against cleanliness?" She spoke not only about the bathhouse raids, but also about the raid of a gay newspaper in Toronto. The police took lists of subscribers and advertisers from the office.

I arrived late to the rally because I had to work, so I stood in the back of thousands of protesters. It didn't matter. Everyone was so galvanized that I *felt* I was in the first row. It was electric. I wish you could have been there. We didn't have the million you had at the demonstration in Madrid, but the energy felt like that of a million people.

Sorry you and Octavio split up, but it sounds like you already know it's for the best. I bet he was easy on the eye, as my freshman roommate from Georgia used to say. But you know, when you start looking for someone to spend your life with, looks and sexiness are only a start. You need more than that to go the distance. I'm beginning to realize that there's a huge difference between intensity and strength when it comes to relationships. I think Ernesto and I had an intense relationship, which got us through six or so months, but we didn't have the strength for the long haul.

I think you and I have that strength. We're family, right? I sometimes wildly imagine that we could even adopt a child together. I think we'd be great parents. I'm not suggesting that you might ever be attracted to me sexually. What I am suggesting is that what we have might very well be stronger than sexual attraction. I'm probably not making any sense. Ugh. Why do you have to be an ocean away? I want you right here in Toronto so we can talk.

Please write to me asap. Let me know you don't think I'm crazy.

Love,

Poppy

~

Professor Warren C. Stoddard
Pearson Hall, Nearing College
Nearing, Vermont 05251

MARCH 9, 1981

Dear Casey,

The last thing I'd have imagined of our correspondence is that I would write to you twice, without a response in between. Somewhere pigs must be flying. Suffice it to say that you have been on my mind, given the political circus in Spain.

My departure from Nearing will be made public on March 15. I have been surprised at how liberating it feels to have made my decision. (Liberating: now that's a word no one at Nearing could possibly associate with me.) I think I told you that I'm moving to Boston to live with my friend, Emory. These days one would call him my companion. I'm eager to attend the upcoming season of the Boston Symphony as well as that of the Opera Company of Boston. (That is, if its director, Sarah Caldwell, can balance her books. She's notorious at spending money the company doesn't have.)

If you should resettle in the Boston area, perhaps we could meet for a cup of tea some afternoon. If you don't return to the area, please accept my best wishes for the future.

Sincerely,

Warren

~

Last night, about five members of the Civil Guard burst into the theater shortly into the show. We all thought they were shutting us down in the middle of another coup attempt, so we were oddly relieved when one of the guards took to the stage and announced there had been a bomb threat. The performance was cancelled while bomb experts investigated. José Luis Gómez came with us to a bar near Sol, where we stayed until midnight.

By now all the major newspapers and magazines have reviewed the play. As we expected, the raves and the pans fell along political lines. *El País* called it "a brilliant example of how Shakespeare can speak to our hopes and fears of the present day," while *ABC* said the production was a "propagandistic bastardization of a great play." *El Alcázar*, the most right-wing of all the newspapers, called for the immediate closing of the National Theater before "one more cent of government money is used in such a revolting manner." You have to wonder if the person who called in the bomb scare got their cue from this newspaper.

While I'm sorry we didn't get to perform the show last night, I can't deny how thrilling it was to be in that cast after the guards burst in. Sure, I was anxious at first, but once I realized what was happening, I allowed myself to take in the enormity of what has been going on these past weeks, of what I have witnessed. It was as if the strands of who I am—actor, scholar, sexual outcast, maybe even activist—had been braided, and knotted with a strand of political danger.

I felt rooted in history before what happened was even history.

～

Dear Warren,

I was touched and embarrassed to have received your second letter before I had responded to the first. I usually try to answer letters right away but I must have put yours in my desk drawer, run off to rehearsal, and forgotten it. Throw in an attempted overthrow of the government, and I hope you'll understand my lapse in etiquette.

The city is slowly calming down, although a day doesn't go by when the coup isn't mentioned. I half expect Juan Carlos to be canonized any day now for drawing a line in the sand with the military rebels. Of course, not everyone is on the King's side. The Fascists and some right-wing newspapers have been merciless in their criticism. But I've been encouraged by the outpouring of support for what he did that night.

As for next year, I might very well end up in Boston. I hope to teach or act or do both. I've toyed with the idea of New York City, but I think the chances of me finding work in the theater are slim, given all the competition. And I would love to have tea and to meet your companion.

Sincerely,
Casey

∾

Dear Poppy,

Thank you for your letter, which I received a few days ago. I want to make sure what I'm about to say is taken the right way: not as a rebuff of you and our friendship, but a validation of it. I do see you as family, just as much as I saw you as family before our strange time together in Madrid. I love that we can rely on each other, that we can tell each other anything, and that we even have the shorthand long-married couples do. I know when you want to leave a party without you telling me. I know that when you fling your hair back, you're letting me know that whoever you're talking to is putting on airs, or that when you pull on your earlobe, as Carol Burnett did on her TV show, it's your way of winking at me. I love our language.

I haven't fully explained what my relationship with Octavio has done for me. Yes, I am better off without him, even though at times my heart feels hollow. Before Spain, I called myself a gay man, but it was Octavio who finally gave me the experience of being one, not just in my mind, but in my body. I now see myself as having desires that go beyond friendship, as essential as friendships are in my life. More importantly, I now see myself as worthy of having those desires met.

You wrote that you "wildly imagined" us raising a child together. Raising a child might be stretching it, but I can see a family of you and me, as best friends. We'll have other families—friends and lovers—that will be different from what the two of us have now.

Please write soon.

Love,

Casey

~

Beltrán, the guy who usually plays Orlando, called to say that his grandfather had died and he couldn't perform. I've been understudying Orlando since rehearsals began. Once into performances, I started running my lines during every walk to the theater. On Tuesday afternoons we have an understudy rehearsal when we do the show without any of the original cast members. Intellectually I felt ready to go on, but I still considered every possible mistake I could make, from forgetting all my lines to falling flat on my back, legs and arms splayed, as if I were trying to make snow angels.

Well, none of that happened. The play ran smoothly. I missed a beat here and there, but it was nothing the audience noticed. The fact is, no one really cares about Orlando. It's a pretty one-dimensional role defined more by youth than anything else.

After the show, everyone came up to congratulate me. Manuel, the actor who plays Touchstone, suggested that we all go out and celebrate my performance, so we went to a bar near the Plaza Mayor. José Luis Gómez asked me if I wanted to play the role until the end of the run. Beltrán has been asking for some time off to rehearse another show that is opening right after As You Like It. I had to bite my lip to keep from smiling too broadly.

My father has been on my mind these past weeks, given the upheaval in Spain. I wonder how involved he would have been in the politics here. He wasn't the kind of man who'd march in the streets chanting slogans. His activism was more peaceful. He'd attend vigils. He'd hand out flyers against the war. He'd talk one-on-one with neighbors, kindly and reasonably explaining why they should vote for McGovern. He was quietly true to his ideals.

I remember the fall when the teachers went on strike just before classes were supposed to start. The whole city was divided between union families and those who said teachers got paid more than enough, given that they had their summers off. The first day of the strike, some parents forced their children to cross the picket lines with them, even though school had been canceled, just to make a point. A few teachers crossed the picket lines as well. Mrs. Grady went to get her classroom ready and the strikers called her a scab. My father supported the teachers (no surprise there) but instead of joining the picket line or lashing out at Mrs. Grady, he stood in front of Sisson Elementary and played Pete Seeger songs on his guitar before he went to work at the tannery.

I should probably run my lines before I go to bed but I'm exhausted. I'll leave rehearsing until tomorrow.

∾

TUESDAY, MARCH 31, 1981   5:15 P.M.

Someone tried to assassinate Reagan yesterday. I listened on the radio in the dressing room with some of the cast. I can't say I was completely removed from what was happening, but hearing the news so many miles from home did distance me from it. Right now no one knows what the motive was. Gustavo's convinced politics is behind it, which makes sense because politics is usually behind assassinations in Spain.

I told him I disagreed. Americans just don't share the same level of passion with much of the world when it comes to the government. Maybe we should, but we don't. Or more accurately, maybe I should, but I don't. Gustavo lost some of his eyesight when he protested the night of the coup attempt. In Belfast, Bobby Sands has been on a hunger strike for a month. And I went to a pro-democracy march. My offerings seem meager.

I received a postcard from Noah Bergen (a.k.a. The Wisenheimer). He's deferred his acceptance to the Fletcher School of Law and Diplomacy to travel this year. He's coming to Madrid in June and wants to have dinner with me. I'll take him to Black & White. It'll be nice to go there without Octavio, but not alone.

∼

Dear Casey,

This must be at least the fifth attempt at writing this letter in as many days. Those versions are now torn up. It was a little cathartic, really. Every time I destroyed a letter I could imagine that the contents in it weren't true. After this letter, which I swear I'll finish and send to you, you'll know exactly what's going on.

In my last letter I said that I "wildly imagined" us having a family. I have to tell you that having a child with you is not as much of a fantasy as I led you to believe. And this is why: I am pregnant. I'm sure your immediate thought is that Ernesto is the father, but that's impossible. We'd stopped having sex a few weeks before we visited his family in Mexico, and there's no way we were about to do anything with his mother and father around.

That leaves me with the news I know you won't like to hear. I'm three and a half months pregnant and you are the father.

When I first learned the news, I thought of not telling you. I considered driving to New York to have an abortion because I'd have to prove my health was in danger to have one in Canada. I actually made an appointment in Buffalo and drove as far as the border at Niagara Falls where I parked and stepped out of the car. I looked across at the Falls, and thought about the amazing continuity in front of me. Second after second, month after month, year after year: the water kept cascading, its dull roar unbreaking. I started to see our baby this way. I started to believe that the steady tumble of water was telling me not to break the continuity of life after life. I decided not to have the abortion. It wasn't an easy decision. I was at Niagara Falls, with honeymooners everywhere. I wanted to be one of them.

I write assuming you'll be father in name only, although I wish terribly that it were otherwise. This pains me not only for our child but also for us—because I don't see how we can remain close friends if our child sees you trotting in and out of my life without knowing who you are. Maybe I'm being too pessimistic. Do you think there's a way we could work something out?

My parents have been supportive enough, although my father seems to have more sympathy for me. They assume the baby is Ernesto's— I haven't told them the truth—so there's been no talk of marrying the father. They'd only see marriage as making matters worse.

Despite all the complications, I do feel great joy when I think about having a child, at least when I'm not overcome with terror. But I really wish we could talk. Please write back as soon as possible.

Love,

Poppy

~

THURSDAY, APRIL 9, 1981   MIDNIGHT

I came right back from the theater as soon as I made my last exit. I didn't even stay for the curtain call. I performed abysmally because all I could focus on was Poppy's letter. If I'd been playing my usual minor role, people might not have noticed. But now I was playing Orlando. I've only had one anxiety attack before, and that was during my father's funeral service. I had another one on stage tonight. I was watching myself act instead of acting, and became so distracted by the watching that I mixed up pronouns. (Instead of "if this be so, why blame you me to love you?" I said, "why blame me you to love me?") I came in late after my cues, and blanked on some lines altogether. Backstage I sat head between my knees, taking deep breaths. When the stage manager brought me a glass of water I thought it was a prop. I walked on stage with a plastic tumbler.

Poppy's letter. Fuck. I haven't written her back yet because I have no idea what to say. Instead of thinking about ways to help her through the pregnancy, I'm hoping—even praying—that the baby she gives birth to ends up being browner than she expected, and that it will be Ernesto, not me, who will be responsible for the child.

What I should do is go to the communications building and call her, but I'm afraid that instead of comforting her I'll keep asking her why she didn't she tell me earlier so we could have talked seriously about ending the pregnancy. I'd have flown to Toronto to go with her, if she needed me. At least that's what I've convinced myself I'd have done.

How the hell can I be responsible for a child? Fuck. Fuck. Fuck. This just can't be. I can barely support myself, let alone a baby. I have to believe it's Ernesto's. Or maybe someone else's, someone Poppy met when she returned to Toronto. Or maybe she'll have a miscarriage. How awful I am to think this.

∿

SATURDAY, APRIL 11, 1981   10:30 A.M.

When I arrived at the theater last night, the stage manager told me that José Luis Gómez wanted to see me in his office. I knew right away how serious this was.

His door was open. Before I had the chance to give a courtesy knock, he looked up from his desk and invited me in. His voice wasn't harsh, but that didn't comfort me. José is never harsh, even during the tensest of rehearsals. When I sat across from him, he offered me some tea, which I refused. I imagined spilling it all over me, on the Persian rug, on José's desk, on José himself.

He got right to the point. The stage manager had told him about my problems the night before, as did the woman playing Rosalind. I felt betrayed, but I can't blame her. I wouldn't want to act opposite me after what happened. He said he was bringing Beltrán back to play Orlando for the rest of the run. I was welcome to return to the role I had before. When he told me to take a few days off before rejoining the production, I knew he was giving me the chance to quit before he fired me from the production altogether. I wish he'd been impatient, unfair in his assessment of me. I might have been able to shift the blame, allow myself to feel pissed off instead of feeling so devoid of spirit.

After I left his office and was approaching the stage door, I saw Beltrán doing stretches against the wall. He looks much more like

Orlando than I ever will. He's taller than I am, with a long, handsome face and ash blond hair in naturally tight curls. When I wished him luck, he said he was really tired of the role, and that he was only returning because of his contractual obligations. He also said it was a bad idea to make an enemy out of José if he wanted to act in Madrid for very long. Then, as if he realized this wasn't the kindest thing to say to me given that José had more or less fired me, he added, "But he likes you, Casey. Really, he does."

I started walking back to the boarding house, wishing I could talk with Poppy. Well, at least the old version of Poppy, the one before she started dating Ernesto, before she came to Spain, before she got pregnant.

Before *I* got her pregnant. That is, if I did.

I decided that if I couldn't talk to Poppy, I'd see if Gustavo wanted to go to the bar next door. The boarding house lobby was empty except for Mr. Good Morning. He was sitting in his chair, eyes closed, accordion at his feet. His cigar stub was on the floor. I touched his knee but he didn't respond. I put my hand in front of his mouth but didn't feel his breath.

I wondered how long he'd been dead, if the men in the pensión had finished their meal and walked right by him, thinking he'd been sleeping.

That Mr. Good Morning had helped me many months ago when the civil guards had detained me in the Parque de Retiro didn't make his belief in fascism any more palatable, but I allowed myself to feel sad, if only for a moment. I remembered him welcoming me when I first inquired about Marianela. He'd been kind to me when the civil guards had arrested me.

I generally don't believe the world sends signals to guide us. I'd be as bad an astrologer as I was a Catholic. Yet I can't help but thinking that the confluence of events these past few days is telling me my time in Spain is over, that I need to travel to Toronto to be with Poppy and our child.

BOSTON

1984–1985

We shouldn't have to be faithful, we should want to be faithful.

—LARRY KRAMER

Dear Grace,

By the time you read this, you'll think it's really hokey of me to be writing you. You spoke your first complete sentence not that long ago: "Gus is *my* dog." There you have it: subject + verb + predicate nominative and a possessive adjective to boot. You surprised me, since we don't even own a pet, let alone a dog named Gus. Your mother told me later that one of your friends at the playground has a dog named Gus. You said your first word, by the way, when you were in the bathtub: "duck." You couldn't stop saying it, and sometimes it sounded like you were saying something else that rhymes with "duck," so your mother taught you the word "bird."

Even when you are able to read this letter, I doubt you'll be able to understand it. That will take some more years. But I need to put my thoughts down while they are still clear, so you know how I was feeling when I left Toronto. Here's the truth. I left your mother and she left me (even though she plans to stay in the city to be close to your grandparents). I'm sure it feels like I'm leaving you as well. At least that's what I thought you were telling me when you saw me with my suitcase the day I left. You started screaming and pushed your fists against your ears, the way you always you do when you don't like something. I'll never forget the day when your mother served you a bowl of Kraft macaroni and cheese, only this time the noodles were a different shape than you were used to.

When people divorce, it's often because they stop getting along, or someone does something terrible to the other, or someone falls in love with someone else. None of this is true about your mother and me. We've loved each other for a long time, long before you were born. We tried to create a regular family once we knew you were about to come into our lives. For much of this time, we were happy in some important ways. We were happy whenever we were with you. We were happy when we shopped for your Cabbage Patch Doll and the Walking

Dog Xylophone to put under the Christmas tree. We were happy just watching you sleep.

All of this is true, Grace. But some other things are also true, and one of those things is that your mother and I should have been brother and sister instead of husband and wife. My attraction to your mother was—and still is—emotional. Physically and sexually I have always gravitated toward men. This difference might not seem all that important to you now, but for most people it's the first law of attraction. Your mother and I thought we had enough love without this attraction to make a marriage.

So now I am in Boston, a few days before I start teaching Spanish and theater. I'm at a private school and living in a dormitory, which will make me miss you and your mother and our apartment near the park even more. My room is dreary. The walls are cinder blocks painted powder blue. I bought some used furniture at Goodwill, and had a futon delivered for my bedroom. Because I eat all my meals with the students and staff, my only means of cooking on my own is a toaster oven the school provides for me.

It's getting late. Now I have to prepare my lesson on Spanish introductions and goodbyes. I'll leave you with a Spanish goodbye that assumes more meetings in the future: *Hasta luego.* I refuse to say *adiós* to you, Grace. I will come to Toronto often.

Much love,
Dad

~

BOSTON   SEPTEMBER 3, 1984

Dear Professor Stoddard,

I'm writing—after far too long, I know—to let you know that I've recently moved to Boston from Toronto. You've been on my mind because not only am I now teaching Spanish, I'm using Sastre's *Muerte en el barrio* in my advanced class. I remember reading it in your course on Spanish Theater at Nearing.

I was wondering if you'd be open to getting together sometime. Last I heard you were planning to retire and move to Boston to live with your companion. The phone book confirms that you've moved here, but I don't know much else about your life.

Please do get in touch with me if you'd like to get together.

Sincerely,

Casey

∿

I've been a very poor diarist these past three years or so—an entry here, an entry there that I tore up before moving to Boston. Now, as I start life all over again, I've decided to start all over again in writing, in marking time.

It still saddens me that Poppy never got the wedding she and her parents had envisioned when she was growing up. Ours was a handful of guests in the historic but small Campbell House. It was cozy enough, but one of my memories of that day was the enormous fireplace that was never lit, which even then felt like a metaphor. I also remember that when I exchanged vows with Poppy, I kept thinking, *I can get out of this if it's too hard.*

Poppy later acknowledged that even as she was saying "I do," she understood there wasn't much cause for optimism. We'd already come to an agreement that I could have sex with men as long as I was discreet and didn't fall in love with them. I slept with a total of five men in three years—the very definition of celibacy for a gay man. My first encounter was with a man at a bathhouse a few weeks after I arrived in Toronto. I hated it. I hated the sex I had with other guys, too. The guilt was too much.

The strain of our marriage got to both of us, but it got to Poppy more. I wasn't out prowling every night but she could read the writing on the wall. Our marriage wasn't working. Now I'm here in Boston. We're both hoping that distance will allow us to move on with our lives.

I'll miss Grace. I'll be there for the big moments in her life, like graduations and birthday parties. But what about those big moments that come unexpectedly, like the first time she rides a bike without training wheels in High Park? Or even the not-so-great things, like having a nightmare and crawling into bed with her parents and describing what she just dreamed?

I've placed a photo of Grace on my desk in my room in the dormitory. I think she looks more like Poppy than she looks like me. I'd like to put one on my classroom desk, but I'm not ready for people to ask questions about my life.

I'm about to start teaching at Chadwick Academy. It's about twenty minutes from Boston, so I hope to have some sort of social life. Sidney Chadwick, for whom the school is named, was a colonel in the Civil War. The school feels pretty traditional, but I think it'll be bearable as long as I keep my nose to the grindstone and mind my business.

I've gotten to know a few people on the faculty who are my age. They seem nice enough. The headmaster is a 50ish former marine named Vernon Reed whose ruddy complexion and broad shoulders make me think he was a football player in college. This is only his second year at the school, but he exudes confidence. He speaks softly, and when he isn't talking, he cocks his head and presses his lips together. I'm not sure what to make of him, although my guess is he's probably a boring but decent guy. At our opening faculty meeting, he had us all go around and say our names, and then said, "There'll be a test on this later," thinking the remark was both funny and original.

Classes start tomorrow. I'm the only Spanish teacher at Chadwick, so I teach all four levels. Auditions for the fall semester play won't take place for a couple of weeks, so I have some time to think about what I want to direct. *As You Like It* comes to mind, but I'm afraid that would bring back bad memories. My screwing up on stage that night in Madrid still haunts me.

I've kept in touch with Gustavo. He's happy the Socialists won the national elections last year. He wants to give Felipe González a chance to enact the reforms he's promised, but he's already disappointed. He wished González governed more like France's Mitterrand, who included Communists in his Socialist government and is nationalizing some industries.

It's almost 11:00, time for me to make sure the boys are in bed with the lights out. I've been doing check-in for three nights now, but it still feels awkward. Everyone knows the other two men in the dorm are straight. The dorm head keeps reminding me that I don't have to knock before bed check. He tells me it's a way to keep the boys on their toes, from getting into trouble. I still knock. I can only imagine what would happen if they find out I'm gay and catch me bursting into their rooms unannounced.

◞◞

SUNDAY, SEPTEMBER 9, 1984   11:30 P.M.

I spent most of this weekend on dorm duty, checking the boys in three times a day, and shuttling them to the movies and to Harvard Square in the school van. I'd never driven anything that big. We survived a near miss of an accident on Storrow Drive. When I got off duty at six this evening, I was wiped out, but I kept my date with Warren Stoddard and his "companion," the word he used when he called the other day.

Emory was a surprise—the total opposite of Stoddard. He's black and quite a bit younger than Stoddard, and taller by about half a foot. He's also all extroverted charm, the last thing I'd say about Stoddard. He's a pediatric dentist in the affluent town of Wellesley. He knew how to keep the conversation rolling when we hit a lull. Not long after I arrived at their apartment I realized that I'd never seen Stoddard without a jacket and tie. I'd never seen him so at ease, either. Emory seemed to tap into a part of him that he kept buried at Nearing.

Emory is originally from Goose Creek, South Carolina (which he calls "Gay as a Goose Creek"). He and Stoddard argued about whether or not Bostonians were aloof, especially compared to Southerners. According to Emory, they've been living in Boston for three years now and still haven't made close friends. Stoddard claims they have plenty of friends, although he could only name two, both widowed neighbors in their building. But Emory is willing to excuse Bostonians. I guess we're at a social disadvantage for not understanding what hospitality means in the South, where you can spend a good hour just talking about the weather. He says that small talk in Boston is deconstructing the latest Harold Pinter play.

⌷ 99 ⌷

We drank gin and tonics, which Emory called the staple of any party, at least until the end of September. In South Carolina, you can serve G&Ts any time other than winter. He then presented a platter with cheese, green and red grapes, and cantaloupe arranged as an autumn leaf. While we ate, we shared a bottle of Spanish wine I'd brought.

Toward the end of the evening, Stoddard started talking about how nice it was for him to be in retirement after teaching for almost four decades at Nearing. He predicted I'd like being in the classroom, which I assumed was a compliment, but with Stoddard, you never know, especially after his riff on how wonderful it was to be *out* of the classroom.

Stoddard had had a few gin and tonics and was slightly drunk. He started gesticulating, which looked like unqualified enthusiasm for him. It was getting warm in the apartment and he brushed his hair from his forehead. That's when I saw it: the tiny purple dot, right below his scalp line. I couldn't bring myself to say anything. If neither of them knew it was there, they'd soon find out. And once they did, they'd understand right away what an ominous sign it was.

When I was in New York City a couple of weeks ago, I saw a number of men with blotches on their faces. I was struck by how they didn't try to conceal them. One guy at MoMA stood in front of the Magritte's *The Lovers*—two people kissing with fabric over their faces—looking out at all of us looking at that painting. I think he was trying to situate himself as part of the piece, and he was, in a way. But he was also defiantly making sure we saw his face, with all its purple-red macules, against the covered faces. The image is embedded in my mind.

I'm trying to convince myself that the purple dot was always on Stoddard's face, some sort of birthmark, but I'm just kidding myself. Kidding myself is how I keep my head above water these days.

~

TORONTO   SEPTEMBER 9, 1984

Casey—

Since we haven't heard from you, I thought I would update you on life in Toronto. Thank you for calling from the airport when you arrived in Boston, but I'm afraid that isn't enough for Grace, who was crying for you tonight. I tried comforting her by bringing out some photographs of you, but she needs to hear your voice. I know it's pricey to call from the US to Canada. You can call collect if things are really tight. Let me know when your phone is installed.

It's still hot here in Toronto, although the heat isn't as ghastly as it was this summer. I'm just grateful that Grace and I still get to spend some time in the park without having to dress in layers of clothing. Speaking of which, Mummy took us shopping on Bloor Street this morning and outfitted Grace for the fall. She bought her this darling Florence Eiseman sweater that looks just gorgeous on her. Even Grace knows how beautiful she looks. She's been parading around the apartment in it all day.

I've started looking for a part-time job. I'm not quite sure what I'm qualified to do after playing mum for three years. I might go back to the bookstore where I worked before Grace was born.

I received a wedding announcement from Ernesto yesterday. He's deep into his PhD in Art History at Yale. He's also marrying a nice Catholic girl from Veracruz. I'm sure his mother is beside herself with happiness. I'm happy for him. I'm also happy I got out of that relationship before it was too late, although I'm not convinced my present situation is that much better.

We're hoping you'll come to Toronto for Thanksgiving. Daddy says he'll pay your airfare.

Please call Grace soon. She misses you.

Poppy

～

SATURDAY, SEPTEMBER 15, 1984   3:00 P.M.

I received a letter from Poppy this morning that has left me deflated. I don't even know what the hell a Florence Eiseman sweater *is*, let alone be able to afford one for Grace. If it weren't for her parents, Poppy would be going through the bins at the thrift store for our daughter's clothes.

She says that Grace is desperate to see me at Thanksgiving in Canada, which is Columbus Day here. I'm sure Grace would like to see me, although I wonder if the need was more on Poppy's part. I'll go, but I can't accept her father's offer of flying me up and back. I need to maintain a modicum of self-respect. It's bad enough that I now have the car he bought for Poppy and me last year.

I wasn't assigned dorm duty this weekend, so after I'd read Poppy's letter, I had brunch at a restaurant called Club Café, in Boston's South End. The clientele is pretty much all gay. I've been looking forward to finding out about Boston's gay scene. This was a first baby step.

Except for Stoddard and Emory, I don't know any gay people in Boston, so I went alone. As I drove, I pictured myself at a table with a single flower, perfectly content sipping coffee and reading the latest installment of *Tales of the City*. I found a parking space a few blocks away. It was warm, and many South End boys wore tight shorts and tank tops. I was no match for these guys.

The front of the restaurant looked like a greenhouse, with its curved ceiling-to-floor windows. A cute maître d' led me to a small table in the middle of the restaurant. It was packed. Women were at their tables and men at theirs: there was little mixing of the genders. I didn't know a soul, but somehow I felt at home, like the first time I went to Black & White in Madrid.

I decided to celebrate my first venture into Boston's gay scene by ordering a mimosa. I sipped and looked at the people around me— some laughing, others in serious discussion, one couple exchanging winks. I took in this scene of everyone just being themselves. I drank my mimosa and let the alcohol do its work.

I'd just been served my eggs Benedict when I saw a face I couldn't quite place. He showed a flash of recognition as well. He walked over to me and smiled quizzically. By then I was able to recall that his was one of many faces I'd seen crossing the quad at Nearing. And it was a handsome face: dark hair, bronze skin. And blue eyes, the killer for me. There's something so unexpected about seeing a dark-haired man with blue eyes that it always slays me.

As soon as he said hello and I heard his deep Texas drawl, I remembered. Dallas Moore. Dallas From Dallas, we used to call him. Or D². Class of '78. His father owned a major whiskey distillery. I invited him to sit down, which he did, after telling me he'd just finished brunch but couldn't pass a familiar face. He told me to start eating. It was awkward as he sat there looking at me. I was relieved when he summoned the waiter for a cup of coffee.

We talked about Nearing: how we missed it sometimes, who'd we'd been in touch with, how often we'd visited. We went on to describe our present lives. I didn't mention Poppy and Grace. It seemed like that was a topic for when we had more time. Dallas said he was in financial services, but didn't offer much more than that.

"This any good?" Dallas picked up *Tales of the City* and fanned through the pages with his thumb.

"It's fun," I said. "It's nice to read about people like yourself."

"I suppose that's true," Dallas said. "But I don't think I'd find myself in there."

"I'm sorry if I made any presumptions," I said. "It's just that we're both here, and I thought—"

"That we both belonged here?"

"I guess so."

"I did, once." He put the book down, shaking his head. "Have you been to San Francisco lately?"

I told him I'd never been but wanted to go soon.

"It's a horror show. Emaciated men walking around the city. Men our age relying on canes to get from one aisle of the grocery store to another. It's demoralizing. Who wants to see all that?"

"It seems to me that seeing all that is part of the bargain when you visit San Francisco."

"I guess," Dallas said. "It's also part of the bargain of being gay."

"It doesn't have to be."

"Don't kid yourself. If you keep having sex with men, you're going to get it. Period."

I know there are guys who preach that promiscuity is what's killing us. Activists like Larry Kramer are doing everything to change gay men's behavior, but I don't think he's asking us to give up sex completely. He wants us to take responsibility for ourselves, to take care of ourselves. But Dallas doesn't think gay men should have any sex at all. Before I had the chance to formulate a question for him (other than, What the hell are you doing here?), he was sliding a pamphlet in my direction. I saw the word "sin" and slid it back to him.

"No, thanks," I said.

"I embraced the gay lifestyle for quite a few years. It made me very unhappy. The drugs, the anonymous sex, the whole thing. But then this AIDS thing hit and I realized that it's a *lethal* lifestyle. God was warning me. It was my last chance to free myself. So I did. Now I try to help other men out."

"I don't need help."

"The problem with most Christian religions is that they've treated homosexuality as a horrible sin. And the fact is, it's just a sin—no worse or no better than lying, say. I'm trying to get that word out. There's no reason to give up God just because you have certain tendencies. I happen to belong to a church that doesn't treat me as a leper. They just see me as someone who has sinned and might very well sin again if I didn't have their support. They keep me on the straight and narrow, so to speak."

"I'm not going to listen to this bullshit. You can leave now."

When he continued to press me, I told him I was going to show his pamphlet to the maître d,' who would no doubt escort him to the door. He finally rose from his chair. When he extended his hand, I reflexively extended mine, then hated myself for obliging.

The veins in my neck were pounding. This restaurant was supposed to be a refuge from people like Dallas From Fucking Dallas. I couldn't finish my eggs, so I pushed my plate away and ordered another mimosa. I started thinking about Madrid, about how Gustavo had moved out when he found out I was gay, but at least he never tried to change me. Dallas urging me to deny who I was felt worse than when Gustavo rejected me because of who I was.

After I left the restaurant, I walked around the city for a while, trying to stay calm. I ended up at the huge reflecting pool behind the Mary Baker Eddy Library. Only a few people dotted the perimeter. Last Wednesday was the eleventh anniversary of my father's death, but I was so busy with school, I hardly thought about it. Now I sat on a bench at the side of the water, took a few cleansing breaths, and tried to recall his face and hear his voice. I listened to his fingers strumming the guitar.

My father would have dealt with Dallas in a far more diplomatic manner. He was remarkable that way. Sometimes I think I failed my father. Not about my being gay. I do believe he would have been on my side. He was always on the side of the underdog. I often wonder where he found the patience. How was he so calm? I usually think of calm as the absence of things: anger, distraction, anxiety. But my father seemed to turn the word "calm" into a presence of its own, something that wasn't accomplished by getting rid of certain feelings, but by embracing calmness as a state by itself. Maybe he was some sort of spiritual master.

After a while, I stopped thinking about my father and opened my novel. I read for about half an hour before I drove back to Chadwick. I don't want to stay in the dorm the rest of the night. There's a movie called *Another Country* playing not too far from here. It's about young gay men at Eton in the '30s. Sounds a lot better than *Ninja 3: The Domination*. Actually, it sounds perfect.

∼

BOSTON   SEPTEMBER 20, 1980

Dear Poppy,

I apologize for taking a week to answer your letter, but I've been busy with school nonstop. And next weekend is Parents Weekend, when I meet with the parents of every one of my students. I've heard a few horror stories, like the parent who brought a stenographer with him to record the entire meeting because the school had already announced that tape recorders weren't permitted.

Life here has been all work and no play, as Jack says in *The Shining*. It's frustrating to devote twelve hours a day to your profession and not have much to show for it financially. I really do appreciate your father's generosity. I just wish we didn't have to rely on it. Maybe someday I'll be named a headmaster and be paid enough to take care of you and Grace myself.

While we're on the subject of headmasters, I'm having a hard time figuring out mine. The other day he (Vernon Reed) showed up to my advanced class and sat in the back row from start to finish. He took notes, even though I spoke Spanish most of the time. At the end he simply said "Thank you." *Thank you for what?* I wanted to ask. It wasn't as if he said it unkindly; he was just vague. At least he tried to praise a few of the boys, although he looked awkward high-fiving them as they left the classroom. He towered over some of them and had to stoop.

I spoke to a couple of teachers here and they told me not to worry. All new faculty are observed a few times the first year. As far as the brief "thank you" is concerned, they told me it was better than just a smile, which is all some of them received. I'm beginning to think that Vernon Reed has no idea *how* to productively critique a class and that his silence or simple "thank you" is meant to intimidate, to keep you guessing. So far, it's worked on me. I interpret his silence as judgment.

I plan to come to Toronto for Thanksgiving, although I'm going to beg off on your father's offer to pay for my airline ticket. I can drive to Toronto in eight hours if I only stop once or twice along the way. I'll put on an Agatha Christie book on tape to make time pass.

I look forward to seeing everyone. Please give Grace a huge hug for me.

Casey

~

SUNDAY, SEPTEMBER 23, 1984   11:30 P.M.

Emory called me earlier this week to ask if I would meet him in town. He said he needed to talk about Stoddard. I agreed to have coffee with him today at a bookstore café on Newbury Street called The Trident. I arrived early, so I walked up and down the street for a while, taking in the window displays of the latest fashion by designers I'd never heard of. I passed a window with children's clothes and wondered if any of the sweaters were by the designer that Poppy's mother liked. I've already forgotten the name.

I browsed for a while at the Boston Public Library. On my way out I stopped downstairs to pee. I was standing in front of the urinal, my eyes directed at the wall in front of me, when I felt someone brush their hand against my thigh. I turned and saw a decent-looking man in his fifties who wrapped his hand around his cock and then started tugging on it. I shook my head no and stared ahead again. I finished quickly.

I checked out a few books and left the library. It had turned cloudy, so I ran to The Trident before the rain started. I scanned the crowd in the café, packed with students and older intellectuals. The ambience felt like the Café Comercial in Madrid, with less smoke. Emory waved to me from a corner table. He hugged me tight. I realized that it had been months since I'd had any physical touch with another man, save for the handshakes I'd shared at Chadwick Academy when the school year started. I returned the embrace.

"Order whatever you want," Emory said. "This is on me."

I tried to object, but just as I opened my mouth Emory stretched his long, thin arm over the table and put a finger to my lips.

"It's on you, then," I said.

I told him what had happened in the Boston Public Library men's room.

"Is that scene still going on?" he said. "I thought that was over by now. There used to be a secret schedule, like between two and four on Saturdays, six and eight on Mondays. Or sometimes men would just take their chances. I had a whore of a roommate when I was in dental school at Tufts. He told me *everything*. At first the stories were titillating but then they got *bor*-ing."

Emory said his practice was going well, or at least the child side of it was. Before anyone signs on for pediatric dentistry, he said, they should take a few psychology courses to deal with the adults in the children's life. I told him the same went for teaching.

"Listen," he said as soon as the waitress delivered our menus. "I know you saw the purple spot on Warren's forehead the other night."

"I tried to look like I hadn't seen anything."

"That was a major failure, honey. The neighbors could have seen your chin drop. What I wanted to say is that yes, it's exactly what you thought it was."

I told him how sorry I was and asked him how Stoddard was dealing with it. The problem, Emory said, was that he *wasn't* dealing with it. Emory's been trying to get him to a doctor, but to no avail. His voice cracked. He waited a bit before regaining his composure to ask me if I'd be willing to join him and Stoddard some evening when we could bring up the issue together. We'd be nonjudgmental, giving Stoddard all the time he needed to talk. We'd explain specifically how we were ready to help.

The invitation felt important, a step toward a meaningful friendship not just with Stoddard, but also with Emory. I'd spent the last few years trying so hard to put my relationship with Poppy on the right track that I hardly worked on any other friendships. And now here was a man I'd only met once, reaching out to me. I decided to reach back to him, and agreed to help.

As we drank our coffee, Emory talked a little more about Stoddard. His childhood in an upper middle-class family was unremarkable. He had a brother ten years older than he was, so they hardly knew each other growing up. That brother had died a couple of years ago. Stoddard was a fairly sad man, Emory said, something I already knew. His sadness was the result of an accumulation of many minor disappointments and letdowns.

"Nowadays there's a focus on *the big event* that screws you up for life," Emory said. "Your uncle sexually abuses you. You see your father beat your mother or your father beats *you* while your mother watches and does nothing. I can't begin to understand how anyone gets on with life after something like that. But there are other kinds of blows. Smaller blows. And I think for Warren, it was one small blow after another. The mocking, the self-hatred, the loneliness. Every day was a dagger."

I'd never thought about Stoddard that way. I just assumed he was born sad, that it was part of his genetic makeup. But I also knew that Stoddard had seemed more relaxed when I had dinner at his apartment. Emory had turned those daily blows and daggers into something more manageable. I wondered how Stoddard made Emory happy. I asked him.

"He just does. How should I know why I fell in love with him more than with anyone else?"

I understood what he was saying. I couldn't say why I was drawn to Octavio while I was in Spain. It made as much sense as it didn't.

I left Emory feeling like I knew him better, probably even better than I knew Stoddard. I was glad to have somebody in Boston who spoke my language.

~

I've been thinking a lot about Stoddard and how Emory said the sadness in his life was a result of an accumulation of disappointments. I'm sure this is true for a lot of people. I don't consider myself a sad person, but if I were, I'm not convinced mine would be an accumulated sadness. And I'd have thought that my father's early death would have put me on a pretty melancholy path. Strangely, it didn't. I miss him terribly at times, but his death hasn't determined who I am. At least I don't think it has.

Tonight another faculty member, an athletic-looking guy named Tony Moretti, invited me out with some other teachers. He teaches physics and runs my dorm. We went to a place called O'Toole's, a bar somewhere between a dive and a decent Irish pub. Two guys from the math department played pool in the corner while the rest of us sat at the bar where *Hill Street Blues* showed on a suspended TV. It had been a long week at school (the expulsion of a popular soccer player, two late-night false alarms in the boys' dorm, flooding from the wetlands on campus), so most of us just stared at the screen. It was nice just sitting with my colleagues.

It was the first time Tony and I had really talked. He'd drunk almost a pitcher of Michelob. We compared résumés, discussed politics (he likes Reagan), and reminisced about our childhoods. We both come from middle-class Catholic families. Our fathers died when we were young. His was killed in Viet Nam.

I wonder how old Tony was when his father died in the war. The idea of a father suddenly disappearing from a child's life seems like the cruelest thing imaginable. My father, and Tony's father, and countless other fathers left, not of their own free will. I had a choice. I was the one who didn't have to leave my daughter but did anyway. I had to remind myself that I hadn't really left, that I'm still in her life. Or maybe I didn't remind myself of this. Maybe it was more like convincing myself.

After a while, I made a move to stand, but Tony grabbed me by the arm and kept talking. Paula, who teaches English, came over and wrapped her arms around him from behind.

"He gets chatty after a few drinks," she whispered to me. Even when soft her voice had a rasp. Her hair was sun-bleached. Sunglasses she didn't need inside rested on top of her head. Her bright red shirt with blue and white parrots made me peg her for a Jimmy Buffet fan.

I told the group I was walking back to campus. Paula asked me to knock on Tony's door in the morning so he'd make it to his 8:30 class. Paula seems to look out for everyone. She'd apparently organized tonight's trip to the pub, just as she organizes most faculty social events. I bet she was a border collie in a former life.

When I got back to the dorm I couldn't sleep. I kept thinking about Grace and how I'd left her to be raised by her mother. Toronto was just too stifling, too confining, and I'd found myself in hiding again. Poppy had gone along with my leaving, eventually finding it the better alternative to thinking of herself as a sad woman married to a gay man.

I've made a list of things I could do to make the situation better for Grace. At the very least I'll ask for a few days off before Canadian Thanksgiving so I can spend more time with her in October. I'll have to come clean about my family situation to Vernon Reed. He asked me if I was married right before he offered me the job. (Is this even legal?) When I hesitated giving an answer, he said that Chadwick Academy liked to support faculty families, and that he tried to find professional opportunities within the school for faculty spouses. I wasn't sure how to take this. Was he suggesting that I get married or that I wasn't welcome at Chadwick because I wasn't married? He gave me the contract anyway, but ever since I've felt like he looks at me with suspicion.

Now I won't even consider a trip to Spain over Christmas vacation, not that I'd have the money. I'll go to Toronto. Maybe I could also line up a summer job there.

Dear Poppy,

I've spoken with the headmaster and he has given me permission to leave campus Friday morning (October 5) and to return two days after Thanksgiving (the 10th). That gives me some extra time. It was a hard sell, but not as hard as I'd expected. Tony (a new friend of mine on the faculty) had told me that if the headmaster sits in the chair next to you, you're golden. But if he sits behind his desk offering you one of the chairs on the other side, then he's going to be hard to budge. He sat behind the desk.

Sometimes when Vernon Reed gets irritated, he covers it up with a smile that tenses at the corners. This only happened once, at the beginning, before I explained why I needed the two days off. I told him Grace was asking for me every night. I threw in a few pleas about keeping the family together, and fibbed by saying you and I were separated rather than divorced, hoping he'd think his granting me the time away might even lead to a reconciliation. In the end, I think he was pleased to help out. He even told me to drive safely.

I have dorm duty Thursday night, so I plan to leave at the crack of dawn on Friday and drive straight through to Toronto. The highways shouldn't be too busy since it's not Thanksgiving Day here, and the Columbus Day traffic won't start until Friday afternoon.

Love to Grace,
Casey

~

Dear Casey,

Man, it took me forever to find out where you were. I knew you were leaving Toronto in August but you never gave me your new address. You weren't going to abandon your dear old roommate, were you? My name is Gustavo, in case you've forgotten me. Ha. Ha. I finally found your old phone number and talked to your ex-wife.

I'm afraid I'm not writing for a happy reason. I thought you'd want to know that Octavio died in August after months of being ill. We all think he died from AIDS, although no one knows for sure. The signs were all there: the weight loss, the blotches on his skin, the sunken eyes. It was awful to watch. Some of the guys here immediately thought they'd been infected because Octavio had sat with them at dinner. I tried to talk some sense into them but it didn't work. It did make me wonder about you. Have you shown any symptoms?

Octavio was alone toward the end, with only a brother from Valladolid visiting him in the hospital on weekends. Those of us who weren't afraid set up a schedule so someone would be at the hospital now and then. We all agreed it was the right thing to do even though Octavio would have nothing to do with us when he was well.

I'm really sorry about this news, Casey, but he did ask me to let you know. I know you two didn't separate on the best of terms, but I guess death changes everything.

I hope you're out there fighting for some sort of cure. They say it may take two to three years before a vaccine, which feels so long. I read in *El País* there's a group in New York that is staging dramatic acts of disobedience. Is this happening in Boston? Are you taking part? I hope so. It would make me proud. I love that I took you to your first protest, even if I was arrested and we had a falling out afterwards.

My news is that I've been dating a woman from Torremolinos recently. I was surprised to find someone who was actually from the place. It has always seemed to me like one of those cities people migrate to, and then don't stay very long. If I spend any more time with her I might end up dropping the "r" from the end of my words. I'll tell you if it gets serious. I wouldn't be looking for something to wear to the wedding quite yet.

All for now. Write back! Some of the guys here still ask about you, but not King John. He returned to his royal England last winter, not to be heard of since. Not that he'd give us the time of day while he lived here.

Oh, I'm officially pissed off at Felipe González, who has turned out to be more moderate than we expected. I've enclosed a leaflet announcing an upcoming demonstration, for old times' sake.

Hugs,
Gustavo

~

MARCH FOR JUSTICE
SATURDAY, 13 OCTOBER
UNIVERSITY OF MADRID
MONCLOA CAMPUS
STUDENT UNION
14:00

• Felipe González promised us 800,000 new jobs. Instead we have an unacceptable 20 percent unemployment rate.
• Felipe González promised a restructured economy that would lift the poor. Instead, he gave us austerity and pension reductions.
• Felipe González promised to keep Spain out of military alliances such as NATO. Instead, González has called for a national vote on the matter.
• Felipe González promised unity. Instead, he has overseen the creation of government-sponsored anti-terrorist groups that have assassinated leaders of the Basque Separatist Movement.

Felipe González ran as leader of the Socialist Workers Party. He needs to start behaving like one.

Please join us in a March for Justice.

∽

TUESDAY, OCTOBER 9, 1984   10:30 P.M.

I leave Toronto for Boston early tomorrow morning so I can be back in time for dorm duty. I'm glad I was able to come for Thanksgiving. Grace really did seem happy to see me. I spent as much time as I could with her, although it was hard to find time alone. We celebrated Thanksgiving yesterday at Poppy's parents' house. They were nice to me, probably because I met them while Poppy and I were in college, so it's a little easier for them to see me in a non-spousal role. I can also see her mother putting on a chipper air because one doesn't make a scene over the holiday, *darling*, and all that. Her cheerfulness seems to become more impenetrable as she gets older. She's also become more controlling over the years. She put signs in the bathrooms asking the men to pee sitting down so as not to splash.

I had a nice chat with Poppy's father, who seems not to bear a grudge. He's a pretty unflappable guy. He's cheery like his wife, but it doesn't seem like a façade.

I wish Poppy and I had gotten along better over the weekend. There were times when she snapped at me for no reason and in front of Grace. Moments like these assuaged my guilt, if only a little, as I imagined us still married and Grace witnessing the contempt her mother has for me. No, contempt is too strong a word. She doesn't hate me. She hates that I left.

On Saturday I took Grace to High Park, a little bit of a hike from the apartment on a cold day, so I hailed us a taxi. Grace almost liked the ride there as much as the park itself. She wanted to play with the taxi meter, and I finally had to put her on my lap and take her in my arms.

Her favorite part of the trip was the section of the park where dogs run off leash. We just sat on a bench for a while, Grace squealing every time a dog came up to sniff her. I thought she'd like the zoo more than she did. Once she found out she couldn't pet the animals like she'd petted the dogs, she wanted to leave, so we went back to the dogs for a while.

She couldn't wait to get into another taxi, and luckily there was a line of them outside the gates of the park. As I was helping her in, her foot gave way and she fell against the curb. She was more stunned than hurt but she did manage to scrape her elbow. I wiped a little blood off with a bandana, straightened out her hair, and off we went. The crying only lasted a minute. All was well.

Or so I thought. When we got back and I told Poppy what happened, she started going on about how she couldn't trust me with our daughter, that she could have gotten killed if a car had come close to the curb. "Unreliable" was the word she used. My translation of all this: I'd proven unreliable to Poppy over the past few years, and now she was afraid I'd be unreliable to Grace.

In the middle of this scene, Grace decided that yes, the fall was traumatic after all, and she started crying again, only louder. She hugged her mother's legs, twisting herself in such a way that all I could see was her long red hair. I began to wonder if coming to Toronto was a good idea after all.

Eventually everyone calmed down. Grace fell asleep on the sofa and Poppy made tea. I sat with her at the kitchen table and we talked, or rather she talked. She'd softened her tone. I was no longer a candidate for World's Worst Father.

Poppy wondered if we should have waited a few years before divorcing, for Grace's sake. She'd been doubting many of her decisions, from whether or not Grace should have worn a heavier coat on a certain day to the amount of television she was watching. She hated relying so much on her parents for money. She wanted to go back to work but was afraid Grace would feel abandoned. Then, in a surprising moment of honesty she said, "And I miss you, Casey. I can't help it. I just do."

I took her hand while she pulled herself together, which didn't take long. She soon withdrew from me, blew her nose into a tea napkin, and apologized for being so emotional. She seemed embarrassed she'd told me the truth, but it was good for me. I'll try to remember that moment the next time she accuses me of neglecting my duties as a father.

Tomorrow I'll make my departure short and sweet. I don't want to open the possibility of another scene and leave Toronto feeling worse than I did before coming here. Poppy talked about coming with Grace to Boston over American Thanksgiving.

I'm looking forward to seeing some of the Chadwick teachers tomorrow. I discovered that Paula doesn't just dress like a Jimmy Buffet fan—she actually is one. She told me that some Buffet fans call themselves "Parrot Heads." Last week she and Tony and I had a few margaritas listening to his music at her place after the girls in her dorm had gone to sleep.

I've been surprised at how sad I've been feeling about Octavio's death, seeing that we weren't speaking when I left Madrid. I'm sorry he died alone. I'm trying not to worry about getting sick myself, since we only had sex a few times, and it was a long time ago. But this morning I woke up with a scratchy throat and immediately thought of pneumonia. I shook off the moment of panic by taking a hot, steamy shower, which returned my voice to normal.

I really don't think Poppy has anything to worry about. We had sex only once, after all.

Time for bed. I have a long ride ahead of me back to Chadwick.

∽

I'm exhausted from dorm duty this weekend. I don't know how I'll find the energy to teach all day tomorrow, not to mention holding auditions for the play. I've had a hard time deciding which play to do. I thought I'd do *The Winter's Tale*. (At Chadwick, the January play is always a Shakespearean production.) The theme of rebirth speaks to me these days, and I find the play oddly healing as I navigate life away from Toronto and do my best to help Emory and Stoddard. But I ended up choosing *Measure for Measure*, a play I think is relevant these days. It's about trying to impose one's own morality on an entire city. It's also about sexual repression as power.

I hope to subtly parallel the religious right's grip on the Reagan administration while cases of AIDS rise exponentially. I've read some of Larry Kramer's work, and he claims he wrote a letter to Reagan official Gary Bauer about AIDS, and Bauer responded that the President was "irrevocably opposed to anything having to do with homosexuality." Meanwhile Jerry Falwell is just like Angelo in *Measure for Measure*, imposing his moral code on the rest of us. And he has Reagan's ear. Reagan has yet to even mention the word "AIDS" publicly.

Stoddard, Emory, and I met Thursday evening for dinner at Locke-Ober, an upscale restaurant in Boston. When we first arrived, I thought Emory had made a mistake: this was the sort of place you went to for a celebration, not to convince someone they might have a serious illness. When I saw the tuxedoed waiters, the ornate woodwork at the bar, the clientele—all clad in suits and elegant dark dresses—I understood Emory's reasoning. This was a place where Stoddard would feel at home. The insistence on proper decorum alone would make it a safe place for him. And because of those very rules of decorum, he would never make a scene here.

We sat at a corner table and ordered drinks. Emory wasted no time: this meeting had been weighing heavily on his mind.

"Warren," he began, his voice quavering. "We've got to do something, dear. You can't ignore that lesion any longer."

Stoddard gave me a quizzical look that I interpreted as "Are you in on this?" But his confusion soon vanished. He brought his hands to his face, then lowered his head. His breathing became louder. I thought he was crying. When Emory reached across the table to him, Stoddard looked up. His eyes weren't wet after all but instead looked dull, a reflection of where exhaustion and relief might meet. Stoddard pulled away from Emory and left the dining area.

Emory and I weren't sure what to do, so we did nothing. If we'd followed Stoddard, what were we supposed to do when we caught up with him? Drag him back to the table? We stayed where we were.

Stoddard returned after about ten long minutes. He straightened his tie as he sat back down.

"It doesn't have to be what you think it is, so I wouldn't go planning any funerals yet." His voice had the flatness I remembered from his classes at Nearing. He could have been telling the class to open their Spanish texts to chapter seven.

"The only plan I want to make is for you to call the doctor," Emory said.

And then, because he'd been trying to be stoic for so long, Emory burst into tears. Stoddard and I held his hands until he pulled himself together. We didn't mention Stoddard's health for the rest of the evening. Emory wanted to talk about anything else, but I had a hard time getting Stoddard's illness out of my mind.

Emory called me Friday afternoon to say that Stoddard had an appointment with the doctor on Monday and that he'd let me know how it went. I can't say that I'm worried about the news because I doubt that the news is actually news at all. But I do have to be careful and not catastrophize the situation. Many people with AIDS haven't died from the disease. Stoddard could be one of them.

Time to prep for my classes tomorrow. Midterms are at the end of this week, so it's mostly review tomorrow and Tuesday. The students are such a mixed bag. In my upper level classes they're reading some of García Márquez's stories and are doing pretty well with them. But my ninth graders are so young, hardly aware of any time other than the here and now. On Friday I taught some geography of Spanish-speaking countries. When I explained that the three major southern cities in Spain were Granada, Córdova, and Seville, I told the class to think of the three American cars as a way to remember them. Cecily (I have to tell her to spit out her gum at least once every class) said, "Wow. I can't believe they named their cities after our cars."

~

Chadwick Academy Drama Department
Audition Notice
William Shakespeare's Measure for Measure

Please be prepared to read from the script. Copies are available in the library on reserve.
WHEN: Friday, October 19, 3:00.
WHERE: Wignall Theater
QUESTIONS: See Mr. Adair

The Play: *When the Duke of Vienna temporarily leaves the city because he considers it too morally corrupt, he cedes his power to Angelo, a harsh puritanical deputy who immediately closes all the brothels and sentences a young man named Claudio to death for impregnating his lover. Angelo then requests sexual favors from Claudio's sister Isabela in exchange for her brother's release.*

Major Roles
Isabela: *A nun. Claudio's sister. Must decide between her virtue and her brother's life.*
Claudio: *Isabela's brother. Imprisoned for unlawful sexual activity.*
The Duke: *A virtuous figure who spends much of the play in disguise to observe Angelo's actions. Fifth largest of all Shakespeare's roles.*
Angelo: *Is asked to be temporary leader of Vienna when the Duke pretends to leave the city. A ruthless hypocrite.*

Supporting Roles
Juliet: *Claudio's lover. Pregnant.*
Mistress Overdone: *Runs a brothel.*
Escalus: *A loyal, wise lord.*

Lucio: *Claudio's friend. A comic role.*
Elbow: *A constable. Comic role.*
Other nuns, clowns, citizens, prisoners.

~

THURSDAY, OCTOBER 18, 1984   MIDNIGHT

A group of us took a break from correcting midterms and went to
O'Toole's. I wasn't in the mood to sit on a stool to watch game five of
the World Series between the Tigers and the Padres. Paula wasn't in
the mood, either. When I joined her at a table, she raised her Guinness
and flung her hair back in that carefree Jimmy Buffet Margaritaville
way I'd grown fond of over the past weeks.

Tony was yelling at the TV from the bar. Paula said he was all wound
up because he had some connection with the Padres even though he
wasn't even born on the West Coast. When the Padres lost the first
game of the series, he took the next day off from school and drove to
Maine to commiserate with a friend.

Paula gulped the last of her beer, slammed down her glass, and
waved the waiter for another. I ordered another pinot grigio. Paula
joked that no one ordered pinot at O'Toole's and why couldn't I just
order a beer? I reminded her that in Spain wine is the drink of the
proletariat and that she'd gone to Miss Porter's and had a debutante
ball. I'm sure she's had her share of very expensive wines. At the same
time, she shops at thrift stores and drives an old beat-up Volvo. I don't
understand the rich.

Just as she was telling me not to take her joking too seriously, cheers
erupted from the bar as the Tigers won the World Series. When Tony
and the others reached for their wallets to pay the tab, Paula signaled
for the waiter. She told him that she was going to pay for all the Chadwick people tonight. I later learned Paula often picks up the tab as long
as everyone pretends they don't know who paid.

Everyone started leaving except Tony, who was hunched over the bar.
I asked Paula if she thought we should go rouse him and head back to
campus. Instead she looked me right in the eye and said, "Marry me."

I laughed so suddenly that wine came out of my nose. I told her she must be kidding; she told me she wasn't sure. It seemed as good a time to tell her I was gay. She said she wasn't surprised at all. She grabbed her beer glass and raised it in a toast. "Me too," she said.

Huh? I thought right then that Paula had more contradictions than anyone I knew, but then she explained herself. It wasn't a real proposal. She said if the head of Chadwick found out about me, she worried he might overreact, maybe even try to "counsel me out," as they like to phrase it, to avoid controversy. Vernon felt so uncomfortable about sex that he'd convinced the curriculum committee to move the sexuality curriculum from ninth to eleventh grade this fall. And he allows parents to opt their kids out of books with sexual content. When some parents in Paula's class refused to let their daughter read *Catcher in the Rye* last spring, Vernon made her come up with an alternative novel. Paula proposed we have dinner every now and then, maybe even go dancing, to cover us both. Let Vernon think we were an item, just to be on the safe side.

At the bar, Tony began to stir. Paula went over to offer him an arm. I wondered aloud if he'd take the day off as he had after the first game. Paula says Vernon just sees Tony as a lovable party jock. He'd never question his judgment. He's too impressed with Tony's degree from Princeton (also Vernon Reed's alma mater), his past as a star football player (also like Vernon), and his camaraderie with many of the Chadwick parents.

There's no way I'll ever fall into Vernon's good graces if I have to drink beer and play football to do it. I remember the summer before I left for Spain, I played volleyball with a group of gay guys on Friday nights. The first time we played, the ball never made it across the net more than two or three times before hitting the ground. We were all being too polite, stepping out of the way so a teammate could return the ball. Instead of "I've got it!" that first hour all I heard was, "That's yours!" or "No, *you* go for it."

I can't imagine Tony ever stepping out of the way for anyone.

Dear Casey,

I know I could simply pick up the phone and call you, but I feel more comfortable writing to you as I did when you were in Madrid. I never let you know how pleased I was that a student of mine received such a prestigious fellowship, to spend the year in Spain. I took great pride in you. I should have told you at the time, but in keeping my sexual feelings in the closet at Nearing, I'm afraid all my other feelings ended up closeted as well.

I'm writing to thank you for coming to dinner with Emory and me to address my health issues. For weeks I'd been able to dismiss Emory's concern about my lesions (now there are two), yet when I was face-to-face with you, I couldn't keep lying to myself. I know I wasn't the most popular professor at Nearing College, not by a long shot, although I do think I could have been named "best organized" if such an award existed. I also considered myself an honest one. I might have lied to myself at times, but I could never tell anything but the truth to a student. It got me into trouble. After informing a girl it was statistically impossible to pass my course when she failed the midterm, the dean called me into his office and tried to persuade me to give her another chance. He asked me how it could be possible to fail a class when there was half a semester left. "This is how," I said and handed him my grade book. I couldn't even do small talk with my students because it seemed artificial: another strike against me. I'd rather get into a discussion about the use of the subjunctive in Spanish than go on about the weather any day.

I did see a doctor and the lesions are, in fact, Kaposi's sarcoma. He knew as soon as he saw me, but he went through the motions of pressing his thumb against the lesion, telling me that if it had been a bruise the skin would have turned white for a few seconds. He did a biopsy, which to the surprise of no one, came out positive for the cancer. Radiation therapy can reduce the size of these lesions if and when they get bigger. I'm considering this option.

The doctor wants me to take the test they have for the AIDS antibodies. At first I decided against it. What good would it do? None of us need any more evidence that I've got the disease. You won't be surprised that Emory wasn't completely on board with my decision. He said that knowing my status for certain was important for treatment. It might even allow me to participate in some drug trials. I did finally see that Emory was right in all of this. I tried to bargain with him: I'd take the test if he would, too. He said he'd consider it.

I'm sounding stoic in this letter, but I will admit to being frightened, sometimes deeply so. I'm doing my best to stick to whatever routines I have left in my life now that I've retired. I've decided to read ten pages of *The Man Without Qualities* every morning, which, given that it's 1,700 pages long, feels like an expression of faith.

Emory is going through a hard time of his own. While we were in the waiting room for the doctor last week, the mother of one of his patients came in. She was pleasant enough, but was clearly shaken when she saw the lesion on my forehead. Two days later she canceled an appointment for her child. The following day two other mothers called to cancel. Emory's afraid word has gotten out that his lover has AIDS.

Before I close, Emory and I were wondering if you'd like to join us for the Boston Symphony a week from Saturday. His sister was supposed to visit us from Charleston so we bought a third ticket, but she's postponed the trip until late November. David Zinman is conducting Elgar and Mendelssohn, so it should be a lovely evening.

All best,
Warren

∽

SUNDAY, OCTOBER 28, 1984   11:00 P.M.

Rehearsals for *Measure for Measure* are going well. More girls showed up for auditions than boys, so I cast some females in male roles. I don't like the idea of girls playing men—it feels too limiting—so I've made some changes to make the roles female. The Duke of Vienna is now the Duchess of Vienna. I'm doing the play in modern dress, and I plan on having Maryanne (the girl who's playing the Duchess) wear a sharp skirt suit. I got the idea from studying Geraldine Ferraro's wardrobe on the campaign trail. With the gender change, a woman will be romantically attached to Isabella (the nun and Claudio's sister) at the end of the play. There's so much going on in the last scene that I'm hoping this will go over Vernon Reed's head.

The play is so relevant today. I just know evangelists like Jim and Tammy Faye Bakker don't follow the rules they try to force on the rest of us. There's no way that the millions they raise all go into their church works. And I bet half these preachers are closeted gay men, even as they publicly scold gay men for having the audacity to have sex. AIDS is God's punishment. Fuck them.

I need to do something useful during this crisis. Emory mentioned an organization in Boston called the AIDS Action Committee that works with people with the disease and tries to inform the public about it. I'm thinking of volunteering once I get more settled in life at Chadwick.

I woke up sweating last night. I panicked until I realized it was the first really cold night of the season, and that the heat was turned on way too high. I felt fine once I opened a window. Other than that, I'm doing a pretty good job pushing thoughts of possibly having the virus out of my mind. It isn't always easy, seeing how often I think about Stoddard. I worry about Emory, too, and whether he'll get sick.

On Friday after school I had tea with Ileana Phelan, the school psychologist. She likes to meet with all new faculty one-on-one both to get to know us as well as to talk about her role at Chadwick. We met in her office, which felt more like a living room. On one wall were shelves of teacups she has collected from her summer travels over the years. There wasn't a desk in the office, just a sofa, rocking chair, and a coffee table.

She started by telling me about herself. She's a first-generation Irish immigrant, but I'd already guessed that from her brogue. Her brothers live outside Dublin in the same town as her parents. She seems to know everything about everyone at Chadwick, and talks about the faculty in the positive light you'd expect from a mother boasting about her children. I get the feeling the school is her entire world.

When she said, "I spent most of last July in Madrid," a door opened up and we had much more to talk about. I told her about my theater project, the coup attempt, my return to the United States. I even told her about Poppy and Grace, hinting that I was gay by saying that Poppy and I should have been brother and sister. I few minutes later I knew she understood because she casually mentioned that one of her brothers lived with a boyfriend. I'm out to two people at Chadwick now, Paula and Ileana. She ended the meeting by giving me Roald Dahl's autobiography, some of which covers his years in a boarding school. She said she gives this book to every new faculty member.

∾

Dear Poppy,

As I write this, I'm imagining you and Grace trick-or-treating. When I was in Toronto for Thanksgiving, she said she wanted to be a bunny, but one of her friends told her that she couldn't be a bunny, that being a bunny was an *Easter* thing. Grace started to cry as she said this. Did she get her wish? If Halloween were on a weekend this year, I'd have driven up to see her. Please take lots of pictures. If you still plan to visit during American Thanksgiving, you can give them to me then.

What I need to say next is difficult for me. I received our credit card bill in the mail yesterday. I was surprised you spent over $2,000 in one day. Or is it a mistake? I'd understand if you needed something like a new oven or furniture, but to spend so much money at Holt Renfrew seems extravagant, given our financial situation. I don't know what to make of this. Maybe you intend to ask your parents to pay the bill. I can't pay it on my salary, and my credit rating is bad enough already.

I was going to ask you this before the bill came, so please don't assume my question is related to our finances. Have you thought any more about going back to work, even if it's just in the bookstore? You said your mother was willing to look after Grace or pay for day care. It would do you good to get out in the world and forget about being a mother for a few hours a week.

With that I'll sign off for tonight.

Casey

∾

When I got home from the symphony last night, Tony asked me if I would take over dorm duty for him. "Victory at Sea," he said with a wink, his code for getting a woman into his waterbed. I felt put out, but I agreed.

At 12:30, I went to corral the boys to their rooms. In the smoker downstairs, five or six of them were huddled in a corner. Behind the guys in the corner was Matty Wheelwright, kneeling with his hand over his mouth, vomit all around his legs. I asked David Lam what, exactly, Matty had drunk or taken, but he wouldn't tell me, so then I addressed all the boys.

"You have to tell me what happened," I said. "Don't fuck around with this. Do. Not. Fuck. Around." I'm usually guarded in my language around the boys, but this was urgent. (Tony swears all the time.) It worked: David finally told me that Matty had smoked some weed and had drunk about a fifth of vodka. I sent him to knock on Tony's door.

He returned and said there was no answer. Jesus. "Victory at Sea" was one thing. Being AWOL when a kid was puking his guts out was another.

I brought Matty to my room, made him sit up in a chair (as much as he could) and called an ambulance. While we waited, I called Vernon Reed to tell him what was going on. I thought he'd be pleased that I'd stepped in and helped Tony, but he sounded anxious, asking details that seemed irrelevant, like who Matty's teachers were. He told me it would have been better to drive him to the ER myself to avoid the commotion of an ambulance arriving on campus.

I understand a headmaster needs to consider what sort of press his school receives, but I feel like Vernon was more worried about the Chadwick's reputation than about Matty himself. He also seemed overly concerned about the reaction of Matty's father, who just happens to be Chief Medical Officer at the nearest hospital (Emerson in Concord), a major donor to the school, and a member of the Board of Overseers.

I called Paula and asked her to mind the dorm while I went to the hospital.

In the ambulance they hooked Matty up to an IV for dehydration. His father was waiting at the ER entrance when we arrived. He officiously told me he'd take care of things from here. He handed me $10 for a taxi he'd already called. It felt like a bribe.

By the time I returned to the school, Paula had directed the boys to their rooms. She was waiting in the living room of the dorm, stretched across the sofa. She sat up when she saw me, and we talked a little about the night. I told her about Vernon's reaction, asked her whether or not I had done the right thing by calling an ambulance. She told me I did, that I shouldn't let Vernon make me doubt that. The last school he ran was an all-boys military high school. It was very top-down. He called all the shots. Image was everything. At Chadwick, unlike at his last school where he had a lot of autonomy, he has to take parent complaints very seriously. Sometimes he goes overboard in trying to appease them, as he'd done with Matty's father.

"I know I shouldn't, but sometimes I actually feel bad for Vernon," she said. "He's a fish out of water here."

She left and I tried to sleep, but haven't been able to. I kept thinking about Matty and whether I fucked up. And I've been thinking a lot about Stoddard and Emory, who treated me to dinner and the symphony tonight. It was enjoyable enough, but Stoddard seemed on edge, as if his diagnosis had just begun to sink in. When he went to the restroom, Emory took the opportunity to tell me that thrush had developed in Stoddard's mouth, and that he was having a hard time swallowing. He's taking anti-fungal medication, and it leaves him nauseous. This explained why Stoddard hadn't ordered a drink, as he usually did. The doctor told him that he should eliminate sugar, which tends to feed thrush.

His mood didn't improve when he discovered that in addition to Elgar and Mendelsohn (two of his favorite composers), the orchestra was starting out the evening with a contemporary Latvian composer named Gundaris Poné. Stoddard announced that he was not going to sit through twenty minutes of dissonance, and that he would join us at our seats after "the noise of a screeching train masquerading as music" was over. Emory and I both decided to stay with him in the café in Symphony Hall, where we all had tea and talked about Tuesday's election.

None of us could even pretend to be the least bit optimistic. There's no way Mondale will beat Reagan. It was bad enough when he beat Carter four years ago, but now there's AIDS to contend with. The lack of government action is criminal.

"At least after all these years with me, Warren is finally voting the right way," Emory said.

Emory looked tired tonight. I can't imagine how hard it must be to worry about Stoddard so much. To top it off, his situation at work is getting worse. Three more parents canceled appointments for their children last week, and one of his dental hygienists quit unexpectedly. He said it was hard enough being a black dentist in a lily-white town, but the AIDS rumors were just making his situation worse. He's considering giving up pediatric dentistry and opening an office for adult care near the South End, where he'd cater to a largely gay, more racially diverse clientele.

I can't believe it's after 4:30 and I haven't slept at all. I got up and tried to read the Dahl autobiography Ileana Phelan gave me the other day, but the words just aren't sinking in. I keep thinking of Irina's line in *Three Sisters* when she panics because she can no longer remember the word for "ceiling" in Italian. Sometimes I panic about forgetting everything except the things I want to forget.

∼

Vernon Reed, Headmaster
Chadwick Academy
134 Pleasant Hill Road
Smythe Administration Building
East Wellington, MA 02421

NOVEMBER 5, 1984

Dear Casey,

I was happy we had the opportunity today to discuss the incident that took place in Wentworth Hall on Saturday. Because I believe clear and concise communication is essential to good governance and relationships at Chadwick Academy, I'd like to summarize what I consider the most salient points of our conversation.

We both agreed that Matty Wheelwright's health was of the utmost importance that evening. We were both also relieved he was released Sunday morning, making his stay in the hospital not more than ten hours. I informed you that his family is investigating a treatment facility in Arizona in case the situation should arise again, warranting further intervention. I am grateful that we were able to inform Matty's parents of our concerns. I thank you for your role in that.

Yet it is because Matty spent such limited time in the hospital that I felt the need to review your response to the incident. As you know, the arrival of an ambulance caused a great deal of worry on the Chadwick campus. Some students found it difficult to sleep given the circumstances. Our school counselor, Ileana Phelan, was up until 2:00 a.m. calming the girls in Appleton Hall. Neighbors were awoken and showed up on campus. The incident was reported in the local newspaper this morning.

You and I discussed the ways in which this scene could have been avoided, while at the same time guaranteeing Matty's wellbeing. Most obvious is the fact that Matty's father is a doctor at the very hospital where Matty was observed. The simplest way to have dealt with the situation would have been to call him. He surely would have been able to care for his son as professionally as anyone else at Emerson Hospital. Even better would have been if you had called me so that I could contact Mr. Wheelwright personally.

I also discussed with you the appropriateness of your language when trying to ascertain from the boys what had happened to Matty. I do understand how anxiety-producing the situation must have been for you. At the same time, swearing in front of the residents of Wentworth Hall is not good role modeling. I admit to being dismayed that instead of immediately acknowledging your mistake, you responded by claiming that your language was no different from what other teachers at Chadwick Academy use. I must take exception to that generalization. I have never had a student complain about a teacher's language until now.

Finally, you expressed frustration that Tony Moretti was not present during the situation on Saturday. I have spoken to him. While he was gracious in apologizing for not being available, I must stress that as dorm head, it is perfectly reasonable that he delegate responsibility to you in his absence with confidence in your professionalism.

I hope you will view this letter as supportive rather than punitive. You are new to Chadwick, and I'm willing to chalk Saturday night up to a typical rookie mistake. In the classroom, you have proven yourself to be a solid teacher. Still, Chadwick Academy is a boarding school, and the standards for one's behavior and professionalism are no different outside the classroom.

Onward! I look forward to your continued presence in the Chadwick community.

Sincerely yours,

Vernon Reed, Headmaster

cc: employment file, Casey Adair

⁓

Dear Gustavo,

I'm sorry I've taken so long getting back to you after you were kind enough to give me the news that Octavio had died. I was saddened but not surprised. He worked as a hustler for quite a few closeted and wealthy men in Madrid, just when the virus was quietly spreading. You're right: he and I ended badly. I'm moved that he asked you to write me about his death.

I feel like I need a Gustavo refresher course in protest and resistance in pretty much all areas of my life. AIDS is at the forefront, of course. A former professor of mine has it. I try to be there for him and his partner, but I feel helpless most of the time. I'm taking the train to New York City in December to demand more research and prevention funding.

I'm feeling pressure at work. Our headmaster is a very traditional guy who'd probably need smelling salts if he found out I was gay. This week he wrote a letter for my personnel file that criticized me for what I felt was doing the right thing. I'm also directing *Measure for Measure* with a contemporary twist, which may not go over well. They tell me contract time comes up in April, so I'll know about my future by then. You know me, though. I'm probably overthinking everything because I'm new to the school and can't afford to screw up.

And what's this about a girlfriend? In your letter you said it wasn't all that serious, but it sounded like things could get serious quickly. I want all the details. I never thought you'd settle down—politics before love, after all—but I guess our priorities change as we get older.

I can't ask you to write back as soon as possible when it took me so long to respond to your letter, so I'll end by saying I can't wait to hear from you.

Big hugs,
Casey

~

Dear Casey,

I was going to talk to you when you called for Grace last week, but I was really worked up and didn't want to yell at you in front of our daughter. I bet you have no idea why I'm mad at you, which makes me madder.

I'll quote directly from your last letter: "It would do you good to get out in the world and forget about being a mother for a few hours a week." Are you kidding me? You think turning off the mother switch is that easy? Maybe you've mastered the art of forgetting about parenting, but when you're a single parent—and let's face it, that's what I am—there *is* no forgetting being a mother for a few hours while you work in a bookstore.

Here is a very short list of the things I'd be worrying about during my "time off" working at a bookstore:

1. Maybe Grace is crying her eyes out or holding her breath like she did a few weeks after you left, forcing me to run cold water over her head in the kitchen sink.
2. Maybe she had a cough this morning. Could it turn into bronchitis and then pneumonia? Could she be developing something chronic, like asthma? And should I have called in sick rather than dropping her off at my mother's?

3. Maybe she's missing me way too much.
4. Maybe she isn't missing me at all.
5. Will my mother know that look she gives me when she really, really wants to sit on a lap?
6. Will spending too much time at my parents' house bring up questions about why they live in such a big place while we're cramped in our apartment?
7. On a related note, will my father quietly promise to get her the dog she's been begging for even when pets aren't allowed in our apartment building?
8. Will Grace accidentally bump into a table and break one of my father's cherished Inuit bear sculptures?

I could go on and on, but I hope you get the picture. There's *no such thing* as forgetting you are a mother. It is *who I am*. And it's hard.

I do my best to keep my spirits up, which brings me to the Holt Renfrew bill. One Friday afternoon I was on the sofa, trying to read while Grace rearranged the furniture in her doll house. And it just hit me. Here I am on another Friday afternoon, a night's worth of TV ahead of me, a weekend with no plans other than brunch with my parents on Sunday. I thought *I can't do this anymore*. I got out of my bathrobe, got dressed, dressed Grace, walked downstairs and hailed a taxi. I told the driver to drive around the block a few times while I decided where to go. After the third time around, I said, "Holt Renfrew."

I took Grace by the hand and headed straight to the women's department. Without even trying them on, I bought three dresses. Then I headed for the shoe department and bought three pairs in colors I'd never dream of putting on my feet. And *voilà*. My weekend. I wore each dress for a few hours. I made three different trips to the grocery store just so I would be seen in public. And you know what? I was happy for a while. I'm good at pretending. I pretended this was me in five years, while I'm still young. I wasn't pretending I was anything specific—no Scotiabank CEO, no budding actress who spends summers at the Stratford Festival—it was just *me*, in gorgeous clothes, feeling I could be desired.

By Saturday night the bloom was off the rose. I boxed everything up and sat down with Grace to watch *Thrill of a Lifetime*, which was sort of ironic. Did we ever watch it together? Contestants reveal something they've always wanted to do, and the producers find a way to make it happen. That night a group of boys played with the Harlem Globetrotters, a businessman prepared sushi, and a couple visited the Northwest Territories and slept in an igloo. I derided them at first. *This is what you most want to do? Make sushi? Sleep in the cold?* And then I started to think, *At least they know what they want to do. That's way ahead of you, Poppy.*

There's also the question of whether or not you infected me the night Grace was conceived. I know the chances of this are slim, even if you do have the virus, which I pray to God you don't. But I'm still scared as hell. I'm getting tested just to make sure. I have no idea if you plan to get tested, so I've taken matters into my own hands.

There. I've said my piece. We won't have a scene when Grace and I visit over Thanksgiving. Any hotels you could recommend around Boston? If it's not too cold, I thought we could go to the Boston Common. Will the Christmas lights be up by then? I also think Grace would like the Planetarium.

Grace asks for you all the time. If you could only call just a little bit more, I think she'd be much happier. She's really looking forward to visiting. She's never been on an airplane, so it's a big deal.

Call or write soon with some hotel names, please.

Feeling less mad at you,

Poppy

PS: I returned all the dresses, and all but one pair of the shoes so this should be reflected on the next VISA bill. I'm asking my parents for the shoes for Christmas, so don't worry about that expense.

$\sim$

MONDAY, NOVEMBER 12, 1984   11:15 P.M.

It was a long weekend (Veteran's Day, observed today) and I've had dorm duty since Friday afternoon. It hasn't been all that bad. Most of the boarders were away until tonight. Twelve of them stayed, and seven of them were girls, so I only had five boys to take care of. On Friday night, I piled both groups into a van and went to the movies in Framingham. Half of them decided on *A Nightmare on Elm Street* and the other half on *Amadeus* (which I'd already seen). I went to see *The Killing Fields*, a movie about Pol Pot's "cleansing" of two million Cambodian citizens. It was staggering.

In bed I started comparing what happened in Cambodia to what's happening right now with AIDS in the United States. I know they're not the same thing. In Cambodia they were dealing with the deliberate execution of a huge number of people. In the United States, the numbers aren't that large (yet) and people are dying not because of direct action. Instead, conscious inaction is to blame. But there is a similarity in the hatred that is driving people to see others as "undesirable," which is what they called the slaughtered Cambodians. If AIDS had begun among a more "desirable" population (straight white men, for example), we'd have a cure by now (and probably a vaccine, too). But because gay men are so "undesirable," especially in the eyes of the present administration, millions of us *could* end up with the same fate as the Cambodians. Hospitals and hospices are becoming our killing fields. And with Mondale pummeled in the election last week, I don't see any real hope for change.

Maybe I'll feel better after I go to New York in a few weeks to protest with some of Emory's friends. They really hate Mayor Koch down there. Well, at least Larry Kramer does, but he doesn't seem to like anyone these days. He hates the *New York Times* for not giving more coverage to AIDS. He hates some of the leaders of The Gay Men's Health Crisis, an organization he founded, because he doesn't think they're in-your-face enough.

On Saturday, Ileana Phelan (the school psychologist) and I took a van full of kids into Boston for a few hours. While the kids did some shopping, she and I spent time at The Trident—the place where I met Emory to talk about Stoddard—and had tea. She and I hadn't talked since the incident with Matty and his trip to the ER. I wanted to get her take on what happened, so I'd brought the letter Vernon had written for my personnel file. She took out a pair of red half-moon glasses and read slowly, looking up at me after every few sentences, which I did not take as a good sign. When she was done she slowly folded the letter and inserted it back in the envelope, but didn't return it to me right away. She held it for a while, as if she wanted to spare me.

"Does he want me out?" I said.

"No. Don't go there yet." Her Irish lilt was charming and made her words go down easier. "It's not a great letter, but I wouldn't say your job is in jeopardy, at least not right away."

She went on to say that Vernon probably wanted a paper trail just in case something else should come up. She didn't call it a "cover your ass letter," which is what it really was. It was written to save Vernon's ass if he fired me and I took him to court. I asked her why he needed a letter like this in my employment file. Was sending a sick kid to the hospital such a crime?

Ileana told me she'd screwed up. At the administrative council meeting a few weeks ago, the subject of AIDS came up. The national association that governs independent schools is suggesting all its members to come up with clear policies around what to do if a student or employee gets sick. There have been some really ugly episodes with hemophiliacs in public schools in the Midwest. Vernon had asked Ileana and the school nurse, along with Chadwick's consulting doctor, to devise a plan.

Ileana said she thought this sounded all well and good, even progressive, far beyond what she thought Vernon would do. But then on the way out of the meeting, he whispered to her, "We won't need to worry about the faculty because we don't have any homosexuals teaching here at Chadwick." According to Ileana, as soon as the words came out of Vernon's mouth, she blurted, "Are you kidding, Vernon? Of course there are." She claims that she never mentioned my name when he pressed her. I'm choosing to believe her.

Now I wonder if Vernon has put two and two together, and if his response to me the night Matty got drunk could be part his trying to have something official in my file, something he could use if my sexuality ever becomes an issue. Ileana assures me that's not the case, that he looked confused rather than angry when she told him not everyone was straight at Chadwick.

"The man has no imagination," she said. "He's led a sheltered life and can't fathom that a different world exists beyond that shelter. He's naïve, but I don't think he's spiteful."

Vernon may well be naïve, but he can be really thoughtless, too. There's a scrawny stray dog that shows up on campus once in a while. Vernon has taken to calling him "AIDS," and when he does it, people laugh. People who should know better laugh. I feel like a coward for not saying anything. Gustavo would want me to fight like hell.

∿

SUNDAY, NOVEMBER 18, 1984   6:45 P.M.

I just got off the phone with Poppy to finalize the details for the trip this week. She'll be arriving early Wednesday afternoon with Grace. I promised to pick them up at the airport. We'll have Thanksgiving dinner at a hotel in Boston. I'm hoping to do a day trip to Rockport on Friday.

Poppy seemed quiet on the phone. I worried that her AIDS test had come out positive, but she said she got the results yesterday and she's fine. I think she's looking forward to the trip, or at least to having some adult company with someone she knows.

She graciously accepted my apology for assuming she could forget about motherhood for a few hours if she went back to work. Then she handed the phone to Grace. Because Grace and I don't talk all that much, when we do talk I feel like she's taken a month's worth of intensive language courses between calls. Today's new word was "typewriter," which made me wonder if Poppy has been polishing up her résumé and may be looking for a job after all.

Last night Paula and I went to a dance bar in Boston called the 1270 because its address is 1270 Boylston Street. At the entrance was a sign that read "Where Two of a Kind Beats a Straight and There's Always a Full House." It was near the Fenway (or the Fens, as some guys call it), where gay men cruise for sex once the sun goes down. Every once in a while, the police sweep through and make a few arrests. The club is also near Fenway Park. Paula said the last time she was at the 1270, a bunch of gay men ran through the entrance in a panic because they'd been chased by some drunk guys leaving the ballgame.

I'd stayed out of dance clubs when I was living with Poppy and Grace in Toronto, so I could only compare the 1270 to the Black & White. What struck me first was how large the club was compared to the one in Madrid. There were three floors: one for gay guys, one for lesbians, and one for bisexuals. There was also a rooftop that overlooked Boston if you wanted to get away from the noise and the crowd. I was surprised Paula hadn't taken me to the sort of bar that played her beloved Jimmy Buffet. She was even wearing her parrot shirt.

She took me by the hand and we went to the floor where the bisexuals were. Over the deafening thump of the music, she explained that we could start the evening off dancing together, then go our separate ways and meet up again at the end of the night.

The strobe and disco lights made it hard to really see anyone until you were up close. Still, I could tell there were more women on the floor than men. A few men were eying each other. I wondered if any of them would end up eying me. With so much going on these past months, I hadn't even considered the logistics of what would happen if I met someone. I didn't even remember to put a condom in my wallet.

We danced for about ten minutes until Paula signaled to me that she was going downstairs where the women were. I walked up to the third floor. I was almost as overwhelmed as I was when I first saw men dancing together in Madrid. It's hard to describe the combination of ease and sexual excitement that hit me. I stood against the wall for a while, taking it all in.

I was wondering if I should ask someone to dance when a guy in a white T-shirt, black leather pants, and a black leather cap walked up to me. Chains hung from his belt loops and a navy-blue handkerchief sprouted from his back-left pocket. I knew there was a sexual code based on a handkerchief's color and which pocket it was in, but I didn't know the details. He leaned beside me against the wall, brushed his hand up against my leg, and nodded for me to follow him. I wasn't ready for this. I shook my head no. He walked away without a word.

I went to the rooftop where cigarette smoke didn't fill the air. It was chilly, so not many people were outside. Two guys were wrapped in a kiss not far from the door. I walked to the edge of the roof and looked out over a lit Kenmore Square and an unlit Fenway Park.

"There's nothing more melancholy than a dark ballpark."

The words came from behind me. A man stepped next to me and put his elbows on the edge of the roof fence. He was dressed in black: sports jacket, T-shirt, pants, shoes. His hair was thick and wavy with occasional touches of white. I thought: if this guy were ten years younger, I'd be swooning.

In a British accent, he introduced himself as "Geoffrey with a G."

Sans British accent, I told him I was "Casey with a C."

He laughed, then reached into his coat and produced a package of Barclays. He offered me one. I rarely smoke, but I accepted. He lit my cigarette with a silver lighter. It was engraved, I assumed with his initials.

"So, where are you from, Geoffrey with a G?" I asked, trying to suppress a cough.

"Across the pond," he said. "Brighton. Just moved here last June. I was desperate to leave Thatcher's England."

"So you moved to Reagan's America?"

"It sounds ridiculous, doesn't it?" he said. "But we know Reagan has a shelf life. He'll be gone in '88. Thatcher could be prime minister for another decade."

I told him that sounded reasonable. I asked him why he found dark ballparks so melancholy.

"I became a baseball fan over the summer. I loved being in Fenway just as much as I loved watching the game. There's so much life there, but it's a different sort of life than you find at a rugby match, where everything goes so quickly. There's a leisure to baseball that I find irresistible. When I look over a dark ballpark, it's very wistful for me. I want to be there, watching the game, being part of the crowd."

We talked a little bit more about baseball, then Boston. He chose to live here because it had a shoreline like his native Brighton.

After Geoffrey with a G and I smoked our cigarettes, he asked me if I wanted to go to a quieter bar, a place called Napoleon's in the Back

Bay. When I told him I was with someone, I saw him twinge just a bit, which gave me a certain amount of pleasure. "My friend's female," I said. "And we just drove here together, but I really should go back with her."

He handed me his business card, suggesting that I call him sometime. He's an assistant director of one of Harvard's libraries. Having a 40-something guy give me his number at the 1270 was not something I'd envisioned when Paula and I planned the evening. He handed me another business card and a pen and told me to jot down my number.

Emory called this morning to say that he thought Stoddard was doing better. The radiation has shrunk the lesions. The bad news is that Emory's patients keep dropping him, to the point where he is now closed on Wednesdays. He tried to put a positive spin on the situation, saying that now he'd have more time to stay with Stoddard, but they both knew he wasn't fooling either of them.

~

The very last place I thought I would find myself tonight was in Toronto, sleeping on Poppy's sofa. But here I am. I got to the airport early to pick up Poppy and Grace. I went to the gate to wait for Air Canada 263. It landed on schedule. The passengers straggled out. No Poppy. No Grace. I went to the Air Canada desk and asked if there was another flight arriving soon. Maybe I had written down the wrong information? No, she said. The next flight landed in the evening.

I found a pay phone and called my number to see if Poppy had left a message. There was one from Paula wishing me a happy Thanksgiving. That was it.

When I called Poppy in Toronto, her mother picked up. She explained how she'd driven Poppy and Grace to the airport. Poppy seemed a little shaky so her mother parked and walked with them to the gate. As soon as they called Poppy's flight, she turned to her mother and said, "I can't do this." She was paralyzed. Some sort of panic attack. It took her mother twenty minutes just to get Poppy to take the first step to leave the airport. She drove Poppy and Grace back to their apartment. Poppy was now in bed; Grace was watching TV.

I asked her what I should do. She didn't hesitate to tell me to come to Toronto. My presence would normalize things, calm everything down. She considers life one long dinner party, and it's our job to get through it without breaking the china. I'm sure she asked me to come so the china breakage would be minimal.

She gave me her credit card number to buy myself a ticket, because "teachers don't make that kind of money." I couldn't tell if she thought we ought to make more, or if not being able to afford a plane ticket was the way it should be. She sent her husband to pick me up at the airport. We didn't talk much along the way to Toronto Center, just a few words about the publishing industry these days and how crazy Canadian politics has been this year with three prime ministers within a four-month period. He said little about Poppy except for acknowledging that she seems to be going through a hard time right now.

He parked in front of Poppy's building. As soon as I entered the apartment, her mother threw on her coat, relieved to be sprung. On her way out, she told me she'd brought Poppy a pot of chamomile to her bed about an hour ago, and I might ask if she wanted or needed anything.

Grace was happy to see me. She insisted on sitting on my lap, outlining my face with her fingers, breaking into a fit of laughter when she reached my nostrils. I hip-carried her into Poppy's bedroom. Her legs felt longer than I'd remembered only a few weeks ago. The light was off. We sat at the end of the bed while Poppy stirred awake.

"I don't know what came over me," she said. "I just couldn't get on that plane."

I told her not to worry, that we'd celebrate Thanksgiving quietly here in Toronto. I'd thought of so many other things that might have gone wrong when I didn't see her at the airport. That she couldn't summon the nerve to board wasn't one of them, but at least it was minor compared to the catastrophes I'd imagined.

Grace pulled the throw blanket off her mother and wrapped it around herself. She asked when we were all going on an airplane. I told her that we weren't sure when, but sometime soon. She pondered this as she played with the blanket. She asked why we couldn't go to the airport right now.

Poppy told Grace that she'd explained why three or four times, but Grace still looked puzzled. Poppy was getting exasperated, so I encouraged Grace to go back to watching TV. When Poppy and I were alone I asked her if there was anything else going on that I should know about.

"You know as much as I know," she said. "I just became overwhelmed with sadness and couldn't move."

The grief that hit me right then surprised me. I took Poppy's hand. I told her that if she wanted to do any sort of therapy together, I'd be willing.

"It really isn't as much about you as you think it is," she said. "Sure, our relationship is part of the issue, but it's not the whole issue. I'm not even sure it's the major issue. My parents have offered to pay for a therapist if I need to see one long-term."

"No," I said. "I'll pay."

"Don't be ridiculous. You're having a hard enough time just making ends meet."

I thought about getting a second job, perhaps working nights at Reading International in Harvard Square. Or maybe I'd take out a loan. My being able to pay for Poppy's therapy started to consume me. I told her I was serious and wanted to help however I could.

She ignored me, instead telling me how lately she'd been taking comfort in visiting the textile stores on Queen Street West. At first, she couldn't explain why going to these stores helped her, only that she would go from bolt to bolt and just feel the fabric: wool, cotton, silk, leather, hemp, linen, chiffon, velvet, polyester, taffeta, denim. She'd close her eyes and bring a corner of the fabric to her cheek. The cotton soothed her. The silk cooled her. The wool scratched her. The taffeta tickled her. The fabric made her feel many different things, something she couldn't do with a depression hovering over her. And yes, while what she was feeling was tactile, sometimes that tactile feeling would hint at an emotional feeling, like when she brought a corner of velvet up to her face and thought its softness not only felt beautifully soft against her skin, it also softened something inside her as well.

After a while, I encouraged her to get out of bed. We sat at the kitchen table with Grace. We had pizza delivered and drank a bottle of root beer. I asked Poppy if she'd be up to Thanksgiving dinner in a restaurant tomorrow, and she said she thought she might. I called a few restaurants and found one that served American Thanksgiving. Someone had just canceled a 6:00 reservation. I booked a table.

Grace was exhausted and went to bed easily. I read from Berenstain Bears. She fell asleep halfway through, and by then Poppy had fallen asleep in the den. I helped her back to bed and selected a pillow and blanket from her closet for my night on the sofa.

Before I went to sleep, I checked for any messages on my answering machine. I listened to an unfamiliar voice that I gradually recognized as "Geoffrey with a G" from the 1270. He was calling to see if I wanted to go to dinner Friday night. I made a mental note to call him in the morning and politely decline.

∾

SATURDAY, NOVEMBER 24, 1984   8:30 A.M.

I just returned from a walk. I started along Lake Ontario, where it was quiet, with only a few other walkers and some cyclists joining me, wearing gloves and tuques. Funny how that was the first word for a knit hat that came to mind. Maybe I'm more of a Canadian than I thought I was.

I left the lake and headed up Bay Street toward the Financial District. No one was around on a Saturday morning. I had a flashback to one day about a year before I left Toronto for Boston. I was walking to my job at the publishing house when I saw a small group gathered at a plaza. They called themselves "Fruit Cocktail," and each one was dressed head to toe as a fruit: an orange with the word "Sunkist" on it, a bunch of grapes, a banana, an apple, and a lemon. Even with their bulky costumes, they managed to form a kick line as they sang something silly. A sign in front of them said that they were raising money for the Gay and Lesbian Community Appeal, so I threw some change into the hat on the ground.

A few months later I learned that they were performing at the Ryerson University Theater. I told Poppy I was out to do some errands, but went to the show first. The group had grown enough to fill the stage. The fruit costumes were gone, but everyone was dressed in what I'd call fruit colors. I remember lots of singing and dancing, and a woman on roller skates. I wanted to embrace the performers' complete abandon, but I just wasn't there yet, and I'm not sure I'm any closer. If anything, these few days with Poppy and Grace have sobered me. I'm beginning to think I should have stayed at least another year until Poppy had secured a job and Grace was in kindergarten.

By the time I returned from my morning walk, Poppy wasn't exactly cheerful, but she seemed to be in a better place. We kept our Thanksgiving dinner reservations at a funky hotel restaurant on Queen West. At first it looked like the design was randomly thrown together: different colored chairs, a few booths, thick red velvet curtains that pooled on the floor, shelving with an odd combination of books and old radios. Then I realized that everything was strangely all of a piece, that this was exactly the look the owners wanted.

The food was great—a buffet with the traditional turkey and stuffing, and lots of side dishes. Grace stuck to the mashed potatoes and cranberry sauce, but Poppy and I ventured into winter squash with spiced butter and Brussels sprouts with shallots and salt pork. I worried when Poppy ordered a vodka martini to start the meal, thinking it might darken her mood, but it had the opposite effect. She was more relaxed and laughed a few times.

Maybe just getting dressed up made us all feel a little better. Grace wanted two ribbons in her hair, then three, then four. And she begged her mother to let her wear a necklace. Even after Poppy triple-looped the string of fake pearls, it was still too long for Grace, and she ended up looking like a flapper. At the end of the meal, Poppy insisted on paying, saying that her parents wanted to treat us to dinner.

I fly back to Boston tomorrow. I don't know if that's the right thing to do.

∾

Dear Poppy,

Thanks again for driving me to the airport this morning. I'm still a little shaky thinking about Grace's breakdown at the gate. She almost made me reconsider and stay an extra day in Toronto, but I knew that we'd just go through the same scene tomorrow—or the next day, or the next—so I left as quickly as I could. I'm sorry if I seemed cold. That was the last thing I was feeling, but I was afraid that if I showed any emotion at all, I'd have turned into one sloppy mess, which wouldn't have been good for any of us.

The main reason I am writing is again to say how important I think it is that you find a therapist. You need someone to vent with on a regular basis. You suggested that my even considering that I could be a cause of your anger was narcissistic on my part, so I won't speculate as to why you are feeling the way you do. I just believe that you're not going to get better on your own.

If you can't bring it upon yourself to find your way out of this depression for your sake, then please think about Grace. I know I'm hardly one to say this given that I'm over five hundred miles away from you both, but I could tell that she misses you. She wants her mother back.

And I meant what I said about paying for anything that isn't covered. That wasn't just talk.

Love,
Casey

∿

TUESDAY, NOVEMBER 27, 1984   6:15 A.M.

I got up this morning around 5:00 and walked around campus for a while. Chadwick has a really nice campus, although in November it can be gloomy with the trees bare. I remembered a poem by John Updike my father read to me, not that long before he died. On my way around the pond I stopped at the library and unlocked the front door. I found *Telephone Poles and Other Poems* in the card catalogue, which rang an immediate bell. I left a note on the librarian's desk telling her

I'd borrowed the book, then came back to my apartment to read the poem.

My father wasn't a big Updike fan, but he did like some of his nature poetry. It was the last two lines that felt most familiar, where Updike wrote of telephone poles: "These giants are more constant than evergreens / By being never green." On my walk all I could see were "never green" trees. I couldn't imagine them with any green, or even any fall colors. Was this what Poppy was going through, unable to see the world as green, and thinking that its lack of green was a permanent state?

Tonight Paula suggested we eat at an Italian restaurant a few towns away. She told me eating at The Chateau (such a weird name for an Italian restaurant) was absolutely a "must-do" for anyone on the Chadwick faculty. The rooms at The Chateau were named after colors: ruby, gold, green, blue. We waited in line for about twenty minutes before a friendly woman with towering blond hair escorted us to a pleather booth in the Gold Room. (And yes, pretty much everything in the room, including the pleather, was gold.) Velvet paintings of famous Italians like Al Pacino, Dean Martin, and Sophia Loren hung on the walls.

Over fettuccini Alfredo (me) and chicken marsala (Paula), we talked about our Thanksgivings. She spent it with her brothers at their family home in the Berkshires. She likes the Berkshires this time of year because it's quiet: foliage season is over and ski season hasn't begun. It's when she feels most at home.

It's been almost three months since I started living at Chadwick and I still don't feel at home in the dorm. The boys can't get enough of Tony. They're in his apartment constantly (except when there's "Victory at Sea") while I play the role of drill sergeant. When I'm on duty, lights are out at exactly 11:00 and there's barely a whisper during study hall. Tony's looser with the rules than I am because he can be. When he swears in front of the kids, he gets a pass. I get a warning letter.

I told Paula my feelings about all this. She explained something called "the golden shoehorn." Once Vernon decides to like you, you're set. He rarely changes his mind because that would mean his original assessment of you was wrong. When Tony arrived, his only experience related to teaching was being a camp counselor. He didn't go to private school, but he'd gone to Princeton and he had done athletics. Vernon took out his golden shoehorn and helped Tony slide into one new position after another: dorm head, head of the science department, chair of the Committee on Student Life. Now there's talk of him becoming Dean of Students.

Vernon walked in on a rehearsal of *Measure for Measure* the other day. We were running the scene where Duke Angelo (Duchess, in this production) solicits sex from Isabela in exchange for saving her brother's life. I've tried to tame things, directing the Duchess to be subtle in her aggression. I've also cut some lines. But it's still clear to anyone who knows Shakespeare what's going on. I've been assuming most of the audience doesn't know Shakespeare very well, and that my casting two women in the leads won't register, the same way most American housewives loved watching Paul Lynde camp it up on *Hollywood Squares* but never for a minute considered he might be gay.

When we took a break, Vernon came to me and said, "So the Duke is a Duchess? That's always the way, isn't it? Never enough boys. They play sports and girls do drama. Last year we did an all-female *Twelfth Night*. It was wonderful. A hard act to follow."

Three more weeks until Christmas break. I can't wait.

∼

BOSTON   NOVEMBER 26, 1984

Casey, my love,

I called you a few times over the past few days. I know you've been busy with family visiting. Poppy and Grace were supposed to visit, right? Warren says he remembers Penelope (that's what he calls her) fondly, although he says this in a vague sort of way, as if he were recalling childhood Christmases so many years ago but forgets what toys he received. He doesn't want to reconnect with her, though. He really can't handle renewing an acquaintance at this point in his life. At least that's what he told me, so I have to honor that, even though I think a few new people in his orbit might perk him up even the tiniest bit.

Right now, his blood numbers aren't all that bad. In fact, they're surprisingly good, given the circumstances. But that hasn't cheered Warren up at all. Christmas is coming—always a downer for him—and then what? Constant medical appointments? He needs something—*anything*—to look forward to.

So, here's my plan. I think you and Warren should have a rendezvous in Spain this spring. Warren and I have the money, and we'll be in even better shape come March when my new dental business is up and running in the Fenway. I'm still furious about having to close my pediatric office, but what can I do? Anyway, you must have some sort of spring vacation, right? I propose you and Warren spend some of that time in Spain. We'll also fly you up to Toronto and get a nice hotel for you so you can spend time with Poppy and Grace. I know Warren's health might make any sort of a trip impossible, but there's no harm in giving him a little hope, is there?

Warren has no clue about my scheming. In order for him to say yes, I need to present a plan *in detail.* I need to say, "This is it, Warren. Take it or leave it. And if you don't take it, I'll leave *you.*" (You do know I'd never leave him, especially now.) I just believe in my heart of hearts that this trip—or just looking forward to this trip—would mean the world to him, even if he's not ready to admit it.

Please think about this, love. But don't overthink because you'll end up entertaining all the reasons you *shouldn't* go and . . . honey, just do it, please. Do it for your favorite college professor. Do it for me. Do it for yourself. Do it for a sick man who'll never have the chance to travel again. I'm really pulling on those heartstrings now, aren't I? Do it, Casey. Do it.

Kisses and hugs,
Emory

~

Dear Casey,

I'm sure you'll think this incredibly forward of me, but I left a message with you before Thanksgiving and have called a number of times since, only to get your answering machine. I hesitated to leave another message because I didn't want to give the impression that I was pressuring you in any way, so I'm giving you the opportunity to respond by letter, which I've always found easier than the telephone.

I'm going to play the hopeless romantic and tell you up front that I've had a hard time getting you out of my mind since our brief but lovely conversation on the roof of the 1270. I'm sure you think I'm quite daft (yes, "daft," a British word I'm hoping will charm you) by being so direct in my interest. I'm thinking I'm a little daft myself. I consider myself much subtler and more urbane than this letter would lead you to believe.

I'm hoping there's been some perfectly explicable miscommunication between the two of us. Perhaps you have lost my telephone number. Perhaps your answering machine broke, and you never even heard my message. Whatever the case, I would very much appreciate a quick note letting me know whether or not you'd like to have tea with me sometime (yes, tea, another attempt at British charm) or whether I should give up entirely on any chance that we might see each other again.

Cheers,
Geoffrey (with a "G," obviously)

∾

BOSTON   NOVEMBER 30, 1984

Dear Gustavo,

I know I'm writing out of turn since I just sent you a letter a few weeks ago, but if anyone can understand the need to break a rule it would be my political firebrand friend. I wonder what you're involved in politically these days. Or has the woman you've been dating taken up all your time? Maybe the two of you are protesting together. I can't imagine you dating someone without political passion.

I read the *New York Times* in the school library regularly, so I'm up to date on what's going on in Spain. It sounds like the situation in the Basque region isn't getting any better, which surprises me. Don't they have more autonomy under Felipe González than before?

I am writing because there's a chance I'll travel to Spain in March and I was wondering if you'll be around then. I think I may have mentioned to you that a former college professor of mine, Warren Stoddard, has AIDS. His partner (Emory) thinks it would do him good if I went with him to Madrid during my spring break. I called him the other day and said yes, and to our surprise Stoddard has gone along with the plan. I don't know for sure whether I'll be traveling since we don't know how Stoddard's health will be. I have the last two weeks in March off, so I could be in Madrid for either of those weeks.

I just finished a novel by an Argentine writer named Manuel Puig, *Kiss of the Spider Woman*. I read they're making a movie out of it. It's not a new book, but somehow Puig slipped under my radar all these years. I found a copy in the foreign-language bookstore in Cambridge. I wonder if you've read it? It's about a serious Marxist (is there any other kind?) and a gay man who share a jail cell. I thought of the two of us, although I think we'd get along better than these two characters if we were ever faced with that predicament.

Write soon and let me know your plans for March.

Hugs,

Casey

~

BOSTON   DECEMBER 4, 1984

Dear Geoffrey,

Thank you for your sweet note and phone message. I've been away for a while and haven't had the time to answer you.

I'm so flattered I made an impression on you that night at the 1270. It was such a brief conversation, and I was a little out of my element. For all I knew, you left thinking I was a complete idiot.

Your offer sounds lovely, but at this point my life is much too complicated to add another relationship, even one that begins over tea.

Yours,

Casey

~

Last night I left Poppy four or five phone messages, each one more desperate than the previous, but she didn't call back. I'd only called to say hello and see how she and Grace were doing, nothing that important, but by 8:00 I was convinced she was in the emergency ward because Grace had been hit by a bus. I finally called her mother. Turns out Poppy was out with a friend (a date?) and Grace was with her grandparents. I felt silly for making such a big deal out of things, but her mother didn't seem to mind me calling, even if she sounded surprised at my concern. At least I got to say hello to Grace.

Tony was right when he said that the time between Thanksgiving and Christmas vacations is hard. I've been getting about five hours of sleep, which makes me impatient as hell with the kids the next day. This morning six of my first-year Spanish students showed up without homework. I chewed the whole class out.

I'm happiest at Chadwick when I'm working on *Measure for Measure*. I tried to move the production date to before Christmas vacation so as not to break up the momentum, but apparently there's a long tradition of doing the show after the break, even if no one remembers the reason. ("We've just always done it that way.") If there's one thing I've learned at Chadwick, it's that tradition trumps everything.

Tradition also has it that the drama department present a musical every spring. After my gender-bending Shakespeare, I suppose I should do something traditional like *Guys and Dolls* or *Music Man*.

I'm glad I'm away this weekend. I take the train to New York City on Friday afternoon and return late Sunday night. I'm staying with Emory's friend Donald, a lawyer who lives in the Village. On Saturday, Larry Kramer is leading a protest in front of Gracie Mansion, where Mayor Koch lives. Koch has done next to nothing to stop the spread of AIDS. He won't even talk to the press about it. Donald and I will go to the protest with some of his friends and then to a candlelight vigil to honor everyone who has died so far.

Is it strange that I'm looking forward to getting away for the weekend when I'll be spending it venting anger and grief? Sometimes I wonder if I even have any right to emotions when it comes to AIDS.

Stoddard is the only person I know well who has it. Okay, there was also Octavio. But I haven't had to nurse a lover, let alone bury one.

I guess all that matters is that I want to be in NYC. The need I feel to be there is more powerful than anything I felt when I protested in Madrid.

∾

SATURDAY, DECEMBER 8, 1984   2:15 A.M.

Emory's friend Donald has been a wonderful host so far. He was waiting for me at Penn Station with a couple of his buddies, Nat and Oliver. We had a quick bite to eat at the Carnegie Deli where the sandwiches and the hair on our waitress were all a mile high. The menu offered plates like "Nosh, Nosh, Nanette" and "50 Ways to Love Your Liver." I settled for a basic pastrami but could barely eat it all. We had just sat down when Donald announced he had tickets to the Royal Shakespeare production of *Much Ado About Nothing* starring Derek Jacoby and Sinead Cusack at the Gershwin. Emory had told him I was a Shakespeare buff, and it just so happened that he could get comp tickets because his brother is the assistant lighting designer.

Donald is in his forties, tall and pale and blond, a wisp of a man, although he doesn't look sick. He dresses in layers: T-shirt, Oxford, sweater, tweed jacket, scarf. I imagined he was trying to appear more substantial than he really was. Even with the sweater underneath it, the jacket looked a little large; its sleeves hung below his wrists. Donald's friend Nat, also thin, is younger with tortoiseshell glasses. The second friend, Oliver, is a bearish black man. No concerns about weight with him. I wonder if this is what it's like to live in New York City these days: a constant taking of inventories whenever you meet a new gay guy, a checklist for sickness or for health.

We talked about the protest and vigil. Nat was involved in the Gay Men's Health Crisis when they ousted Larry Kramer last year because they thought he was too confrontational. Nat agreed with this assessment at the time, but now believes Kramer was right, that the GMHC should be much more activist. He corralled people for the demonstration because he wishes he had defended Kramer earlier. Oliver reminded him that we're all operating with blindfolds on, that beating ourselves up for what we might have done differently is fruitless. Oliver's no-nonsense demeanor makes me think he'd be a good high school teacher. I guess that quality also helps when you're an attorney who does pro-bono work trying to keep landlords from evicting tenants with AIDS.

We kept talking politics all the way to the Gershwin. The show was great. I loved how Beatrice and Benedict were complete intellectual equals. The set was stunning: mirrored floors and glass panels everywhere. The production got me thinking about directing *Much Ado* at Chadwick someday. I could set it in the 1920s, with Beatrice as a suffragette.

After the show, the four of us had a nightcap in the Village at a gay hangout called Julius. It looked like a Western saloon: long wooden bar, wagon-wheel chandelier, and an enormous gold cash register. The place was packed. When Donald ordered us a round of drinks, he brought his mouth to my ear and said, "This is all on me." I wondered if he was flirting with me. Then I assumed he was just being generous and kind—the sort of qualities I'd expect from one of Emory's friends.

Nat and Oliver took a taxi back to their place while Donald and I walked to his narrow two-floor apartment. A spiral staircase made of black metal led from the living room to the bedroom.

We weren't in the apartment very long when Donald announced his intentions by unbuttoning his shirt to reveal his pale, hairless chest. He said something like, "You're here. I'm here. It's Friday night. It doesn't have to be complicated."

And it wasn't. At first it was almost businesslike, and for a moment I thought about Octavio. We removed our clothes, even folding them before we sat together, naked on the sofa. I put my wallet with a condom inside on the side table, just in case I needed it, but we ended up playing pretty safe. Donald kissed me on the neck, skipping my lips all together, and quickly went down on me. After a while, I reciprocated, skipping his lips *and* his neck.

As I took Donald in my mouth, I noticed that mixed in with his dark blond hair were a few strands of white, reminding me that there was at least a fifteen-year age difference between us. His age did get me thinking about Geoffrey with a G, and why I'd been so quick to turn down his simple request for a date. I didn't think twice about sleeping with Donald, so what was the difference?

The most obvious answer is that sex with Donald tonight wasn't emotional but it also wasn't an anonymous one-night stand. It was a type of sex I wasn't used to: pure, in a way, very much in the moment, no worries about what would happen next. When we finished, Donald gave me the option of sleeping on the living room sofa or upstairs with him. I chose the living room.

I feel mostly calm as I write this, except for the looming question about Geoffrey, and whether or not I said no to him too soon.

∾

(ON THE WAY TO) BOSTON   DECEMBER 9, 1984

Dear Gustavo,

I must be violating every rule of etiquette by writing to you for the second time out-of-turn, but I'm feeling such a connection with you right now that it's impossible to keep quiet. Yesterday morning I was released from a New York City jail. I was arrested at a demonstration held in front of the New York City mayor's mansion to protest the lack of response to the AIDS crisis.

Right before the demonstration, one of the leaders briefed us on some rules for nonviolent protest. He told people to put away their umbrellas, because if the police came, anything we held would be seen as a weapon. We then formed a line along the fence and across the driveway.

At first things were low-key, especially compared to the demonstration you and I went to in Madrid. We walked back and forth with our signs ("Living with Aids, Dying from our Mayor" in English and Spanish; a photo of Mayor Koch with the words, "I'd Fight AIDS If I Only Had a Heart"). One guy took about half a dozen pairs of handcuffs out of his backpack. He cuffed himself to the metal gate and urged others to do the same. The only thing that I was thinking was,

"I have to do *something*." I grabbed one of the handcuffs and locked myself.

I didn't think about being arrested until I was attached to the fence, and I realized that without keys, the cops would have to come and remove us, which is exactly what they did. I lay limp, not resisting, but not helping either. They cut my handcuffs off only to slap another pair on me.

I ended up in a jail cell with some of the other guys from the demonstration. Between the paperwork and it being a busy Saturday night, we weren't released until this morning, but only after we were formally charged with disorderly conduct and trespassing. I took the next train out of New York to Boston. I'm writing you this letter as we pass Hartford, Connecticut. My court date isn't until January, but our lawyer thinks we could come to some agreement before then.

While I was in jail, I thought of you a lot, Gustavo. I thought of you bloodied as they carried you away during the demonstration you organized in Madrid. I thought about how you lost your vision in one eye while protesting the attempted coup. Your courage anchored me this weekend. I thank you for that.

Time to sign off. I promise I won't write you any more letters until you write me back.

Hugs from your friend,

Casey

∼

NEW YORK, NEW YORK   DECEMBER 6, 1984

Dear Casey,

It's been quite a while since I've been in touch with you. From what I hear, you and Noah (The Wisenheimer) lost contact after you spent the night with us before you left for Spain. He did say he tried to get together while you were living in Madrid, but that for some reason it didn't work out.

I've always thought you were such a sweetie. Remember when you brought me flowers at the end of your and Noah's freshman year?

Who ever heard of presenting flowers to the mother of a roommate? What a mensch you are.

I remember so much of that year with great fondness, how you visited us in New York for Thanksgiving, how you seemed so tickled whenever we'd invite you to dinner when we were visiting Noah. He used to speak of you with such kindness, long after graduation.

Yes, I did say that Noah *used to* speak of you. I'm heartbroken to tell you that my dear Wisenheimer passed away last weekend. I would have called if I had your number. As it was, I could barely get the Alumni Director at Nearing to give me your address. If I'd been thinking clearly, I might have gotten in touch with you before Noah died, but everything happened so quickly.

I know I can trust you to keep what I'm about to tell you between the two of us. When I contacted the Alumni Director, I told her that Noah had died after a long illness, even though his death was (mercifully, people keep telling me) quick in relation to most AIDS deaths.

I'm sorry to write you with such sad news, but I thought you would want to know. He really loved living with you at Nearing. You know, once his father and I got used to the idea that Noah was a homosexual, we sort of hoped you two might connect again. You'd have made a great son-in-law.

I do hope you are healthy and well.

Love,

Margie Bergen

∾

Dear Casey,

I appreciated your letter and phone call, checking to see how Grace and I were doing since you left. When we spoke, Grace was doing better, but the past few days, she's been on edge again, and has developed a nervous tic of puffing little bursts of air that make "pop" sounds. I've tried to get her to stop, but it's just getting worse. If this keeps up, I'll take her to the pediatrician.

Did I tell you I decided to get back into singing, and have started taking lessons? My teacher is from Quebec. He's stern when we're in class but a sweetheart otherwise. In fact, he and I were having dinner the night you called my mother. I guess you could call it a date—my first since Ernesto, really. I work with Antoine alone an hour a week, then spend two hours in a small choir he conducts. I had to audition for both, which gave me confidence that I've needed. I sang "Kind of Woman" from *Pippin*, the first Broadway show I ever saw. I went with a summer theatre school I attended in Ottawa. After I made it through the song, Antoine said, "Lovely, but rusty." *Rusty?* I wanted to say. *How can you be rusty at 26?* He told me not to worry, that he would help me get the kinks out of my voice. I'm singing better already.

I've been remembering how we sang at Nearing. All those musicals? You've always said you were miscast as Sky Masterson. You weren't "cool enough," is what I remember you saying. Well, I thought you were cool enough. And it was fun to play Sarah Brown to your Sky and pretend to fall in love with you for a few hours.

Let me know your Christmas vacation plans. It'd be great if you could visit for more than a few days.

Poppy

~

Dear Mrs. Bergen,

I'm not quite ready to call you "Margie" yet, so I hope you won't think I'm being too formal in my greeting. You and your husband (along with Noah, of course) were nothing short of family to me while I was at Nearing. I think of you often and how you took me under your maternal wing during my freshman year.

I was so very sad to hear about Noah's passing. I can only imagine how hard it must be for you and Mr. Bergen to remain silent about the facts of his illness. Whoever told you that his quick passing was a blessing was right. I doubt this is any consolation, and I know I'm sounding incredibly clichéd, but it's good to know he didn't suffer longer than he did.

Noah was a wonderful friend and roommate. You're right, he was a wisenheimer, but he could also be incredibly kind and considerate. Did I ever tell you that he would occasionally make my bed when I was in too much of a hurry to get to my history seminar? Or that he planned a small surprise birthday party for me even though I'd forgotten his birthday a month before and didn't so much as give him a card?

If you're ever in the Boston area, please look me up. I'd love to see you and Mr. Bergen. Until then, I send you my deepest condolences.

Love,
Casey

∼

BOSTON   DECEMBER 10, 1984

Dear Geoffrey,

The last person you might want to hear from is me, since it took a number of phone messages and then a letter to get me to respond. I'm sorry for the delay as well as my turning down your offer to have tea with you. When I wrote, I was overwhelmed with work and family obligations. I'll explain if you are kind enough to let me take back my initial answer.

You have my number. I promise to call back this time. I'd very much like to have tea with you.

Yours,
Casey (with a "C")

∼

THURSDAY, DECEMBER 13, 1984   11:30 P.M.

I can't wait for vacation. Every minute feels like a battle in the classroom. Attention spans are shot. Any enthusiasm for academics has disappeared. Half of the kids show up stoned, even to my 8 a.m. class. And right in the middle of yesterday morning's disaster of a class arrives Vernon Reed. He was smiling, but there was something fake about it, something I didn't trust. He didn't even arrive to observe the class from the beginning. He came in fifteen minutes late.

I was still feeling emboldened by my weekend in New York City. That's the only way to explain the chutzpah of asking him to leave. I didn't make a scene. I greeted him at the door, and said, "This isn't the most convenient time. Would you mind returning another day?" His grin turned to a frown before I even finished my sentence.

There was a note in my mailbox this morning to make an appointment with Vernon's secretary for a conversation. I talked to Cathy this afternoon. I like Cathy. She dresses impeccably—she's the only woman on campus who wears nylons—and she's always professional, at least on the surface. But her eyes, do they tell all. When I approached her desk, she opened them wide, sucked in some air, and pulled her head back as if to say, "I think he's as much of an idiot as you do."

We couldn't find a time when Vernon and I were both free within the next day or two, so I kicked the proverbial can down the road and told her I would meet him after vacation. She brightened at this. Her eyes telling me, "Good for you."

"And listen, Casey," she whispered as I about to leave. "It's not just about yesterday. He's all worked up about that play you're doing."

The play? When Vernon visited our rehearsal, he looked a little puzzled, but not upset. I assumed he didn't understand the Shakespearean text, let alone what I had done to the play with the casting. I wonder if he talked to a disgruntled parent. Fuck it. Whatever complaints he received will be countered by the amazing performances the kids are giving.

I told Paula about Vernon's nonvisit and his note to me. I think she's getting as fed up with him as I am, and she has a reputation of being a steady presence at Chadwick. I also told her about my weekend: the protest, the arrest, and even sex with Donald. She agreed that I probably didn't have to worry about news getting to Vernon about my short stint in jail. Besides, he's consumed right now with the search for a replacement for the Dean of Students, who's leaving in January. I'm sure Vernon will take out his golden shoehorn so Tony can slip into the role, but he has to *look* like he doesn't have a favorite, and even that takes time.

The one bright spot over the last few days was that Geoffrey received my letter and called me. He seemed not to care that I'd rebuffed him. He proposed having dinner on Saturday. I agreed, even though I was expecting the original invitation to have tea. I want this to be a date in small letters, not capitals.

∼

SUNDAY, DECEMBER 16, 1984   3:30 P.M.

I'm loving (or at least I was loving) being at school relatively alone. This morning I walked around campus and didn't see another person. A couple more inches of snow fell late last night. Just the right amount: not enough to keep me inside but enough to make it appear as if I had started life anew. And then, a few hours ago, Vernon Reed appeared at my apartment door. He wasn't wearing his trademark smile.

He barely waited for me to step back to let him in. I offered him a chair but he refused. He paced the floor, walking over some books, T-shirts and an empty coffee mug with unnecessary exaggeration.

"How well do you understand Chadwick Academy, Casey?" he finally said.

"Why would you ask that?"

He explained that at Chadwick there were two types of contracts. There was the contract I signed in August, and then there was an unwritten contract, a *moral* contract, the contract that binds us as members of the "Chadwick family." Apparently, it was this second contract I wasn't following. I asked him for some examples.

He cited my tendency to eat alone, making other faculty members feel uncomfortable. A parent who complained I had told a class that the hardest thing about Harvard was getting in, but having a big donor in the family helps. Another who was upset at my "inserting sex into Shakespeare where it doesn't belong." And then I turned him away at my classroom door a few days ago.

"There are just some things we assumed you'd *know*," he said. "It's like good manners. We don't expect to have to spell them out. Look,

I'm trying very hard to make your tenure here successful. Very hard. But you have to meet me halfway. I really don't want these slip-ups to becoming a rehiring issue."

And with that he extended his hand, wished me a Merry Christmas, and left my room.

It's taken me a while to calm down. I do think I'm in better shape than I would have been only a month or two ago. The protest and arrest in New York were liberating, and I've carried that feeling into my life back in Boston. I can't say that I'm immune to any of Vernon's dealings with me, but I do feel stronger. I'm becoming more like Gustavo every day.

Last night I had dinner with Geoffrey at a place called the Harvard Bookstore Café on Newbury Street in Boston. It was his suggestion, and a logical one, coming from someone who works in a library. I got there early. The bookstore in the front of the café was filled with Christmas shoppers. While browsing, I came upon a collection of Alan Ginsberg's poems from 1947 to 1980, so I bought it. As a hardcover, it was a little pricey, but I decided that it could be an appropriate reward for protesting at Gracie Manor.

Geoffrey arrived just as I was buying the book. He wore a tweed coat and jeans. His hair, wavy and thick, was perfectly out of place.

When he saw my book, he told me he was a great fan of Ginsberg. He participated in a group reading of "Howl" when he was in university. I didn't tell him that I'd never read "Howl," let alone seen it performed, and that I'd bought the book to get to know an unfamiliar poet.

He'd made reservations for us in a corner of the restaurant. He offered me the seat facing the bookstore, which I appreciated. If the conversation lagged, I could people-watch.

I shouldn't have worried. Geoffrey had such an endless array of topics that I wondered if they were part of a first-date repertoire. I told him about the past few months: the school, that horrible morning Dallas From Dallas tried to convert me at brunch, the protest. I figured I'd save Grace and Poppy for another time. We ordered cocktails, then wine with our meals. He paid. The whole evening was so easy that I assumed we'd go back to his apartment, but instead, after we left the restaurant (and it was snowing, couldn't get much more romantic), he hugged me and said he had a great time, but that he had to get up early. He hopped on a bus, waving goodbye just before he deposited his fare.

Wait a minute. Wasn't this the same guy who tried to pick me up a few weeks ago? The guy who wrote to tell me he couldn't stop thinking about me? Had I said something? Done something? I wasn't ready to call it a night, even if the rest of the night would be spent without Geoffrey, so I walked a block over to Boylston Street to Buddies, a gay bar Emory had told me about.

I inched and elbowed my way to the bar and ordered a whiskey. Everyone was flirting with each other. I thought about approaching a guy who stood at the far end of the bar, but I didn't have the energy. Not just the physical energy, but the sexual energy. I was thinking about Geoffrey. I finished my drink and started the long walk towards North Station.

On the train, I tried to read some of Ginsberg's poems, but my mind started to wander, so I closed the book and looked out the window. The snow whirled in gusts. I thought more about Geoffrey: the shadowy stubble around his jaw and chin, his softly wrinkled Oxford shirt, his black leather boots that zipped up the side. I found myself wishing he were next to me on the train. I was missing him, but without the obsession that became too familiar with Octavio. That I simply missed him came as a relief.

∾

BOSTON   DECEMBER 19, 1984

Dear Geoffrey,

Just wanted to send you a quick note wishing you happy holidays and to let you know that I enjoyed our dinner Saturday night. I hope the snow didn't slow down your trip home too much. I imagine the ride must have been postcard beautiful.

I'm planning to visit family in Canada over the next week or so, but would love to get together again when I return. Maybe this time I can treat you.

Cheers,
Casey

PS: I'm loving Alan Ginsberg's poetry. "The tongue and cock and hand and asshole holy?" Wow. It was all Robert Frost and Emily Dickinson when I was a student, and that includes college. My high school English teachers wouldn't even touch Walt Whitman.

~

Poppy called this morning to tell me she was spending Christmas in the Canary Islands with Antoine, the music teacher she's been seeing for less than a month. She wants Grace to stay with me.

I lost it. I just barraged her with questions, from sarcastic (*Why didn't you wait until the 23rd to tell me?*) to sincere (*Don't you think it'll be hard for Grace without all of us together on Christmas?*).

Finally she said, "Why can't you be happy for me this once?"

We didn't come to any resolution. I walked around campus a few times to think. Her question resonated more than I wanted it to. I always thought I wanted her to be happy. I thought her happiness would make my life easier. And I still think that. But here's the truth: I do resent having to take care of Grace. I still resent that night in Madrid when Grace was conceived. And maybe more than anything, I really resent that Poppy just told me she was going ahead with the pregnancy. She never asked my opinion. Just like she just told me she was going to the Canary Islands.

After my walk I called Paula for advice. She's in the Berkshires now with her family. When she told me I should take Grace, I knew right away she was right. But it's already December 20. I don't even know how we'd spend Christmas Eve. Where am I supposed to get the money to buy her all the presents her grandparents would have provided? What about a Christmas meal? Can I even buy a turkey at this late date? I have no idea how I'll pull this off, but I'll try.

~

Grace will be arriving late Sunday afternoon. Poppy will accompany her to Boston, then fly to Las Palmas where she will meet Antoine. Grace will be with me until New Year's Day. At least that will give me a few days to prepare for classes, work on the set for *Measure for Measure*, and write college recommendations.

Once Poppy and I settled the schedule, I drove to Harvard Square to look for some presents for Grace. (Wait. Do I have to buy a tree now as well? I don't even have any ornaments.) There was still some snow on the ground from the storm the other night. That, along with the wreaths hung in the windows of the stores, began to put me in something resembling Christmas spirit. The city of Cambridge hung a light configuration resembling an abstract star from one side of the street to the other, which captured my mood more than anything else. It was a sort of Christmas decoration, for my sort of Christmas spirit.

Wordsworth—the best bookstore in the Square—was mobbed. I found my way to the children's section and started leafing through a Dr. Seuss book. I picked up *Doggies*, a book on counting by using the number of dog barks. It looked promising, but was it too young? Jesus, I thought. I'm a teacher. If I don't know my own daughter, I should at least know the answer to a question like this, shouldn't I?

I looked around at the shoppers with their lists. I wanted to approach them. Would they mind buying two of everything? It had gotten tight in the children's section and I'd been bumped into too many times when I gave up. I grabbed a copy of *Make Way for Ducklings*. I waited twenty minutes in line for a cashier, hoping that my credit card hadn't reached its limit.

If it had, the clerk didn't know. He cheerily put the book in a bag, then sent me around the corner to Bob Slate's when I asked about wrapping paper. I immediately fell in love with this stationery store and its creaky wood floors, pens and pencils of any style imaginable, and shelves packed to the last inch with paperclips, legal pads, ink pads, rubber stamps, all sizes and colors of envelopes. And wrapping paper. I bought a roll with polar bears on it and drove back to Chadwick.

$\sim$

Dear Casey,

Thank you for your note and your Christmas wishes. I also had a lovely dinner on Saturday. I didn't mean to make such a hasty exit on that bus, but examination period at Harvard is insanely busy, and we've also been short-staffed because of a nasty cold that's been going around. I was at my desk at 8:00 in the morning, on a Sunday, no less.

I'm glad you would like to get together again. Why don't you call me when you return from your travels?

Cheers and Merry Christmas,

Geoffrey

PS: Enclosed is a short book of letters between Alan Ginsberg and his lover, Peter Orlovsky. I found this browsing in Glad Day last night after work. If you don't know the bookstore, we should go sometime. They sell exclusively gay and lesbian books.

～

SUNDAY, DECEMBER 23, 1984 6:30 A.M.

Yesterday I drove to Lexington Center to get Grace a few more gifts. There's a little bookstore tucked away off the main street that I like to go to. I ended up buying *But Not the Hippopotamus* because the drawings looked fun. As I was standing in the very long line, I became overwhelmed with everything on my to-do list, as well as the things I had no idea even should be *on* the to-do list. I didn't even wait for the woman to print the receipt. I wanted out of that store immediately. I wanted out of the pressure that had been building since Poppy called to tell me about her trip with Antoine. I wanted to be on the plane to Toronto, where Christmas would be pretty much taken care of and all I needed to do was show up.

Poppy once told me that whenever her mother got stressed, she'd bake cookies. One time her parents were planning a vacation to Halifax. They were supposed to stop in Quebec City for the night, just about the halfway point of the thousand-mile drive. Poppy's father was getting testy and anxious because he didn't want to drive at night, and it was already late morning and everything still wasn't packed. That's exactly when Poppy's mother decided to bake cookies. The baking was therapy for her mother, something she did at the most inopportune moments so she could distract herself from those very moments.

A distraction. That's what I needed. But I can't bake cookies, even the frozen-dough kind you buy in a roll and slice on an oven tray. So I impulsively called Geoffrey from a payphone, which ordinarily would have been stressful all by itself, but I couldn't think of anything else to take my mind off everything I had to do. I fully expected to leave a message on his answering machine. I fought the urge to hang up when he answered on the second ring.

I thanked him for his note, and told him that I'd love to have dinner with him after Christmas. Would the day after New Year's work? He agreed right away: he was taking that whole week off. Just as I was about to hang up he said, "I guess you're calling long distance. I'm impressed."

He didn't know my plans had changed. I wasn't sure how to respond, so I didn't. He asked me if I was okay, if he'd said anything wrong. And that's when I lost it, right there in the phone booth talking to a guy I'd only gone out with once. I blurted everything that had been going on the past week and then, because Geoffrey didn't have the faintest idea who Poppy was, or Grace, or why they lived in Toronto, I gave him some of the backstory, still blubbering, still a mess.

Finally I said, "I'm sorry, Geoffrey. You just got me at a bad time," and he reminded me that *I* was the one who'd gotten *him*. He didn't say this in a bitchy way. Then he said, "I think you and I should have coffee this afternoon."

I protested because I had too much to do: complete my errand list, clean the apartment for Grace, wrap Grace's presents, figure out what to cook for Christmas dinner. Geoffrey listened patiently. He tried to convince me that a cup of coffee in Harvard Square might calm me, actually make it easier for me to get things ready. And besides, he could help, especially with the meal planning. He was a good cook.

I agreed. I drove into the Square and met him at Café Pamplona where he was holding a table. As soon as I saw him, I knew having a drink with him would relax me. It was already relaxing me. He was in a gray tweed sports coat, black T-shirt, and jeans. A gray scarf. Nothing I'd consider all that fashionable (although who was I to talk, in my moth-eaten green sweater?) but what his style did look like was thoughtful. Instead of throwing on the first thing he saw when he woke up this morning, he'd spent some time thinking about his choices. That seemed deeply mature to me. Geoffrey's maturity, which had made me standoffish when we first saw each other at the 1270, now felt like exactly what I needed.

I sat across from him and thanked him for meeting me.

"Just talk," he said. "Tell me more about yourself. Pick up where you left off on the phone."

I had no idea where I'd left off, so I started at the beginning again, at least the beginning as I saw it, which was Poppy's Christmas visit to Madrid four years ago. I told him about having sex with her, and how the night had led to Poppy's pregnancy. I told him about marrying Poppy and living in Toronto, how out of place I felt. Once I'd finished it would have been only polite of me to ask Geoffrey to tell me more about himself, but I was too tired. He'd absolutely helped me feel less tense and anxious than I was before I arrived, but once I allowed myself to relax, all that was left was exhaustion.

Geoffrey started telling me about himself without my asking, which made me respect him. Spent as I was, I was glad he quietly insisted that the conversation be a two-way street. I knew some of the basics of his life, but he hadn't told me he'd been married in the mid-'60s to a Belgian woman he'd met while she was studying in London and he was working at the Royal Holloway Library. They divorced a couple of years later, once Geoffrey came out as gay. He and his ex-wife haven't spoken for years.

I tried hard not to envy the simplicity of his divorce, but I couldn't push my thoughts away. My life *would* be simpler if Poppy and I hadn't slept together and she hadn't gotten pregnant. That's the truth, a truth I really don't want to acknowledge because actually writing this thought down implies that I'm unhappy that Grace is in my life. A decent father would never say that.

I do love my daughter. Just not in the way people expect of a father. I imagined a deep paternal urge would propel me into the role so powerfully that instincts I never knew I had would guide every interaction with my child. This has not been the case. At work, I didn't check my watch twenty times a day, counting the minutes until I could see Grace. I liked it when I held her to stop her from crying, but what was missing was a profound need to keep her from crying, a feeling that I could never be happy as long as she wasn't. I want to feel that need. I want to worry about her more than I do.

I want to be for Grace who my father was for me.

I said none of this to Geoffrey. I refocused on our conversation when he asked me what Grace and I were doing for Christmas. I told him I planned to cook. Food shopping was on my long list of things to do today, and I thought I'd swing by the Star Market on the Watertown line. That's when he invited Grace and me to his apartment for dinner. I instinctively but politely declined, but he told me to take a deep breath and hear him out. He said I'd have Grace Christmas Eve, Christmas morning, and the rest of her stay here. Wouldn't it be a nice break to let someone else do the cooking on Christmas Day?

I had a flurry of questions, including how to explain his presence in my life to my daughter.

"You tell her I'm your friend," Geoffrey said. "It's pretty easy."

I wasn't sure if he was clarifying our relationship for my sake or sincerely offering advice. "That's it?" I asked.

"What it is, right now anyway, is the truth," he said. "It's something she'll understand. Don't make things any more complicated than they are."

He wrote down directions to his apartment on the back of cardboard coaster, telling me to come at two o'clock. For the first time since Poppy told me she'd be going to the Canary Islands, I was feeling like I could handle Grace's visit.

That was yesterday. This afternoon I'll be at the airport waiting for Grace and Poppy.

~

Dear Casey,

I'm sure this holiday card and letter will be a surprise, coming from your old Scrooge of a Spanish teacher at Nearing. I'm surprised I'm writing it myself. Or to put it better, I'm surprised at my need to write this letter.

As you know, I'm a literal man. I appreciate the concrete. Throughout my life, I have been guided by my head rather than my heart. I'm faithful to facts, not emotion. Yet if you were to ask me to list exactly what you have done for me these past months, I probably could come up with a few items, mostly centered around having dinner with us. What has been most important is not the items on that list, but my knowing you were there. I know I also speak for Emory when I say that your mere presence in our lives has made this extraordinarily difficult time a little bit easier. Thank you.

Emory and I would very much like to see you in the new year.

With warm wishes for a happy Christmas,

Warren

~

Dear Casey,

I'm so impressed with what you did in New York City to call attention to the AIDS crisis. You are doing something truly important and daring. Remember, I marched with hundreds of people in Madrid. It sounds like you are holding the torch of justice with a far smaller crowd. I admire you so.

And to think that you might be in Madrid this March! I'll absolutely be here. My relationship with the woman from Torremolinos has gotten serious. Her name, by the way, is Sofía, like the Spanish Queen. I thought I might be able to keep what's going a little secret until you arrived, but I just have to tell you. I'm going to be a father like you! The baby is due in June. You may not believe this, but I couldn't be happier. I always thought that having a child would turn my entire life around and that I'd be miserable. Having a baby on the horizon *has* turned my life around, but in ways I never could have imagined. I can't remember a time when I've felt so grounded, so stable.

The political news here is not good. There's evidence now of government death squads. The latest was the shooting of a Basque politician and doctor, Santi Brouard, as he walked out of his medical clinic. They shot him on the anniversary of Franco's death. Sadly, this was not a surprise.

Write back as soon as you know anything more about coming to Spain. Sofía and I can't wait to see you.

Big hugs,

Gustavo

~

TUESDAY, DECEMBER 25, 1984   11:00 P.M.

Christmas night. Grace is here, asleep. I picked her up at the airport Sunday and took her to Dunkin' Donuts for a donut and hot chocolate. She couldn't stop giggling as she ate. I assumed she was so happy because this was the type of breakfast Poppy would never let her eat. Once we left the donut shop, I remembered *why* Poppy would never let her eat that type of breakfast. Grace couldn't stay strapped in the car seat. Her sugar high kept her squirming the whole ride home. When I sat her on the sofa with me, I let her open one of her book presents so I could read to her, but she still couldn't sit still until all of a sudden, she could, and once she did, she fell quickly to sleep. She didn't wake up for almost two hours.

Grace was happy just to do a few errands with me after that. I took her to the bookstore so she could pick up some more books. And, sugar be damned, I bought a couple of small Table Top apple pies at Star Market. We had an early dinner, listening to Alvin and the Chipmunks singing Christmas songs while we ate. We watched *Rudolph the Red Nosed Reindeer* at 7:00. Grace fell asleep again. I watched my favorite holiday movie, *Christmas in Connecticut*.

Today Grace and I went to Geoffrey's apartment for Christmas dinner. Everything was homemade. And it was a traditional British

Christmas dinner: a roast goose, brussels sprouts with chestnuts, mashed potatoes, braised red cabbage, bread sauce, cranberry sauce, and pudding. For Grace, Geoffrey added some raw carrot sticks and peanut butter sandwich quarters with the crusts removed. He even stuffed a stocking with candy and crayons for her. She spent much of dinner doodling on construction paper.

His apartment was small, with lots of bookshelves, but he'd still managed to put up a tall evergreen. He'd decorated it in small white lights, dozens of red bows, Victorian dolls, and silver musical instruments. Grace headed straight for the tree when we arrived and pulled off one of the bows. Geoffrey told Grace to wear it in her hair, which she did.

The man is good with children, or at least with Grace. When she wasn't looking, Geoffrey snuck an envelope under my dessert plate. In it were two tickets to a production of *Uncle Vanya* in January at the Huntington Theater, as well as a note on stationery bordered with holly. Geoffrey had written about how happy he was to be sharing Christmas with Grace and me. He also reminded me that soon after we'd met, I'd told him of my love of Chekhov. He ended the note by writing, "Getting to know you has been the best part of moving to the United States."

I'd been so focused on Grace that I hadn't even thought about buying Geoffrey a Christmas present. I insisted on treating us to dinner before the show.

Grace nodded off after dinner. As Geoffrey and I were putting away the dishes, he turned to me and gently pressed his lips against mine. It felt more significant than if we'd had sex. There was an intimacy about kissing that said, "OK. This isn't just going to be about getting each other off."

After we finished cleaning up, Geoffrey suggested we take a walk to the Boston Common to see the Christmas tree, which was almost fifty feet high. It was donated by the city of Halifax. Geoffrey told us the history: around 1920, there was an explosion in Halifax that wiped out a good part of the city. Boston sent a train with provisions to help the survivors, and that Christmas, Halifax sent a tree as a thank you. Sending a tree each year has become a tradition.

Grace squirmed out of my arms when she saw the tree and ran toward the low fence surrounding it. She turned to Geoffrey and me, stomping her feet and laughing. I was happy she was happy.

~

Paula returned to Chadwick last night after having spent Christmas in the Berkshires with her family. It was a relief to have some adult company for a while. I filled her in on the last week after Grace went to bed. I told her how Vernon came to my apartment the first day of vacation with his list of grievances. She said he was under pressure because the fund drive wasn't anywhere near its goal. And—surprise, surprise—Tony will be named Dean of Students in January.

After a few Brandy Alexanders she confided that she gave a great deal of money to the school every year. It's one of the reasons Vernon treats her so well. After another drink or two, she told me her father founded a very successful company that made imitation crabmeat. When he died, he left the business to Paula's brothers, and left over three million dollars to Paula. She teaches because she loves it, not for the money, obviously.

Late this afternoon Paula took us to Beverley, where a friend of hers, Zack, owns a small farm and offers hayrides. Grace fell in love with the two horses (Jack and Millie), so Zack let her pet them while everyone boarded. When it was time to leave, I hoisted Grace into Paula's arms at the back of the wagon. I was about to jump onto the wagon myself when the sleigh bells jingled and the ride began without me. I yelled for Zack to stop but he didn't hear me. I had no idea why some of the passengers were laughing. Couldn't they see what was happening? Did they have any idea what it felt like to watch your child riding away from you?

I ran after the wagon. Paula offered me her arms as I leapt to the metal step. I tumbled into the hay, then grabbed Grace and wrapped my arms around her. I rocked her. I hummed "Jingle Bells" to soothe her, even though I knew she didn't need soothing.

I thought: This is that paternal feeling, that *him* feeling. That instinct I didn't think I had.

~

Dear Casey,

You and Grace left my apartment an hour ago. The high spirits the two of you brought into my home have begun to wane, as if someone were dimming the Christmas tree lights. But what a lovely Christmas it was, thanks to the two of you. My first in the United States! Grace is one of the cutest children I've ever met. I can't imagine having a more enchanting daughter.

All of this brings me to acknowledge that there is something I've neglected to disclose about my life. When I told you about my having been married in my twenties, I may have led you to believe that there were no children in the picture. In a way, that's very true, but it doesn't mean that there haven't been children in my life, specifically a daughter. My ex-wife Camille gave birth to her about a year after we married. I stupidly believed that having a child would make it easier to ignore my sexuality, and therefore save our marriage. It didn't, and not too long after that, Camille and I divorced.

For some time, I remained active in Karleigh's life, not that she'd remember a moment of my involvement now. I'd swing by on my way to the library, often in time to see Karleigh wake up. I'd visit again on my way home. For a while, the arrangement worked. At least I thought it did, until one evening Camille asked me to stay after she'd put Karleigh to bed.

Camille returned often to her native Bruges, especially after our divorce. During one of those trips, she reconnected with a former beau of hers from school. They rekindled their romantic relationship.

She wanted to return to Bruges where she would live with Mathis. Eventually they hoped to marry. She proposed we make a clean break: I would be relieved of any obligation to Karleigh, completely giving up my role as her father. She convinced me that this would be best for everyone, especially our daughter. She'd grow up with one father,

Mathis, who would adopt her. The next day, I called Camille to say that I would agree to her proposal.

So many things played into my saying yes. I was young, and had no idea where my career would take me. I knew I wanted to keep working in a university library, but at the time, jobs were scarce. Where I was working offered limited opportunities for advancement. I was also coming out. I don't think Camille completely understood what being gay really meant, and I could sense her uneasiness about me playing a major part in Karleigh's life. I knew that because of her parents, Camille didn't have to worry about money. But mostly I was scared—of not having a future, of not being a good enough father, of pretty much everything.

There's considerably more to say, but I won't say it now. I couldn't continue to pretend to be the childless figure you imagined me to be, especially after Grace won my heart today.

Merry Christmas, dear Casey.

Geoffrey

~

THURSDAY, DECEMBER 27, 1984   9:15 P.M.

This afternoon Grace and I took the train to the Children's Museum in Boston.

A cold, wet rain was falling all morning, so I dressed her in the yellow slicker and rain hat Poppy had packed. Grace had to keep pushing the hat—Paddington-style and red—from covering her eyes.

"It's like Hallo-*ween*," she said.

Shortly after the train departed, Grace shimmied out of her seat to say hello to a girl sitting with her parents opposite us. When the train stopped at the next station, Grace fell. She held tight to my leg and began to cry. I hoisted her on my lap. I was relieved when she calmed down. And that I needed her to calm down.

I took out a plastic bag of sliced apples from my backpack and gave one to Grace. She took a bite, then thrust the piece toward me and said, "Now, *you*." We went back and forth like this for a while, until the bag was half gone. It was the sort of moment I could never have had with her if we hadn't spent the past few days together. I'm feeling everything I thought I was supposed to feel about Grace for the last three years.

And this: These past days there were times when I looked at Grace, when I held her, and I was overcome with sadness. This sadness wasn't just because of what we had missed together. It was also a sadness—maybe heartbreak is more like it—of holding a child in a world that could so easily hurt her, knowingly and unknowingly, in which she was so fragile. Maybe that's another part of fatherhood.

As we were getting off the train, Grace told me she wanted to see Geoffrey and his tree. I explained that he wasn't home, having no idea whether or not I was telling the truth. I didn't get the letter from Geoffrey until we returned to Chadwick tonight. I didn't even take off my coat before I sat and started reading it at the kitchen table.

Geoffrey has a daughter. Or I guess it's more accurate to say, he had a daughter. He is a father, but he's not. His kindness towards Grace makes sense now, not that it didn't before, because I think Geoffrey is a kind person. He would have been nice to Grace even if he hadn't agreed to give up his child years ago. Yet I sensed something more than just hospitality on his part when he handed Grace the Christmas stocking, when he laughed as she pulled the ribbon from the Christmas tree.

I remembered when I first met him, how I envied the simplicity of his life, or at least the seeming simplicity of it. I guess his life is still simpler than mine, but now I understand at what cost.

I can only imagine the guilt I'd have felt if I'd made the decision Geoffrey had made. Yet I can't say for sure if I wouldn't have done the same thing if Poppy had offered me the chance to cut my ties to her and Grace completely. That is, before this week. Now I can't imagine not having Grace in my life.

∼

MONDAY, DECEMBER 31, 1984   2:00 P.M.

Grace just went down for her nap. I hope she sleeps for a couple of hours. She's been cranky lately. I think she's had a great time here this week but she's also been overstimulated: Christmas at Geoffrey's, snowstorms, rainstorms, the hay ride, maybe one too many videos.

Yesterday Poppy called from the Canary Islands. At first Grace didn't seem interested in hearing from her mother at all, so I talked to Poppy for a while. She gave me a pretty rosy picture of the past week in the Las Palmas. I got the sense she was trying to impress me. The resort, she said, was breathtaking. The food was the best she'd ever eaten. The weather was perfect. The beach was the cleanest and longest she'd ever seen.

When I finally was able to get Grace out from in front of the TV, she held the receiver next to her ear and said nothing. Not even a "hello, mommy" or a giggle. I could hear Poppy asking her if she was having a good time, what Santa had brought her for Christmas. I tried to prompt Grace into saying something, anything, to her mother, but her jaw just tightened. When Poppy said goodbye, Grace dropped the phone on the floor and ran back to the TV. I picked the receiver up.

"Jesus," Poppy said. "Does she even remember me?"

I explained how tired she was, how we'd been doing a lot these past days. I did not mention Geoffrey, but did tell her about our sleigh ride.

I hung up feeling relaxed until Grace decided that she really did want to talk to her mother after all. She burst into tears when I told her she couldn't. The more I tried to reason with her, the more insistent she got, so I let her cry it out until she let me hold her.

There's a New Year's Eve celebration in Boston tonight with lots of things for kids, but I'm not sure taking Grace would be smart. When I was her age, my father would sometimes drive me around during the holidays to see all the lights on the houses. Later this afternoon, Grace and I will drive to Lynn and Nahant and walk along the beach. Then we'll ride through the North Shore and look at the Christmas decorations.

∾

BOSTON   JANUARY 1, 1985

Dear Geoffrey,

I'm sorry it has taken me so long to respond to the letter you wrote after Grace and I left your apartment on Christmas Day. I was going to write you to thank you, not just for such a wonderful dinner, but also for the kindness you showed Grace and me. The tickets to *Uncle Vanya* were beyond generous. Grace adored the stocking you gave her, and has asked me to return it to you so Santa can refill it next Christmas.

I'm also grateful that you told me about your daughter, especially since you could have easily kept her from me. It makes me believe that whatever you and I turn out to be, at the very least, we'll be close friends. I'm glad I called you right before Christmas and that you convinced me to meet you for coffee, where I spilled everything out to you.

The whole issue of fatherhood has been whirling around me these past weeks. I heard from a friend of mine in Madrid that he's about to become a father. To my surprise, he's embraced the role completely. With Grace's visit, I'm embracing the role much more naturally than I ever thought I would. And now there's your story, perhaps the most poignant of all. I sometimes wonder how different motherhood is. Would your ex-wife ever think about allowing you to raise your daughter without her presence? Does Poppy ever wish that she was the one who had moved from Toronto, leaving me to essentially raise Grace as a single parent?

In your letter, you suggested I call you. I plan on doing that soon. For now, Happy New Year, Geoffrey. Thank you for helping me understand why Grace's presence meant so much to you.

All best,
Casey

~

WEDNESDAY, JANUARY 2, 1985   10:30 P.M.

This morning I got a call from the lawyer who's defending me and the other protesters arrested in front of Gracie Mansion. The plan was for him to represent us at the hearing in New York City later this month, but in order to do that, the DA has to agree. In the lawyer's words, "the DA is being a real prick" and won't sign on to any of us missing the hearing. He's a real right-winger who was a Goldwater delegate to the '64 Republican Convention.

It's bad enough that I have to take a day off from school and trek down to New York again. What's worse is that my hearing falls on January 25, the opening night for *Measure for Measure*, which means I'll have to keep my fingers crossed that the hearing is in the morning, so I can fly back here by 6:00. The lawyer still thinks the worst that will happen is we'll all have to pay a stiff fine. But I'm panicking, asking myself what if such-and-such happens (like my lawyer being wrong about the worst-case scenario) or what if such-and-such doesn't happen (like the judge not considering a plea deal).

I'd do anything to talk with Gustavo right now.

Grace's departure yesterday was hard. She refused to get out of her pajamas all morning, and I gave up trying to persuade her. I bundled her up without changing her clothes and carried her to the car. The first thing Poppy said when she saw her at the airport was, "Didn't Daddy dress you?" When I explained what was going on, she softened a bit, and even acknowledged that she'd done the same thing a few times.

It didn't take Grace long to say, "We saw Geoffrey!" When I told Poppy he was just a friend, she didn't buy it for one minute. I could tell she was hurt. Whether it was because I didn't tell her about Geoffrey before Grace did or because she was feeling jealous, I don't know. I hurried us to one of the airport restaurants, a deli marginally more upscale than Burger King.

Poppy relaxed after a glass of wine. Waiting for our food, I taught Grace how to turn the paper wrappers on straws into projectiles by tearing of the ends and blowing. Poppy even got into the game, sending a wrapper my way, hitting me in the eye. She and Grace laughed. Poppy might have laughed a little too hard. When she reached across the table to get a second straw, I saw that one of her fingernails was purple.

"So stupid," she said. "I slammed it in a car door."

Our food arrived and we ate in silence. Both Poppy and I knew that she wasn't being completely honest about the bruise. Grace was oblivious to any tension between her mother and me as she ate the hot dog I'd sliced into pieces for her. (I've got to say it felt close to triumphant, me preparing Grace's meal with her mother at the table.) I took out some crayons and paper from my backpack (another small triumph: me, bringing something to occupy Grace) and placed them in front of me. I was hoping to lure her into my chair, so that I could take her seat next to her mother. Between eating and drawing, I thought she might be distracted just enough to give Poppy and me some time.

It worked. As soon as she saw the crayons, Grace wriggled off her chair and came to me. She alternated between eating her hot dog and taking the crayons in her fist. After a while, she got drowsy. I picked her up and held her, her chin on my shoulder.

I leaned into Poppy and we talked quietly. When I pushed her on how she'd bruised her finger, she said, "Tell me about Geoffrey and I'll tell you about Antoine." She asked why I was so afraid to tell her who this Geoffrey character was. She wasn't some dainty flower that was going to wilt in despair at the thought of me having a boyfriend. I maintained Geoffrey was "just a friend," because, at this time, we'd only gone on one date. I told her I liked him. It felt good to confide in her; it didn't matter that she had demanded it from me.

"Now you," I said.

She said she was embarrassed, that she had had every intention of pretending that she had the most romantic time imaginable, but that there was something about sitting with Grace and me that made her open up.

Soon after Poppy arrived in Las Palmas, Antoine told her he'd met Renata, a pretty young Spaniard who had shown interest in him. When Antoine told Renata he was waiting for Poppy to arrive, she suggested that the three of them spend time together. At first Poppy didn't understand what Antoine was asking of her, but then she did, and told Antoine that a three-way wasn't her thing.

Antoine persisted for the next few days until Poppy finally acquiesced. They arranged a dinner date, to be followed by a rendezvous in Renata's room. After the meal, Poppy said she really tried to go through with it, but after taking off her bra, she froze. She returned to the room she shared with Antoine. Antoine stayed with Renata.

The next morning, Poppy packed her suitcases. She booked a room on the other end of the city where she planned to spend the rest of the vacation alone. A quiet few days of reading and tanning on the beach. Antoine would have none of it. He followed her out the door to the taxi, begging her to stay while at the same time cursing her for leaving. She hopped into the taxi. He slammed the door and her finger was caught.

I said something stupid like, "I was really worried about you going away with someone you barely knew."

She said, "Would you stop talking to me as if I should be under twenty-four-hour psychiatric care?" She was confused and lonely and made an impulsive decision to spend a week with some guy she hardly knew. That's all. She'd just made a mistake. She had a bruised finger, that was it. And it wasn't intentional. I'd bruised her too, she said, just not physically.

I wasn't sure comparing the two of us was fair, but I didn't say anything. I decided to be grateful that she told me anything at all.

~

SATURDAY, JANUARY 5, 1985   11:30 P.M.

The kids arrive tomorrow. Paula and I went to O'Toole's to mark the end of vacation. We sat at the bar to catch the TV news, which I'd been ignoring, mostly because I didn't want to hear about the preparations for Reagan's second inaugural or the retrial of Claus von Bülow. We found a booth.

As we were ordering a round of drinks, the school counselor entered the bar and looked around. We waved her over. A waitress brought Ileana a menu shortly after she slid into the booth next to Paula. Ileana said she was missing her native Ireland recently, so she ordered shepherd's pie and a Guinness. Paula and I ordered burgers.

We had a few drinks before the food arrived, which meant that Ileana, who usually isn't much of a drinker, told us a few things she probably shouldn't have. She thinks Tony drinks too much but Vernon won't even listen to her. He told her that she should try to remember what it was like to be young, jokingly suggesting she might be out-of-touch, which she took as criticism of her work as school psychologist to teenagers. As she spoke, her voice started quivering. She said everything had been building up for weeks. Chadwick was getting to her. And it wasn't just Vernon. She said it was horrible being an outsider at the school.

"But you're not an outsider," Paula said. "Far from it."

"That's how you see it," Ileana said. She went on to explain how everything about her—her accent, her being an immigrant, her inability to understand the subtleties of Boston culture—separated her from everyone. She told us about the first time she set foot on campus, for her interview. It was February and it was cold. She'd bought a camel-hair coat, which had cost her a lot of money, because she thought it would impress. She walked into the headmaster's office—Vernon Reed wasn't in charge yet—and before she had a chance to open her mouth he said, "Hmm. Camel-hair. You might want to rethink that. Only the Irish wear camel-hair around here." The headmaster—a man named Roger Gifford who was so aggressively affable that he earned the nickname Jolly Roger—boomed laughter after his comment, even as Ileana's face dropped.

Since that first day on campus, she felt like she was always saying the wrong thing, missing a joke everyone else got. The whole campus was like a swamp. On the surface the water looked pretty smooth, but there were alligators lurking right below, and she didn't see them until she did something "not very Chadwick." She's been here four years and still doesn't know what "not very Chadwick" means. I can't say that I do, either.

She left the bar before Paula and me. All this time I'd been thinking that Ileana felt right at home at Chadwick, that the school actually *was* her home. Paula thinks for the most part this is true, but that Ileana, like the rest of us, is feeling beleaguered these days.

~

MONDAY, JANUARY 7, 1985   10:30 P.M.

Tonight at dinner Vernon looked bewildered when I told him I'd never read any John LeCarré. He was doing what is done all the time at Chadwick. He valued the knowledge he had above all other knowledge, and judged people's intelligence solely by what *he* knew. This attitude was evident from the very first day I set foot on campus for my interview. There were no signs to tell me where to go. I had to guess where the headmaster's office was, guess where the parking lot was, guess where the classroom buildings were. The message was clear: if you don't know the answer to these questions, you don't belong here.

When I was living in Spain I was feeling low one afternoon so I went to see a Marx Brothers movie at an old revival theater. It was *Horse Feathers*. There's a scene in the office of a professor (played by Groucho) with a student (I think it was Chico). Groucho is getting some papers in order, and at one point asks, "Where's the seal?" Chico leaves and returns with a live, flapping seal. In Spanish the word for a paper seal (*estampa*) and the animal seal (*foco*) are completely different. There's no pun involved for Spanish speakers, but they still laughed at the absurdity of a seal appearing for no reason whatsoever. I remember thinking that I was probably the only one in the theater who got the intended pun. I also remember that I started feeling a little smug, a little wiser than the rest of the audience.

I realize now that just because I understood the real joke didn't make me smarter than anyone else. It just meant that I knew something the others didn't. At Chadwick, they don't recognize that their intellectual snobbery is based in large part on whether or not you get the seal joke.

∼

BOSTON   JANUARY 4, 1985

Dear Casey,

I'm writing this in a hurry since I'm about to leave for the airport on very short notice. My mother has taken ill and I'm flying to England this evening to be with her. It was completely unexpected since she was in perfect health. My father says it's a stroke, and that they're not sure if or when she'll regain consciousness.

I don't know how long I'll be away, but I doubt very much I'll be home in time to see *Uncle Vanya* with you. I'm very disappointed. I hope you'll understand and that we can have dinner and go to the theatre when I return. Please invite a friend to go with you to the play. I wouldn't want the tickets to go to waste.

Everything is happening so quickly that I've barely had time to pack. Thankfully, my supervisor at the library was extraordinarily understanding and told me to take all the time off that I needed.

I'll write to you from Brighton and let you know how things are and how long I anticipate I'll be out of the country.

Yours,
Geoffrey

~

Dear Casey,

I hope you got the message I left saying that Grace and I had arrived safely in Toronto. It was snowing as we touched down. I had Grace look out the window and imagine she was in a snow globe. She got a kick out of the baggage claim carousel. I had all I could do to keep her from jumping on it for a ride.

She's been moody since we got home. She didn't sleep well last night. She kept asking for you and that guy who is "just a friend" of yours. I'm not sure sending Grace to Boston was a great idea after all. It's too much of an adjustment for a child her age to make. It's bad enough when kids of divorced parents have to split their time between houses, but our daughter has to split her time between countries.

Oh, who am I kidding? The truth is that Grace has been difficult lately not just because she's three and a half years old, but also because she really did have a nice time with you. Why is that so hard for me to tell you? I wanted her to have a good time. I would have felt terrible if the trip had been a disaster. I guess in my insecurities I wanted to hear about just one misstep, one small blemish on the week, but everything Grace says is all rah-rah. She keeps asking me when she can go back. And whoever Geoffrey is or will be in your life, she seems to adore him. I also have to say that it feels unfair that you get the Parent of the Year Award for being with Grace a few days.

I'm really beginning to wonder if this arrangement is working for Grace after all. Would it be such a bad idea for us to move closer to you? My life is going nowhere here in Toronto. And I wouldn't want to move too near you. I've actually been toying with the idea of returning to Nearing to work there, maybe in admissions. Then Grace would only be a little more than two hours away from you. Visiting would be a whole lot easier.

I really hope you'll be able to see Grace again soon.

Poppy

∿

I feel bad for Geoffrey having to deal with a sick parent, but I'm also afraid that our relationship, which was just about to take off, has been grounded. I have no idea when it will resume, or even if it will resume. As I read his letter, a creeping panic lodged in my bones. What if he never comes back? I think of him most at night, lying in bed and wishing he were beside me. And we haven't even reclined together, let alone slept together.

He told me to take a friend to the theater with the Chekhov tickets he bought for Christmas. It only makes sense for me to invite Stoddard, if he's feeling well enough. I spoke to Emory the other day who said Stoddard now has "good days and bad days," and then added a little grimly, "but don't we all?" Overall, though, Stoddard is doing okay, and he and Emory are hoping he'll be well enough to go to Spain in March. His doctor says it's still possible, but March is two months away, a long time with this disease.

Good days. Bad days. We rarely know when they are coming. There are exceptions, though. One day I do know is going to be bad is the day we present *Measure for Measure*. I've been debating how to handle my absence while I'm in New York City. Paula has offered to cover two of my classes, which means I might be able to get away without telling Vernon.

We have our first run-through of the play Monday night. The casting of the duke as the duchess has caused hardly a stir with the

182

cast. The girl playing the duchess—she's really good, and I wrote a recommendation for her for a summer theater school—hasn't been at all fearful of seducing the nun (Isabella) in exchange for the release from jail of Isabella's brother. And the girl in the role of Isabella doesn't seem uncomfortable either. It's playing out as it should: the idea of using sex as the carrot for keeping her brother out of prison is what horrifies Isabella. The gender of the assaulter doesn't matter.

~

Dear Poppy,

Thank you for your letter that I received the other day. I'm sorry to hear that Grace is having a hard time adjusting to life in Toronto after her week here with me. By now I hope she's settled in. The two of us did have a very good time over the holidays, so I'm glad about that. I just wish the transition wasn't so hard for her. Maybe we can arrange something different next time: I could fly back with you to Toronto and spend a day or two, or you could spend a day or two down here. We'd then be able to spend time with Grace rather than passing her off quickly at the airport.

I do think that solutions such as this are more practical than you completely uprooting yourself from Toronto and living in the United States, even if you are considering a job at Nearing. It's at least a two-and-a-half-hour drive from here to the college—longer than it takes to fly to Toronto. Besides, I'm not certain that I'll be hired a second year. I could be looking for a job again. There are a lot of schools around Boston, but it's a tight-knit community. Vernon Reed could easily sabotage my job search with a few phone calls. I might have to look outside the area.

I'll block out some time—even if it's just a weekend—to visit you and Grace. The play I'm directing goes up in a little over a week. After that, I'll have more free time. I'm supposed to go to Spain with Stoddard the first week of my March vacation, but could come to Toronto for the second week.

I hope you've been able to recover from your time in Las Palmas with Antoine. I'm assuming you've stopped taking lessons from him. Have you found a new voice teacher? It would be a shame if your experience with Antoine got in the way of you pursuing music again. There must be hundreds of possibilities in a city like Toronto.

Cheers,

Casey

～

SATURDAY, JANUARY 19, 1985   11:15 P.M.

Spent most of yesterday afternoon with the costumer for *Measure for Measure*, a woman in her 70s who has been dressing Chadwick actors for decades. On my way back to the dorm I passed Tony. He walks differently now that he's Dean of Students. It's like he's been given the deed to Chadwick and he owns the place. The golden shoehorn might have made an easy slip into his black loafers, but the blue blazer, the red tie, the white shirt, the khakis—it's all perfectly suited for him. He's doing exactly what he's supposed to be doing. His rising star was inevitable.

I just got back from *Uncle Vanya*, which I attended with Stoddard instead of Geoffrey. At dinner he talked about his health. His doctor advised him to gain as much weight as possible, not just for his own health, but so that officials at the Madrid airport wouldn't suspect he was sick. There's so much panic about AIDS that people have been denied entry at a number of borders. Stoddard doesn't look as bad as some of the men I've seen walking in Boston or New York City. He's gaunt, but Stoddard has always been thin. Radiation treatments have kept the sarcoma at bay. There are a few marks on his face, but they can be covered. He asked me if I knew anything about makeup, given my work in the theater. I told him I'd come over some night and show him how to put some on. So for now, our trip is a tentative go.

Emory has moved his dental business to the South End where he treats adults instead of children. Even in Boston's gay neighborhood, where they should know better, he's had a hard time building a client base because people assume many of the men who go to him are sick. He now explains his sterilization procedures to every new patient.

Emory took the test to see if he had the antibodies and it came out inconclusive. They want him to take the test again in a few weeks. Stoddard asked me if I had taken the test. I told him that I hadn't, that I've had no symptoms whatsoever, and that I'm careful whenever I have sex, which hasn't been much of an issue since I moved to Boston. I'm not sure my answer completely put his mind at ease.

I told Stoddard about Geoffrey. I still remember how he taught the use of the Spanish negative: *El dinero es todo. El amor no vale nada.* (Money is everything. Love isn't worth anything.) It's hard to believe the Stoddard I've come to know is the same Stoddard I knew in college. When I asked him tonight if he really believed what he told us in class, he snickered. "I guess I did. At least a little. Today I'd probably say you need both love and money to get by." Then he added, "Be careful in sex, but don't be careful in love." The words hung there for a while, a piece of advice and a regret.

He said he loved Emory. He considered himself a lucky man, and yet he couldn't help but think that he'd only allowed himself to be just so lucky. He'd never quite allowed himself to love Emory the way that Emory loved him. He'd been careful in love. It was in his DNA to be cautious. He would have been just as cautious if he'd been born heterosexual.

I'm not sure why Stoddard thinks I can succeed where he didn't, that I can remove the protective armor he'd worn with Emory, but I'm going to try.

~

WEDNESDAY, JANUARY 23, 1985   11:45 P.M.

We had a dress rehearsal for *Measure for Measure* tonight. The lights, the costumes, the music (I picked one of Schubert's string quartets) and a few invited audience members really threw some of the actors off. Strangely, most thrown off were the actors who'd had little difficulty in rehearsals leading up to tonight. The stage manager had to feed lines to Isabella and the Duchess of Vienna.

After rehearsal I talked with Maryanne, who's playing the Duchess. The whole experience of playing the Duchess as falling in love with Isabella has made her begin to question her own sexuality. Well, not quite begin to question, she said. She'd been questioning for a while. Playing the Duchess had confirmed what she'd already known. She wondered if it was time for her to come out.

I tried to strike a balance with Maryanne, neither encouraging her to do something she wasn't prepared to do nor discouraging her to be who she was. I said, "I'm so glad you're discovering who you are." Maybe that was spineless, but I was a little less cowardly when she asked me, "Come on, Mr. Adair. You know something about being gay." Smiling, I said I did know a lot about being gay, without saying I actually was.

I've been thinking a lot about Stoddard's advice about not being cautious in love. What I'm discovering is that I think I've been instinctively cautious because I'm afraid the alternative is being reckless. So last night—after the horrible rehearsal and not knowing whether or not I'd dealt with the Maryanne situation well—I did something reckless, or at least it was the most reckless thing I could have done in my very cautious world. I called Geoffrey at his Boston phone, even though I knew he was in England. To make matters worse, I left him a message. "Just calling to say hello." Once I said the words, I would have done anything to erase them. I could only think of how desperate he'd think I was.

It turns out that he didn't think I was desperate. He checked his messages a few hours later and called me back. He was afraid that I never got his letter explaining that his mother was sick and that he had to travel to Brighton. I was tempted to say I hadn't received his letter and that after not hearing from him for over two weeks, I decided to see what was up. Suddenly—at least in my mind—I could go from a desperate, insecure boyfriend to Mr. Cool as a Cucumber, casually checking in after two weeks of silence.

I decided to be truthful. I told him that I did get his letter, but immediately asked about his mother's health so we wouldn't have to deal with how strange my calling him was. The doctors have advised Geoffrey to look for hospices. His father is a mess, and Geoffrey has had to do all the arranging of medical care. His parents had one of those marriages where the labors were divided in the most traditional of ways: his father earned money, and his mother did everything else. Geoffrey worries how his father will manage when his mother is gone. Geoffrey's younger brother lives a little over two hours away in London, and has been able to visit on weekends, but between his job and family, it's hard for him to spend more time in Brighton.

As I was about to commiserate with him, he asked, "So why did you call, Casey?"

"I don't know," I said. "I just did."

"You just called because you wanted to call even though you knew I wasn't there?"

"I know. It sounds nuts."

"Actually," he said, "I think it sounds sweet."

I would have hugged him if he'd been with me. I thanked him for understanding. Then I told him we should probably get off the line before he ran up his father's phone bill.

~

FRIDAY, JANUARY 25, 1985   7:30 A.M.

I'm at the airport waiting for my flight to New York, which leaves at 8:00. Paula was kind enough to drive me this morning. On the way she said that she knew all my expenses were covered, but just in case some of them weren't, I should let her know. She'd like to help me. She'd been donating money to a group that works toward AIDS prevention and the care of people with AIDS. Supporting me in my protest would be just another way to contribute to the cause.

She also gave me a couple of Valium for today, one of which I took in the car. I'm still a wreck. I didn't get more than two hours of sleep last night, and that was in bits and pieces. Rehearsal went marginally better than the night before. The actors have settled into their roles again—Maryanne in particular got her stride back—but I'd really hoped the lighting crew would have had their cues down by now. If I can make it back to Boston early enough, I might be able to do a quick tech review before the show goes up.

~

Waiting for another plane, this time the 6:30 to Boston from New York. I found a payphone to call Paula and ask if she would hold the curtain until 8:15, which might give me enough time to make it to the theater. I've taken the second of the tranquilizers she gave me.

What a day. The cases on the docket were so backed up at the courthouse that my hearing didn't start until 1:30—three hours after the scheduled time. While I waited, I watched some of the proceedings from the back row. The judge looked old enough to be Vernon Reed's father. He also looked a little like Vernon, which did nothing to calm me down. He tended to mumble, and a lot of what he said I couldn't hear. I did gather that he was mostly dealing with arraignments for all sorts of crimes that had taken place last night—burglaries, assaults, weapons charges. Chaining myself to a fence seemed like a parking violation compared to what these guys had done, or at least I hoped it would seem that way.

At noon, the judge broke for an hour-long recess. I hadn't had breakfast, and while I wasn't hungry, I decided it would be a good idea to eat something. I found a Chinese restaurant that also served American breakfasts all day. At the table beside me were some guys who had been in the courtroom. They were planning a protest in the courthouse when our cases came up. They wanted to disrupt the proceedings until the guards had no option but to carry them out in handcuffs.

This made me nervous. I just wanted to get my hearing over with and then get the hell out of Dodge. I used to love New York, but this experience has colored the city for me, and as I sat in the restaurant, all I remember thinking is, "I want to be on that plane back to Boston and I don't care if I ever visit this city again."

I didn't eat much. I left the restaurant before the group and walked back to the courthouse. There were only a few people in the courtroom when I arrived, but many arrived right before 1:00. The bailiff announced my name. As I walked, I felt what little food I'd eaten for lunch begin to stir and rise from my stomach. I swallowed hard. When I reached the judge, I pressed my hand against his bench to steady myself. His look told me to back off. *Immediately.* I stepped back and found myself next to a man in a dark suit who I assumed was my lawyer.

The judge, still mumbling, spoke in a voice just loud enough for the two of us to hear. He said I was lucky the court system was so clogged that he didn't have the time nor the energy to deal with what he called my "childish prank at Gracie Mansion."

"So, I understand you're a father," he said, looking at a piece of paper. Without waiting for my response, he continued. "Why the hell are you chaining yourself to a fence rather than doing what you're supposed to be doing? You mean to tell me you took a weekend away from your child to do something so idiotic? Start being a father, for God's sake."

The words hit me so hard that I could only nod. He offered to reduce my disorderly conduct charge to trespassing, but warned me that if I ever did anything so irresponsible anywhere near New York, my luck would run out. For now, I was to pay a $500 fine. My lawyer asked for a minute alone with me. He took me aside and said, "Take it." We approached the judge and I accepted his offer. I looked over his shoulder as I spoke, avoiding eye contact. He instructed me to follow a cop to a side room so I could sign some papers.

As we were exiting, the large double doors to the courtroom swung open, slamming against the walls with a bang that echoed through the chambers. The group from the restaurant barged in, chanting, "We die. They do nothing," and "They say get back. We say fight back." Some observers in the courtroom applauded, others just looked bewildered. The cop, annoyed that I had stopped following her, pulled at my shirtsleeve.

As I was signing the papers, the pen slipped out of my hand. The cop said, "It's only a fine, buddy. Relax." I finished. My signature looked like it belonged to an elderly person. I could still hear the demonstrators as I left the courthouse. I hopped in a taxi and came straight to the airport.

I keep thinking about how Gustavo has taken a break from political action because he's about to become a father. I fled the scene in the courtroom to avoid any more problems with the police. I've tried to rationalize my actions. Staying out of further legal trouble is what's best for Grace. She doesn't need to have a father in jail—even if just for a month or so—and it's obviously not in her best interest to have a father who's unemployed. Staying with the demonstrators would have ended any chance of a teaching career.

Fatherhood. Activism. Teaching. Geoffrey. I don't know how to be true to everything that's meaningful in my life.

~

Vernon Reed, Headmaster
Chadwick Academy
134 Pleasant Hill Road
Smythe Administration Building
East Wellington, MA 02421

JANUARY 26, 1985

Dear Casey,

It pains me to write this letter because throughout your time at Chadwick Academy, I have wanted nothing more than for you to be successful. However, I cannot in good conscience ignore what occurred last night.

First, I would like to review what took place:

1. You arrived late for the performance of *Measure for Measure*. While I realize you only missed the first twenty minutes of the production, any tardiness when it comes to attending a student presentation that you directed is unprofessional.
2. You left campus for an entire day of the production without informing the administration. You canceled two of your Spanish classes and failed to provide substitute coverage for your lunch duty.
3. Your interpretation of Shakespeare's play was inappropriate for a group of high school aged students. A homosexual reimagining of Shakespeare seems best suited for adult theater company, not teenagers.
4. When Maryanne announced to the audience that you had "helped her discover who she was" by your example, it was clear to

everyone in the theater that this cast knew about your sexual preference. Your decision to share this information with her was a clear and inappropriate crossing of boundaries.

I have concluded that the following response to these events is appropriate and fair:

1. Nathaniel Cooper, Chair of the Arts Department, will be responsible for the spring production.
2. You are also relieved of your duties as advisor to your five advisees. I would ask that you consult with our school counselor, Ileana Phelan, about which teachers would be appropriate matches for these students.
3. You are relieved of all dormitory responsibilities.
4. You may continue to teach your Spanish classes. However, your employment as a Spanish teacher is contingent upon living off campus. You have two weeks to find an alternative housing situation. As a gesture of good faith, the school will supplement your salary by $1500 for housing expenses that were previously covered by residence in the dormitory.
5. You are on probation for the remainder of the academic school year. You will be required to meet with Ileana Phelan once a week as both a means of support as well as an evaluation of your class performance. I trust you see Ileana as a fair-minded, neutral player in this unfortunate episode. Please refer to the Faculty Handbook for further explanation of probationary status.

Other issues might arise in the coming days. Students and parents will no doubt have many questions. I would ask that you refer these questions to me rather than address them yourself. I believe the school should speak in a unified voice on this matter.

Lastly, despite the difficulties of the past days, it is important to remember that I, along with the entire Chadwick community, want what's best for you. At the same time, your position as a role model is cause for concern. The adolescents under your charge are in the process of forming adult identities. These identities are informed by peers, parents, teachers, and the media. It can be a very confusing time. The public acknowledgment of your sexuality is likely to add to that confusion, making your role as a teacher problematic. This is not to say there is no role for you in education, but you might want to reassess what that role is. There are many rewarding administrative positions in which you could ably serve and be yourself. Please know that I am available to discuss your future.

Sincerely,

Vernon Reed

Headmaster

cc: Employment file, Casey Adair

Ileana Phelan, School Psychologist

∼

Dear Mr. Adair,

We are the parents of Becca Hartmann, class of '88. Becca worked on the stage crew for the school play on Friday. We spoke briefly with you at intermission.

Although this is only her first year at Chadwick, Becca has felt very much at home at the school. We have been most impressed with the academic and social offerings available to our daughter.

It is because of our affection for Chadwick that we feel the need to express our concern about your production of *Measure for Measure*, and, more specifically, the events that followed. While we hardly claim to be experts, we are subscribers to the Philadelphia Theater Company and understand that directors have a degree of artistic license. Being exposed to differing interpretations of plays—especially the classics—can, in fact, be one of the most exciting aspects of frequenting the theater. Still, radical departures from the intention of the playwright can be needlessly upsetting to the audience or in some cases even dangerous.

We feel that directors must take especially good care when working with young people. As we witnessed when the young woman playing the Duchess of Vienna admitted her homosexual proclivities to an unsuspecting audience, the interpretation of a director can easily become a lesson for young students. The line between a director's personal take on a play and proselytizing is easily blurred. We fear that—intentionally or not—this occurred with *Measure for Measure*.

Homosexuality is a sensitive, controversial, and above all personal matter. We believe that discussions about the topic are best left within the family in order to respect all cultural and religious values. We were fortunate to have been present Friday night and were able to balance the lesson presented to our daughter over brunch the next morning. Specifically, we found the following bible passages extremely helpful in our discussion: Jude 1:7, Leviticus 20:13, 1 Corinthians 6:9–10.

We would like to stress that none of our criticism is personal. From what Becca has told us, you seem like an extremely nice person. In no way do we want you to interpret our questioning as an assault on your character.

Yours sincerely,

David and Constance Hartmann

cc: Vernon Reed, Headmaster

∾

CAMBRIDGE, MA   JANUARY 27, 1985

Dear Mr. Adair,

I am the father of Maryanne Duffy. I am writing on behalf of myself and my wife, Tina, to express our feelings about the production of *Measure for Measure* and its aftermath.

In all honesty, while we were proud of Maryanne's performance as the Duchess of Vienna, we were quite taken aback when she announced her sexual orientation after the production. We should also say from the start that we hold no ill will against you for the role you played in Maryanne's public acknowledgment.

We decided it best that Maryanne come home for the weekend so we as a family could discuss the ramifications of Friday's performance. These discussions were challenging. Neither my wife nor I slept easily Saturday night.

When we had breakfast with Maryanne Sunday morning, things began to clarify for us. We remain concerned about the life our daughter will have if, in fact, she leads a lesbian lifestyle. Yet during our conversations, our daughter was as confident and mature as we have ever seen her. In short, she was herself. We both have decided that it is our job to adjust to this new "self" Maryanne has become. We will do our best to support her.

We are aware that our initial reaction to Maryanne's revelation stands in contradiction to what she has learned about social justice in our family. Tina is a labor representative, while I am a professor at Harvard who teaches a class on the African American migration north. I tell you all this because I suspect Maryanne will come to you to describe what happened here at home. I want you to have as clear a context as possible.

We have come to see Maryanne's speech on Friday as more courageous than self-indulgent, more sincere than attention-grabbing. Her journey will not be at all easy for our family—and we are not convinced that the journey she began on Friday night will be the journey she ultimately follows—but we do feel the need to thank you for your role in encouraging a discussion about our daughter within our family.

Sincerely,
James Duffy III, PhD

∼

CAMBRIDGE, MA   JANUARY 27, 1985

Dear Mr. Adair,

Hi. Maryanne here. Just wanted to thank you for giving me the strength to come out to everyone Friday night. It was sort of scary, but I kept thinking about how together you seem as a gay guy. Plus, I pretended I was still the Duchess of Vienna when I spoke, so it didn't feel so personal. I'm kind of nervous about going back to school in the morning. My roommate was a little freaked out by what happened, but I think we're good enough friends that we can work things out.

I can't say that my parents were totally cool about my being a lesbian, but as far as parents go, our talk was OK. My mom works with labor unions, so I wasn't surprised when she told me to remember that all real struggles in life were class related. She played the Marxist card. It's kind of funny if you think about it.

Anyway, thanks again. I can't wait to do another show with you. I've been doing a little reading about plays with lesbians and am rooting for *The Children's Hour* before I graduate.

Love ya,

Maryanne

PS: Not that I'm religious or anything, but I was wondering if I could keep the cross that the Duchess wore around her neck in the show.

∾

WEDNESDAY, JANUARY 30, 1985   11:15 P.M.

I had dinner with Stoddard and Emory Monday night. They told me to bring Vernon's letter and contract with me. When I got there, they introduced me to a friend of theirs, a gay lawyer with the alliterative name Mason Merriweather. He and Emory were undergrads together. He wore a tweed coat and bow tie for this very informal dinner. And Docksiders. And khakis. And horn-rimmed glasses.

Mason Merriweather glanced over the letter and then told me that I might have a case against the school, but it could be tricky because my contract has a morals clause, which allows Vernon to fire me if he feels my personal behavior goes against community values. Also, I wasn't technically fired, so it would be hard building a case. Because Vernon had offered compensation for what it would cost to live off campus, I couldn't plead any financial harm. Despite all this, Mason thought we should go to court, especially since chances are slim that I'll be offered a contract for next fall. I think he saw an opportunity to handle what might be a high-profile case, just the sort of thing that the press would love.

I told him I needed some time to think. We went on to have a nice evening, with Emory cooking another great dinner. Stoddard got tired after we ate and we all encouraged him to go to bed. Emory, Mason, and I had another glass of wine. We talked about the trip to Spain and how Stoddard was going to need lots of down time while we were in Madrid. That's if he's able to go at all.

Some of the kids at school are being mean to Maryanne since she came out. Ileana has organized some group discussions around being gay. She's trying to dispel myths about gay people, and I think she's doing a good job. I think Vernon is allowing her to go ahead because he doesn't want to look too homophobic. He's covering his butt. That's a strange sort of progress, I guess. But I doubt he's comfortable with what Ileana is doing.

Geoffrey called again from England to say hello. I told him everything that had happened at school, including having to leave the dorm. He suggested I move into his place while he was gone. "Take some time and get your thoughts together," he said. I was really touched by his gesture. I told him I would take him up on his offer if I needed to. It feels like a strange leap into the relationship to be living in his apartment.

Now I have to decide whether to proceed with a lawsuit to remain in the dormitory. I must say that living in Geoffrey's apartment is much more appealing than staying on campus. The question is whether I want to pursue legal action out of principle. Or maybe I'd be doing it for Maryanne.

~

BOSTON   FEBRUARY 3, 1985

Dear Gustavo,

It would mean so much to me to talk to you about everything I've been questioning these past weeks. Who else could I confide in about the challenges of being a father and an activist? Can you ever be good at both?

My court appearance for demonstrating at Gracie Mansion went well. I was only slapped with a fine for trespassing. I have no idea what happened to the other guys. I dressed in a white shirt and tie, shamelessly playing a game I thought I had about a 50/50 chance of winning. I guess you could say that I won, since someone is paying the $500 fine for me. And nothing goes on my record.

Sometimes I doubt if getting involved in the protest did any good at all. I've come to understand that demonstrations are only as effective as what its participants are willing to give up. Bobby Sands and the Irish Republican prisoners were willing to give up their lives. That's why they captured the attention of the world. Martin Luther King gave up his freedom in a Birmingham jail. What did I give up? Nothing. I'm not even paying my own fine.

The headmaster at Chadwick has told me to leave the dorm because a student came out and cited me as a reason. My job next year is really at risk. I talked with a lawyer the other night and he wants me to sue the school, although whether we'd win is uncertain. But it would draw attention to how vulnerable gay people—especially gay teachers—are to being fired. Massachusetts is a left-leaning state, but even here there's no law to prevent employment discrimination. I really would love to hear your feelings about all this.

I hope you and your girlfriend are having fun getting ready for the baby. Have you picked out any names yet? Still hoping to see both of you in March.

Hugs,
Casey

∿

TUESDAY, FEBRUARY 5, 1985   6:00 A.M.

I had the first of my weekly meetings—one of the stipulations for my staying at Chadwick—with Ileana Phelan yesterday. I think we both were wondering why we were having the meeting at all. I decided that Vernon had arranged our meetings not because he thought I'd feel more comfortable with Ileana, but because of how uncomfortable he'd be with me every week. That, and the notion that any issue with a gay guy should immediately land in the psychologist's lap.

Ileana asked me if I'd been getting any more pushback since the night of the play. I could have told her about how a few people on campus pretend not to see me, how some staff members avoid eye contact at all costs. Instead I told her about the many supportive letters my colleagues had written, the parents who told me that every child needed a role model. She seemed genuinely happy to hear this.

Ileana said that Vernon had hired a new dorm parent, someone he described to her as "a burly guy ready to keep the boys in line." He's arriving February 20, so today I looked at the classified ads in the

Globe for a studio apartment somewhere near the school, but didn't have much luck. Even the smallest places are more expensive than I can afford. During my bout of insomnia last night, I had a glass of wine and I called Geoffrey. It was ten in the morning in England, a perfect time to reach him.

He answered right away. He told me that while it was hard to see his mother so ill, what he was mostly feeling these days was bored. His father has become so depressed that he sleeps most of the day. Geoffrey spends his time reading and working on jigsaw puzzles at the kitchen table.

I approached the subject of living in his apartment delicately. The minute I mentioned it, his voice became charged with energy. I simply had to move in. It was the only solution. I assured him that I'd keep looking for a place while he was away, and that I'd be ready to move out as soon as he returned to Boston.

"We'll deal with that when the time comes," he said.

His kindness momentarily overwhelmed me. I tried to control my voice. I didn't want to hang up but knew I had to. I'd already called Toronto twice this month and couldn't afford a huge phone bill.

~

Law Offices of Mason Merriweather & Partners
360 Commonwealth Avenue #3
Boston, Massachusetts 02215

FEBRUARY 6, 1985

Dear Casey,

I very much enjoyed meeting you the other night at dinner, and I'm keen on discussing your lawsuit further. After some consideration and consultation with my partners, I have decided that yours is just the sort of case our firm would do *pro bono* because the outcome has ramifications for state and perhaps even federal law.

If you would like to proceed, and I very much hope you will, please call my office so that we can arrange a consultation. In the meantime, please save any communications you have received from the school regarding your situation. I would further ask that you document your interactions with the headmaster and other administrators in writing. We will also need a copy of the faculty handbook.

I look forward to hearing from you.

Sincerely,

Mason Merriweather, Esq.

~

Paula was a great friend today by helping me move into Geoffrey's apartment. She also offered to store some things of mine that I wouldn't need, like my stereo system, TV, and VCR, since Geoffrey already has these. His apartment is small and I don't want to clutter the place, especially if he comes home before I find a new place to live. I called Poppy and told her I had a new phone number without providing an explanation. I was grateful that she didn't push for details.

Once Paula and I carried everything up the stairs, I brought my suitcase into the bedroom. I wasn't sure where to put my clothes. It seemed too intrusive to mix my underwear with Geoffrey's in the top dresser drawer. Since there were no extra hangers—and not a lot of room for many more—I hung my shirts over Geoffrey's. I only had a few pairs of shoes, but I couldn't see anywhere to put them where they wouldn't cause me to trip. There didn't seem to be room for me at all. And everything was so tidy. His socks were folded, not rolled into a ball like mine. His polos were arranged in the drawer with the precision you'd find in a high-end clothing store. In his shoes, he'd inserted cedarwood shoe trees; inside his sneakers he'd stuffed fabric dryer sheets.

I wondered if it would be better to get a room at the YMCA instead of disrupting the order Geoffrey had so painstakingly created. And what about the sheets? Was I supposed to change them or sleep in the ones he'd slept in? I put my suitcase on the bed.

Paula hugged me from behind. "It'll be okay," she said. "It might even be great. Relax."

I followed her to the kitchen where she took a bottle of wine out of her backpack and poured us each a glass. We sat in the living area, which seemed bigger now that the Christmas tree was down. After

Paula and I clinked glasses, she told me how sorry she was about the way Vernon had treated me. She paused to collect herself while she was talking. I wasn't sure if anger or sadness had taken hold. I realize now it was probably both. She said she wouldn't renew her contract next year. She reminded me that she wasn't just leaving Chadwick. Her large yearly contribution to Chadwick's fund drive would be leaving with her. That, more than anything, would speak to Vernon. It might even get him to rethink how he'd responded.

I tried to get her to change her mind. I said that I couldn't imagine Chadwick without her. I didn't want to be the cause of her leaving.

"It's not only about you," she said. "Sure, it's a lot about you because you're my friend and I hate what's happened. But it's also a lot about Maryanne and any other kid at the school who's gay. I'm not feeling very good about keeping quiet all these years."

It was cold and windy, so we decided to grab some pizza right next door instead of exploring the neighborhood for a cozy restaurant. The overhead fluorescent bulbs gave me a headache. At the same time, the harsh light seemed appropriate for a day in which reality seemed so stark. I'd been asked to leave my place and Paula was going to leave Chadwick. I was about to start living in the apartment of a man I didn't think I knew very well.

We were both exhausted from the move so we didn't talk much. I did fill her in on the possibility of a lawsuit against the school. She wholeheartedly supported taking Vernon to court. By leaving the school, she was taking a stand not just for me but for some sort of greater good. I should do the same, she said. She made a good case.

Sometimes I wonder if Paula and I would have had the sort of relationship I had with Poppy if we'd met in college. Pre-pregnancy, of course. I'm actually glad that we met after college. When you take sexual attraction out of the picture, things become a lot simpler. Although sometimes I wonder if you can ever take sexual attraction completely out of the picture.

I'm back at Geoffrey's apartment, sitting on the sofa, where I think I'll sleep tonight instead of in the bed. Geoffrey has a shelf of British movie videos. I've never seen *The Lavender Hill Mob*. I think I'll put that on before I go to sleep.

Dear Mason:

Thank you for taking the time to talk with me about the legal possibilities regarding my employment situation. I now feel I have a more thorough understanding of the issues involved.

I have decided that I would like to proceed with the lawsuit. I am persuaded by your argument that my case might bring an unfair situation into public light. I understand that winning our case is by no means a certainty.

I appreciate your offering your services *pro bono*, as I hardly have the financial resources to fund a legal case myself.

Please advise as to how we may proceed.

Sincerely,

Casey Adair

~

TUESDAY, FEBRUARY 12, 1985   11:15 P.M.

I really want to see Grace, so I'm glad I'm flying up for the long weekend. Poppy has bought us tickets to *Cats* for Saturday afternoon. I'm not wild about cats even when they're sleeping, so I'm still not completely sold on the idea of them singing and dancing.

Geoffrey sent a bouquet of flowers yesterday, to celebrate my moving in. It was incredibly sweet of him. It made me miss him. I've been so caught up in what's going on at school that I haven't really had time to think about anything else, including Geoffrey. He called the next night, just to make sure the bouquet arrived, but I think that he was using the flowers as an excuse to talk with me, which I found endearing.

His mother has been transferred to hospice care. It's a matter of days. He'll stay in England for a bit after she dies to be with his father, but he wants to return to Boston as soon as possible. When he said he wanted me to stay in the apartment with him, I didn't commit, but at least I didn't immediately list all the ways things could go wrong or how I might be making an irreversible mistake. I was just grateful. I started envisioning a life with him: reading the Sunday

Times together, learning how to cook from him, arguing about space, having sex.

I'm supposed to have my second meeting with Ileana tomorrow. I don't think she's a bad or deceptive person at heart. I see her as someone who tries to be friends with everyone, so her loyalties are divided between the faculty and Vernon. Yet when push comes to shove, I think she'll take the side of the school, and for her the school is personified in Vernon Reed. The school is her life. I guess there's something admirable in her faithfulness. It's like a monogamous marriage. I can see her at Chadwick for another twenty years, maybe 'til death do they part.

∼

SATURDAY, FEBRUARY 16, 1985   11:00 P.M.

I'm in Toronto. Being with Grace has reminded me of our time together over Christmas, which then got me thinking about Geoffrey. I woke up around four this morning and did something that wasn't terribly smart. I called him from Poppy's phone, knowing she'd see the number from England on her next bill.

Geoffrey didn't answer. I got dressed and walked right to the bathhouse, open all night. Without thinking I paid for a room and towel. I took off my clothes and went to the Jacuzzi where some men were soaking and others groping each other. I slid into the steaming water slowly. A blond bearish guy inched his way over to me, rubbing his hip against mine, then running his foot up and down my shin. I wanted him in the worst way. All I had to do was look at him and I knew we'd be in the tiny room I'd rented. Even a sigh would have given him the signal. And yet I didn't do anything. I started thinking about Geoffrey. I shimmied away from the man and left the Jacuzzi. Strange: I'm being true to someone I haven't even seen naked.

Poppy was sitting on the sofa in her bathrobe when I returned. She was drinking wine and reading a novel.

"Welcome back. I thought we were all in for the night." Her eyes were still glued to the book.

"I thought so, too," I said. "I couldn't sleep."

She shut her book. I think she smelled the chlorine on me because she said, "The bathhouse raids have stopped. At least you don't have to worry about that."

I told her the truth: I'd gone to the bathhouse because I hadn't had sex in the longest time, but that once I was there, I started thinking about someone else, and found it impossible have sex with a stranger. She went to the kitchen and poured another glass of wine and handed it to me. When she sat on the sofa again, she crossed her legs, deliberately revealing her thigh.

Fuck. Did she think that *she* was the person who kept me from having sex in the bathhouse? How stupid could I be? But her flirtation was strangely seducing. Maybe I was just horny and the possibility of a release with someone I knew so well seemed appealing. Or maybe I wanted to prove once and for all that I'd made the right decision moving to Boston.

Whatever the reason, I joined her on the sofa. I touched her knee and she immediately leaned against me, her head on my chest, her arm around my neck. What followed wasn't unpleasurable, but it wasn't satisfying, either. I was glad that we both realized how awkward the situation was before I even unbuckled my belt.

"I'm not feeling anything," she said.

I was going to tell her the same. Then it came to me that this was her moment of revelation, not mine. I'd had that realization years ago.

"I think that's good," I said.

She ran her index finger around the rim of her wine glass. "I don't know why it took me this long to understand, but it does feel better."

The sun was beginning to rise. Poppy turned on the TV. We watched the early morning news like so many other people in Toronto.

∽

TORONTO   FEBRUARY 19, 1985

Dear Poppy,

I'm writing you from the airport as I wait for my early morning flight back to Boston. I know I have a tendency to see things between us as rosier than they actually are. So when I say that I felt a positive shift in our relationship over the past few days, I don't mean to imply that we've hit any sort of tonic chord that has settled things once and for all. Yet I can't help but think that we're in a better place now than we have been in a very long time.

It meant a lot to be able to tell you about everything that's been happening at school and how I came to be living in Geoffrey's apartment. The last time we talked about him, I was confused as to where the relationship was going. I can't say that I'm no longer confused, but I do see a clearer path ahead.

I was glad to hear that you've started seeing the guy from the bookstore. He sounds like a sweetheart. We're both dating Brits! And they're both into books.

My flight has just been called so I'll wrap up. Just know that I leave Toronto grateful that Grace is in our lives. I'll absolutely look at March for another trip to see you both.

Love,
Casey

~

WEDNESDAY, FEBRUARY 20, 1985   2:15 A.M.

Strange to think that just this morning I was in Toronto. It feels like a lifetime ago. I drove straight from the airport to school. I was in my classroom by 9:00. The return trip felt like a victory, as if my life has started to fall into place for the first time in a while.

But the big news isn't that I made it to class on time. The big news is that Geoffrey was waiting for me at the apartment when I got back this evening. His mother had died last Friday. He said the best way for him to heal was to be with me.

I told him how sorry I was that his mother had died, that I'd never get the chance to meet her. I told him I'd do anything he needed. After that I had no idea what to say. A million thoughts went through my mind, from "I'll have to find a new place soon," to "It is so damn nice to see him."

He was in his bathrobe. I had never seen his bare legs before, and tried not to stare. He handed me a glass of wine and told me to sit down on the sofa. He said he'd tried to get in touch with me over the weekend but that I hadn't answered. He decided not to leave a message because he was afraid that if I heard he was coming back, I might find a new place to live before he even landed.

"I wanted you here," he said.

It's hard for me to write about what happened next. When I was in Spain, I took few photos. I knew that the experience of looking at them later would never match what had happened in real life. I've also learned by writing this journal that words can only approximate reality. Sometimes when I read my entries from Spain or even this past fall, the experience feels diminished, like I'm rereading a novel I fell in love with as a child but don't find engaging as an adult. This is why I'm going to limit what I write about this evening. Geoffrey and I finally slept together. It was about sex and not about sex. It was passionate and comforting. Foreign and familiar. The minute I think of a word to describe the two of us together, I come up with an opposite word that feels just as real.

Geoffrey is sleeping now while I'm still awake. I've stopped thinking of him as fifteen years older than I am. Now I see myself as fifteen years younger than he is. It's like I'm now the one who needs to prove something, to convince him that the age difference isn't all that much.

I don't know where we go from here. I worry I'll be in the way. I'll drop his favorite coffee mug on the floor, shattering it to pieces. I'll sleep late one Saturday and he won't be able to make the slightest noise in his own home until I wake up. I'll track snow into the living room. I'll make him make room for me: my books, my clothes, my records, my mood after a draining day at school.

But for now I am here.

~

TORONTO   FEBRUARY 19, 1985

Dear Casey,

I've read your letter a number of times. I can't say that I disagree with much of what you've written. For the first time in a while, I feel optimistic about the two of us maintaining a friendship. It will never be like the one we had in college, but I found myself letting go of some of my anger this weekend. At that moment when we both realized (well, when I realized, at least) that there was nothing romantic between us, a burden lifted. I was bearing all the responsibility for keeping you connected to Grace and me. The problem was, I was trying to keep us connected through some outdated image of a Disney movie romance.

Before we get too far ahead of ourselves, I have one more thing I need to tell you. I've resented the way you've tried to pathologize me since you moved to Boston. You turned everything I did that was the least out of the norm as a sign of emotional instability. In fact, I was just responding to my situation. Overusing the credit card, jetting off with a man I hardly knew to the Canary Islands—these were maybe not the smartest things I've ever done, but they weren't signs that I was mentally ill. They were signs that I was human. A complex, messy, contradictory, emotional human. And I had to laugh when you gave me advice like, "Try to find another music teacher." Seriously, Casey. Did you really believe that poor-little-old-me didn't think about that? Being a gay guy doesn't give you a pass on sexism.

I'm not sure you've spent enough time thinking about how *you* have been reacting to our lives changing. Or maybe you haven't reacted. You've thrown yourself into your new job. You've carried a political torch, getting arrested in the process. And now you're in the middle of a lawsuit with the school. What have you actually felt these past months?

Now you have reason to resent me for psychoanalyzing you. In the end, what matters is that we've moved forward, which is good for everyone, especially Grace.

Love,
Poppy

~

SATURDAY, FEBRUARY 23, 1985   1:00 P.M.

Geoffrey has left the apartment to play squash with one of his library pals at Harvard. It's nice to have the place to myself, even if I have to write on the kitchen table instead of a desk. We're getting along fine living in the same small place. I'm vigilant for any sign he wants to be alone. Sometimes I think I know he wants to be by himself before he does. I watch for him to go through magazines on the coffee table and throw out the ones he's already read. Or he might move a stray fork on the kitchen counter to the sink. That's when I go down the street to the library and correct papers. Or I'll put on my Walkman and curl up with a book in the bedroom.

I'm still getting used to sleeping with Geoffrey. I listen for his quiet gurgle, the softest trumpet sound he makes when his lips aren't completely sealed. I think about him—his past, the wife and child he'll never see again, the mother he just lost—and I can feel the pulse in my neck. I wonder how long it will be until he wants to be alone more than an hour or two, when he starts needing days or weeks without me. I think about Stoddard, about death. I think about the age difference between Geoffrey and me. If he dies at 70, I'll only be 55, and on and on. Then I realize it's not really death I'm thinking about after all. It's a future with Geoffrey.

Poppy and I wrote letters that crossed in the mail. We both agree that we're in a better place today than we were even a week ago. I'm encouraged by that. She did give me some advice in her letter, along with a mild scolding for, in her words, "pathologizing" her behavior. She implied that I'm afraid to get too close to Geoffrey. She has a point, although she doesn't know that Geoffrey has returned and that at least for now we're living together, which makes it hard *not* to deal with emotion. She doesn't know I'm up all hours thinking about him and me—the two of us—as a couple.

∼

BOSTON   FEBRUARY 28, 1985

Dear Casey,

It was wonderful seeing you last night, even if (and Warren agrees) I overcooked the pasta just a bit. I used to just throw a piece against the kitchen wall and if it stuck, I knew it was done. Warren would have none of it. "We can't have food flying around the kitchen as if we were in a high school cafeteria," were his exact words.

We loved meeting Geoffrey. What a charming guy. So easy on the eyes. And so intelligent! I've never met anyone outside the business who was able to talk about dentistry so knowledgably. A real renaissance man.

I hope I'm not stepping out of bounds when I say that the two of you seemed wonderful together. He had a hard time keeping his eyes off you even as we plunged into such gripping topics as new methods for root canals. You also seem pretty sweet on him. You deserve all of what is happening given what you've gone through these past months at school. We're both so happy for you.

As I promised, I've enclosed the itinerary for your trip with Warren. It's very light, for obvious reasons. I do believe he's stabilized and that the trip won't take too much out of him, as long as he takes time to rest.

It's been very touching to see Warren get excited about something. We can't thank you enough for bringing such joy to us.

Love you, Darling,

Emory

~

Today I was grateful to get in my car and drive not only to an apartment off campus, but to one where Geoffrey welcomed me with a glass of wine. I sat next to him on the sofa, his arm around me, and started to explain what had happened. I didn't get through the first sentence. I wish I could say I cried in a Diane Keaton sort of way, which means that you cry but are always on the verge of snapping out of it, or the way she cried in *Annie Hall* when she looked like she was making fun of her crying, listening to an inner voice say, "Well, it's really stupid to be crying *now*." But it wasn't that way. I felt more like Brando in *Streetcar*.

This morning Paula officially informed Vernon that she wouldn't be returning next fall. She said that she was upset at the way I'd been treated. He begged her to stay at least another year but she refused. "Don't you get it?" she asked. "Don't you see that what you do to Casey you do to me?" When she left, he called me into his office and implied

I'd turned one of "Chadwick's finest" against him. It was the first time I think I've seen him with his guard down. No tight smile. No cock of the head. His voice, usually steady to the point of monotone, quavered.

I left his office certain I wouldn't have a job by the end of the day. Between my third and fourth period class, I told Paula. She turned on her heels and marched right back to Vernon and gave him hell for taking her resignation out on me. She threatened to quit immediately.

Vernon summoned me to his office again, his cautious old self back.

"I've given it some thought," he said. "I think Chadwick Academy might have been a little too hasty in asking you to leave the dormitory."

I knew immediately this was about Paula's annual donation. If I were a different person, I might have sat back and savored every minute of Vernon's about-face. I could see other people in my position barely able to hide their glee. They'd be taking mental notes to describe in detail how Vernon was humiliated into making nice with me. But when he asked me if I'd like to return to the dormitory, all I could think about was how I wanted out of the whole mess. I ended the meeting.

When I told Geoffrey about the day, he said, "Well, you bloody well better not be thinking of moving back into that dorm."

That's all he had to say to make me realize that I wasn't alone in this. A writing teacher at Nearing once told us that she thought people misunderstood "write what you know." She believed that writers often interpreted the adage to mean write what you know *about*, when really it was suggesting that you write what you know is true, not factually but emotionally. Tonight was like this for me. Intellectually I knew that Geoffrey would be with me during this whole Chadwick mess. Now I think I know this in a more profound way.

Geoffrey and I also talked about something we'd been avoiding for a while. He wants us both to take the AIDS test together. He made it clear that he'd never consider bailing out if I tested positive. "I'm way past the point where I can retreat," he said. I told him that I needed to think for a while.

～

Dear Casey,

My God, I've been a poor correspondent! Please forgive me, dear friend. My life feels even busier than when we were roommates at Marianela and I was studying, editing the newspaper, and organizing protests. I've been hired by the University of Madrid to teach a course called "Protest and Democracy." You met me as a political radical who went to jail protesting the establishment. Now I'm on the faculty of the establishment teaching a class not on how to organize and make your voice heard, but how we *think* about those people who organize and resist. I feel like I've sold out.

Right now my focus is on providing our baby with a comfortable life. Working at the university helps me do that, so I'm more grateful than anything else.

While you're in Madrid, would you be willing to give a lecture on your experience in New York City and being arrested during the protest? I'd really love my students to hear a first-hand account of someone in the thick of a movement. They've grown tired of my own stories. I'd love for them to hear something new.

Also, Sofía and I had planned to get married after the baby was born, maybe sometime late summer or early fall. Now that we know you're going to be here in a few weeks, we're reconsidering. Would you be up for attending a very informal wedding ceremony in March? We're thinking twenty guests, tops. Nothing fancy. Let me know if this works for you!

Hugs,
Gustavo

～

MONDAY, MARCH 11, 1985   10:15 P.M.

Stoddard has taken a turn for the worse. His breathing became irregular this morning. Emory took him to his doctor, who was concerned that he had developed PCP, the pneumonia that comes with AIDS. The doctor ordered a biopsy of his lung. They're also running some blood tests. We won't know the results until tomorrow. He'll be at Mass General for at least a couple of nights.

We always knew the trip was tentative, but Stoddard had been holding steady. Pneumonia is different. Emory mentioned something about an intubation procedure if the oxygen levels in his blood drop much lower. At the end of the phone call Emory insisted that I leave for Spain on Friday as scheduled. I told him I wouldn't even think about going without Warren. But it's not just about Stoddard. I can't imagine leaving Emory right now, either.

I'll go to Mass General tomorrow to see Stoddard after my last class. But I feel the need to talk to him now. How bad is he? Is he on a breathing machine? And what the hell was this intubation Emory had mentioned? I should have asked him more questions.

When I moved into Geoffrey's apartment I didn't take much with me but I did bring my letters from Spain and the ones I'd received since I started teaching in Boston. They were in a manila envelope I'd stuck behind Geoffrey's boxed set of Proust on the top of the bookcase.

I placed my correspondence with Stoddard in chronological order. Not even two years of a life was in the pile, yet as I began reading, it felt like the full life of a friendship. There was an arc in the relationship, from our early letters—mine sounding eager, his sounding annoyed—to those of sad gratitude for the circumstances of our reconnection.

I'll need to call Gustavo. I dread giving bad news, but he needs to know right away that I won't be coming.

∿

Nearing Alumni Magazine
Winter/Spring 1985
Obituaries

Dallas Burnet Akins '78, who lived in Dallas, Texas, died on January 10, 1985. At Nearing, Dallas was affectionately known as "Dallas From Dallas" or "D²." He is survived by his parents, Preston and Loretta, and his siblings, Hunter and Jolene, along with many aunts, uncles, and cousins. Dallas came to Nearing from St. Mark's School of Texas where he was a member of the Hiking Club, the Young Republicans Club, and played for the basketball team. Prior to his illness, Dallas lived in Boston. He was planning to attend University of Texas School of Law.

Noah Allen Bergen '80, who lived in New York City, died on November 28, 1984, after a long illness. He is survived by his parents, John and Margie, and his sisters, Rachel and Hannah, along with a number of aunts, uncles, and cousins. Nicknamed "The Wisenheimer," Noah came to Nearing from the Horace Mann School in the Bronx where he was salutatorian of his class. At Nearing, Noah was a member of the Debate Club and the International Relations Club. Before his illness, Noah was studying for his Master's Degree in Foreign Policy at the Fletcher School of Law and Diplomacy in Medford, Massachusetts. Noah's passions were chess and understanding different cultures. He spent his post-graduate year traveling through Europe and the Middle East, trying to understand how we are all connected.

∽

TUESDAY, MARCH 12, 1985   7:00 P.M.

This afternoon I visited Stoddard in the hospital. He was hooked to an IV. At the entrance to his room, the nurses suggested I wear a hazmat suit to protect myself, but I said absolutely not. I was visiting a friend, not walking into a chemical disaster zone. I couldn't imagine standing beside Stoddard without an inch of my skin showing.

The test results had come back late this morning and confirmed that Stoddard does have PCP. He was much more alert and lucid than I'd expected. He shimmied himself up and reached for a pink plastic cup from his bed stand. Without saying a word, Emory left the room.

"The trip is off. I'm not going without you," I said.

"We're not going argue about this, Casey." He used the stern, professorial tone I hadn't heard since my Nearing days. It took everything for me to oppose him.

"I said I'm not going," I said. "Not now, anyway. Maybe if you get better."

"There will be no getting better." He let the r sound hang in the air, thick and intimidating.

"We don't know that."

"Oh, for God's sake, be honest, will you?" he said, his energy and annoyance rising. He then softened. He told me he liked getting the letters from me when I lived in Spain, especially the ones that described Madrid just as I was discovering it. He felt like he was discovering the city for the first time, too. So he thought it'd be nice for us to visit the Madrid he got to know when he was young. That's one of the things he had wanted to do when we went to Spain.

He handed me a list of places he wanted to see with me. Now it was going to be without him. When I got back from Spain he wanted me to give him my impressions. I wondered if he was being honest himself, if he really thought he'd still be alive by then. I unfolded the list of places he'd written down. He ended the list with "best wishes for a wonderful vacation and beyond."

"And beyond?" The words called up the ominous sound of the timpani in 2001: A Space Odyssey. I looked at him, waiting for a wink, an upturn of the lips, any sign that acknowledged the melodrama of the phrase. He didn't respond.

Then I remembered: I'd read the phrase last night. It was in one of his early letters, when he was attempting to cut short our correspondence. "And with that I shall return to my work. I wish you good luck in all you do this year and beyond." There it was again: "and beyond." Asking me to go to Spain on his behalf sounded like Stoddard's last wish.

I said yes, I would go.

He thanked me, then insisted Geoffrey come too, that he should take his place. This seems unlikely. Geoffrey already took a month off from the library when his mother was dying. I can't imagine him being able to go to Spain on such short notice.

~

I'm airborne right now, Stoddard's empty first-class seat beside me. Geoffrey will be with me on the way back. He was able to get Thursday and Friday off after all, so he'll meet me in Madrid next week. For now it's two first-class seats for myself.

Emory drove me to the airport. Stoddard is in stable condition. He might make it through this bout of pneumonia, but the doctors aren't willing to give us the odds. He'll be in the hospital for at least another week. That is, unless some other illness shows up between now and then. And there are so many illnesses: lymphoma, tuberculosis, meningitis, and on and on.

"I guess it really was crazy to think you and Warren would ever go to Spain together," Emory said as he walked me to the gate. He said he should have known what to expect as soon as Warren was diagnosed. He came from a long line of realists. Pray for the best and prepare for the worst. Somehow, preparing for the worst was always the wiser advice. The praying, he said, never seemed to work. He should have learned by now.

Still, I'm not sure Emory has really prepared for the worst, for Stoddard's death. I'm not sure I have, either. It's strange that I know Stoddard better than I knew my father. Stoddard: the man who'd kept such a distance from me when I was his student and when I first arrived in Spain. I'm sure I've gotten to know him in a way I didn't know my father because I'm older than I was when my father was alive. He could only tell me so much about his life. But there's something more than this, I think.

My father was a kind man—maybe the kindest man I've ever known—but his kindness was a sort of one-size-fits-all. When I remember him with other people, I see him display the same warmth to the world that he showed me. He sometimes brought homeless people to our house for dinner. He didn't make a big deal of it. He'd just ask my mother to put another setting on the table. He treated these strangers just like he treated us.

What I realize now is that there really wasn't anything fatherly about his affection. I didn't know this when I was growing up, which

I suppose was a good thing. Every child wants to feel like there's a special reservoir of love that's tapped just for him. I'm learning that my father had a single reservoir for everyone.

I'm not ungrateful. I'm lucky he was kind, that he spent the time he did with me. Still, in thinking about my relationship with Stoddard, not to mention my role as Grace's father, I've been questioning whether I've been specific enough in loving. The answer is probably not all the time, although I think I've gotten better these past months. Reconnecting with Grace at Christmas, meeting Geoffrey, and getting to know Stoddard during his illness have all hit distinct, very different, emotional chords in me.

～

MONDAY, MARCH 18, 1985   6:00 P.M.

After I checked into my hotel Saturday morning, I walked down to the Gran Vía. Nothing really felt new. Because *my* life had changed so much since I left, I assumed Madrid had changed along with me, which, as I write this, couldn't sound more self-centered. I'd also read about *la movida*, a countercultural movement that's a reaction to the oppression of the Franco years. I did pass a movie theater with an Almodóvar movie playing. Almodóvar's the poster boy for *la movida*.

But mostly things were the same. People still head to the bars for their *churros y chocolate* in the morning and late afternoon. They still walk around the statue of Don Quixote before dinner. They still have drinks at the Plaza Mayor. The blind still sell lottery tickets on street corners.

Saturday afternoon I went to the Prado, following Stoddard's request that I see the works of El Greco. The paintings informed me about Stoddard in some ways I'd already known. It was the darkness, mainly. But I didn't get how Stoddard connected with the drama in the work—all that chiaroscuro—nor did I understand why Stoddard was attracted to such religious work. As far as I know, he's not a religious man. I finally decided it was the secular pieces he wanted me to consider, like *The Nobleman with His Hand on His Chest* that depicts a man not unlike Stoddard: somber and honorable.

Yesterday afternoon Gustavo and Sofía were married in a short ceremony at the Parque de Retiro. Only a handful of people were invited: a few of Gustavo's colleagues at the university and Sofía's two brothers and her sister. Her parents, who live in Cádiz, didn't attend because she got pregnant out of wedlock, which seems to me the very definition of ironic.

In some ways Sofía seems like just the woman for Gustavo, yet in others she seems very unlike him. She's bold and opinionated, as he is. At the same time, she works for Agatha Ruíz de la Prada, a popular fashion designer in Madrid known for her use of bright colors and familiar shapes like triangles, circles, and stars. Sofía wore one of her designs to the wedding: a white dress with a hem lined with large red hearts.

After the ceremony Gustavo and Sofía invited us to a cozy restaurant near the park. He'd hired a small group of medieval balladeers to come and sing halfway through the meal. Gustavo and Sofía danced while everyone clapped. When the song was over they sat next to me.

"Sofía's brother over there?" he said. "He's gay, too. We thought you two might have a dance together. Who knows what else will happen?"

"You're too shy," Sofía said to me as the band started up again. She waved her brother to our table. He approached me with an obligatory smile. We made small talk (he was an investment consultant and modern art collector) as we danced awkwardly, not knowing which of us to lead. We parted before the music was over. I was again left wondering why straight people assume that any two random gay men would fall for each other. But I give Gustavo and Sofía credit for trying. It was a sweet gesture.

"I've met someone," I told them when I returned to the table. "His name is Geoffrey."

Gustavo seemed genuinely happy. He called for the waiter to bring a bottle of wine. He topped off everyone's drink and toasted me and Geoffrey.

This morning I guest-lectured in Gustavo's class, "Protest and Democracy." Ten minutes into my talk, students were peppering me with questions, some of which I could answer ("What did you hope to accomplish by protesting in New York City?"), some I couldn't

("Do you think the protest worked?"). The class applauded when I finished.

As the students left, Gustavo hugged me. He said the lecture was inspiring, not just to the class but to him as well. He looked wistful when he spoke.

"Maybe someday I'll be on the front lines again," he said.

"I'm sure you will," I said.

We walked out of the building together. I went back to the hotel. Gustavo went home to pack for his honeymoon. Nothing extravagant. He and Sofía are taking the train to Seville tonight where they'll stay for a few days.

∼

THURSDAY, MARCH 21, 1985   3:00 A.M.

Geoffrey is somewhere over the Atlantic as I write. I haven't given much thought about what we'll do once he's here. I'm more interested in spending time with him and not so interested in how we spend it. I haven't felt that way about someone since Poppy and I were in college.

Wednesday morning I got up early to take a three-hour bus ride to Salamanca, another place on Stoddard's list, where I visited one of the oldest universities in the world, built sometime in the twelfth century. Stoddard was a guest lecturer there in the early '70s. He said teaching in that classroom was one of the highlights of his life. There was a spiritual quality to the place, a sense that it was still inhabited by all the great Spanish writers who attended or taught there: Cervantes, Unamuno, Fray Luis de Léon, Góngora. There were no desks, just long, narrow wooden tables with backless benches that looked original to the building. I pictured Stoddard giving his lecture at the dais, which was more like an altar.

Stoddard also told me to visit the Casa de Conchas (House of Shells), which was (not surprisingly) decorated with hundreds of stone shells on the outside. It now houses the university library. I've decided that Stoddard liked it because—as I've learned this year—his outlook on life isn't completely bleak. He leaves room for whimsy.

∼

Geoffrey is on the bed naked, sleeping quietly. He's already grown accustomed to taking his afternoon siesta.

We just had sex for the first time since he got here. I expected us to have at it as soon as he arrived yesterday morning, but Geoffrey was tired. Also, our meeting at the airport was awkward for reasons I'm still trying to figure out. We said little to each other in the taxi. It was like we were both holding secrets we were so afraid of revealing that we didn't talk at all. I think I might have set the wrong tone. As Geoffrey stepped out of customs, I put on my cheeriest smile and said, "Welcome to the Forum!" It was a ridiculous greeting. I'm not even sure anyone calls Madrid "The Forum," despite what the travel books say. I came across as an eager tourist guide, welcoming someone completely unfamiliar.

At dinner that night, I said, "I'm learning a lot about Stoddard."

"Really?" His voice was soft. The jet lag and wine had made him a little woozy.

"Or at least I think I am. I was thrown off by the Goya exhibit at the Prado. How can you love both *Saturn Devouring His Son* and the painting of everyone playing blind-man's-bluff in the countryside?"

"You went to the Prado without me?" His tone was more melancholy than accusatory.

"I'll go again with you," I said.

"That's okay," he said, although I wasn't sure it was. "I was there a few years ago."

This morning we took the subway to the pensión where I used to live. It's a two-star hotel now, so no one I knew was still there. I was surprised at how little I felt for the place. We didn't go inside, but we did have some churros at the bar I spent time in during the coup attempt.

When we headed back, I hopped on the subway without noticing that Geoffrey had lagged behind me. The doors shut just as we both realized that he was still on the platform while I was on the train. He looked panicked, like a child who'd strayed from his parents. I wasn't sure whether to get off at the next stop or stay on until Sol, near our hotel. And if I did stay on, should I wait at the stop or meet Geoffrey back in our room?

I decided to go back to the room. I got naked and slid under the sheets, waiting for him. Funny how such a brief and harmless separation made me long for him more than I did when he was an ocean away. He looked relieved to see me in bed when he arrived. He undressed and joined me. We kissed for a long time.

"I'm sorry I've been acting peculiar," Geoffrey said when we paused.

Peculiar. Such a Geoffrey word.

"What's going on?"

"I don't know. I guess I'm feeling a little out of place. This was supposed to be between you and Stoddard. I don't want to be a placeholder."

"Never," I said, tracing his lips with my finger. We kissed some more before I put my hand between his legs.

When we had sex, some distance between us remained, but it was something of a turn-on. I felt like we were discovering our bodies for the first time.

Tonight we're going to the Plaza Mayor. Tomorrow we'll go to the zoo, which is also a place Stoddard wants me to visit. He's given me specific instructions to visit the gazelles, which seems, well, peculiar. Tomorrow night we'll go to a zarzuela. Our last night in Madrid.

∿

SUNDAY, MARCH 24, 1985   8:00 A.M.

Geoffrey has left the hotel to get us breakfast. Our cab to the airport arrives in an hour. When I confirmed our flight, I was told that there was a mix-up and Geoffrey and I won't be able to sit next to each other. This feels like a summation of our time in Madrid: together, but not together. We did have a nice time. But we were constantly adjusting to each other in this new landscape called Madrid.

I've been thinking about some of the relief sculptures I saw at the Prado. There was a Roman one, a marble of a satyr tending to a fire. It was created in 25 BC. The artist had chiseled just enough to give you a rough idea of the scene. Then there were other, more detailed pieces, like this second-century relief of Prometheus and Athena. Every fold in their robes was sculpted, every muscle perfectly toned. Madrid allowed Geoffrey and me to see ourselves in some sort of relief, but we're more like the satyr. The contours of who we are have started to become clear, but it'll take a while before the details emerge.

We went to the zoo yesterday afternoon. It was chilly out, but Geoffrey insisted we get snow cones anyway.

"It's what we always did when I was a kid," he said.

"I don't remember going to the zoo," I said.

"Wait. I thought you had the Father of the Year. Why didn't he take you?"

"Just wasn't his thing."

Geoffrey recoiled. I knew I sounded defensive as soon as the words came out of my mouth. He looked around to make sure we were alone before he took my hand.

"I'm on your side, you know," he said.

We went to see the gazelles. They trotted across their terrain like ballet dancers, then darted around so that it was impossible to predict where they would go next. I could be reading way too much into it, but I have a theory about why Stoddard wanted me to see them, what I was supposed to learn about him from them. Formal, graceful, ever aware of good form, but now and then he can surprise you with a gesture or word that's unexpected.

The zarzuela last night was lots of fun, more so for me than for Geoffrey, who doesn't understand Spanish. But as we were leaving the theater he said, "I liked the music and the dancing a lot."

"I'm glad," I said. "I was beginning to think you were getting bored."

"Never," he said.

"I have an idea," I said. "Let me take you to this bar where I hung out when I lived here."

Going to Black & White was not on Stoddard's list of things to do, but I decided to put it on mine. The vibe was different from when I was there last. There was something forced about the way guys were laughing. These days going to a gay bar is a way to get your mind off the disease that's killing us, but at the same time it's a place where the disease is staring you in the face: the guys that were too thin, the couple with lesions on their necks, the thirty-something guy (or maybe he was only twenty and just looked older) who rushed to the men's room not to fuck but because he was having a bout of diarrhea.

I didn't feel at home. I wanted to be in the bar where Octavio fucked me in the bathroom stall, where none of us were thinking whether or not we'd be alive next year. Where the men didn't tire from dancing after only a few songs. Where some men didn't dance at all.

Geoffrey and I danced.

"This is our first time," he said.

He was right. We kissed.

After the dance I told Geoffrey I wanted to get a good night's sleep before our flight today. It was time to go home.

TORONTO

MAY 6, 1985

These are the days that must happen to you.

—WALT WHITMAN

I haven't had the time or desire to write in my journal since my trip
to Spain. Things have recently settled down—I think I found an apartment this morning—so I'm hoping to start writing again this month.

At the end of March, I met with Vernon Reed. I was stunned when
he produced a contract. He told me I could sign it right there in his
office or I could accept the year's salary and not return to Chadwick
after graduation. There was a nondisclosure agreement to sign if I
took that option. He explained all of this without raising his voice.

"Two years' salary," I said.

He agreed.

"I hope you know I never wanted this to happen," he said.

"You didn't want it to happen this way," I said. "But you wanted it
to happen."

I didn't even consult the lawyer. I just signed it. I promised to drop
the lawsuit. I promised not to talk to the press. I promised not to visit
the campus.

That night, I talked with Geoffrey. I told him I wanted to return to
Toronto to be with Grace. He supported me with the understanding
that he might move here when his library contract was up for renewal.
We also promised to talk twice a week on the phone, which we have
done. That weekend I left Boston, all my belongings in one car. A few
days later, Geoffrey called me with the news.

Without telling me, he'd taken the test for the AIDS antibodies.
The results came back positive. The doctors have been encouraging,
although it's hard to believe them. One doctor gave Geoffrey info we
already knew: how not everyone who has tested positive has come
down with full-blown AIDS, how he might not see any symptoms for
many years, how there could soon be some medical breakthrough that
would benefit him.

Geoffrey goes to the Fenway Community Health Center for a blood
test every few weeks. His T-cell levels have remained normal. Getting

his blood drawn almost produces more anxiety than anticipating the results. In the waiting room there are men clearly close to death, along with others like him who are newly seropositive. "It's like I'm looking at Shakespeare's stages of man, only everything is accelerated," Geoffrey said. Men of his generation now look like they've skipped middle stage and have leaped to "dotage and death."

I realize I'm writing about Geoffrey's positive status in an oddly dispassionate way. That's only because this was one of those rare days when I was able to eat three meals without feeling nauseous after at least one of them. I often skip lunch because I don't want to take the chance of heaving during an afternoon audition. I'm getting thinner while Geoffrey gets fatter. The doctor told him to put on weight. The heavier he is, the longer it will take for him to get AIDS skinny.

Weight change is the least of it. I now read the obituaries every morning. I check the lymph nodes under my arms four of five times a day. I replay every single moment of every single sexual encounter I've ever had. I try to remember any drop of semen, blood, even saliva (although I know that's not logical) that might have entered my body. Everything has changed over the past few years. I feel like I've been evicted from my own life and have yet to find another to occupy.

I keep myself busy. I prepare for auditions. Tomorrow I try out for a small role in a Canadian play at a place called the Factory Theater. I also do a lot of crosswords, my new obsession. I stick with them until I've filled in every single box. *Just one more letter to completion. To perfection.* The letter comes to me. I fill it in. The momentary satisfaction is overwhelming until I remember Geoffrey still carries the virus.

I read. Sometimes I get on the subway with a book, no destination in mind, because it's easier for me to read when there's nothing else for me to do but sit. And when I have some sense of moving forward.

I bartend at a gay dance club called Boots. Working at night gives me the daytime to audition. It also occupies me at night, the hardest part of the day.

I answer the phone at the AIDS Committee of Toronto where once in a while I think I'm getting used to seeing sick young men, until I have to run to the men's room because I've come to my senses and realize I'll never get used to seeing sick men so young.

Everyone I know knows someone who has the virus. Or someone who has died. The other day Poppy got a call from a high school classmate who told her a friend of theirs had jumped off the Golden Gate Bridge after he learned he'd tested positive. Even Poppy's mother knows someone. The nephew of one of her bridge partners is in hospice care. Her friend told her that he has a rare form of anemia that is rarely curable. I don't know if Poppy's mother actually believes this, but she does go along with the charade.

I was finally tested the other day and will get the results next week. Geoffrey thinks I'll be fine. Since the two of us have always been safe, there's little chance that he transmitted the virus to me or vice versa. He said the idea that he might be responsible for my getting sick would drive him deeper into despair.

Now I just have to wait. Everyone says that waiting for the results is the hard part, but I'd rather be waiting than learn the bad news. Waiting's the hard part only if you find out you don't carry the virus.

Stoddard died April 16. I was getting ready to take Grace to the park when Emory called. I'd thought about what I was going to say when the time came, but when he told me, I blathered on with every cliché ever said to anyone who has survived a spouse: "You were such a good partner to him. At least he's not in pain now. Is there anything I can do?" Emory said he was thinking of moving back to South Carolina.

When I suggested he shouldn't make any big decisions for a year, that it might also be hard to be a gay man in the South, he said, "In Boston I'm gay *and* black. At least in Goose Creek I know exactly who to avoid. In Boston, I have no idea who to trust."

By then I'd wrapped the telephone cord around my chest. I wished I had wrapped it around my mouth before I blurted my advice to Emory.

"I get it," I said.

And then, maybe to suggest I didn't get it, he said, "Remember when the two of us met in that café last fall? I told you that Warren didn't have this one big event that threw him off course. What got to him was one small blow after another. Well, that's what Boston has been like for me. I'm moving because I'm tired of all the small blows."

After I hung up, I told Poppy to take over for Grace. I hopped on my bicycle and rode. I was glad it was raining. I wanted to be wet, to be aware of my skin, my presence in the world. I thought about Emory. His friends have told him that activism might help him in his grief. What is activism, anyway? Is there anything more activist than what Emory has been doing these past months caring for Stoddard? Sure, he wasn't protesting or attending candlelight vigils, but in the truest way possible, he was on the front lines. If that isn't activism, I don't know what is. When Geoffrey gets sick, I'll be in Emory's shoes, caring for a lover. That might be the only type of activism I can handle as well.

Emory followed Stoddard's wishes and didn't hold a memorial service. Just as well, I suppose. I've tried to imagine what I might have said if there had been a service. I've come up blank: Warren would have hated any display of affection at any sort of memorial.

We took Grace to see Mr. Dressup on Saturday. I didn't know who he was, but Grace told me (about ten times) that he was on TV every morning and took costumes out of his Tickle Trunk. She was so excited driving over that I had to move to the back seat and calm her down. It was a lovely moment, especially since the day before, Grace had turned on me. Out of the blue she started yelling, "Dead Daddy!" I've been thinking about death so much these days that for a moment I wondered if she could read my mind or—much more likely—she'd overheard Poppy and me talking. I decided it was the culmination of a toddler's anger at her father being gone for so long.

At least I've returned to her. For the most part, I like being in Toronto. I'll soon have my own apartment, with an extra bedroom for Grace. I have enough money from the settlement to last a long time. I've shot two commercials and have auditions for two plays next week. But it's not as if I've moved to some Shangri-La. I'm still working things out with Poppy. My boyfriend who may soon get sick is five hundred miles away. At times my daughter resents me.

Sometimes being here seems like something I need to get through. A lesson to be learned. A cleansing. Maybe an atonement.

That's when I don't feel I'm avoiding things at all. That's when I feel I'm facing my life, maybe for the first time.

Acknowledgments

While writing may be a solitary act, getting a manuscript into shape and publishing it is often not. I have some people and organizations to thank.

Years ago, the Thomas J. Watson Foundation awarded me a travel grant. I used it to live in Spain and study theater. You could say that the birth of this novel goes all the way back to that award.

I began this novel at my residency at the Millay Colony. I am grateful for the month I spent there. I'm also appreciative of the time and space I had at the Toronto Writers Centre. I'm deeply appreciative of the many wonderful people at the University of Wisconsin Press: Dennis Lloyd, Jackie Teoh, Adam Mehring, Kaitlin Svabek, and Jennifer Conn. And thanks to the Bennington MFA community, especially Cat Parnell, Amy Hempel, Alice Madison, Askold Melnyczuk, and Brian Morton.

Akin Akinwumi at the Willenfield Literary Agency is the perfect agent: kind, supportive, and most importantly, honest. Gordon Mackeracher told me about Toronto in the '80s. His sharing of this experience was invaluable. My sister, Alicia, is a rock and cared for our sick mother while I was five hundred miles away and writing this book. She made this book possible.

I hope the real-life Poppy, who left us way too soon, would howl at the irony of her name being given to this character.

I've been lucky enough to have some true believers: Ed Burdekin (who first told me I could write), Jen Haydock (whose enthusiasm for my work seems to know no bounds), Jennie Rathbun (whom I met twenty-five years ago in a writing class taught by the amazing Mameve Medwed, also a believer). Joan Wickersham also gave me her wise advice on the manuscript. Thanks also to Michele Karlsberg and Vince Ciarlo for spreading the word.

My writing group has sustained me for many years. Marcella Larsen, Debbie Michel, and Laura Kung Taylor offered me almost monthly criticism and support. There simply is no way I would have finished this book without their encouragement. Claire Cook may not be in this writing group, but she also helped me a great deal, both with the manuscript and with social media.

And finally, thank you to Bruce. Here's to twenty-five more.